CORE FOUR

The One

SARA BURWELL

Copyright © 2025 Sara Burwell
All rights reserved
First Edition

PAGE PUBLISHING
Meadville, PA

First originally published by Page Publishing 2025

This is a work of fiction. Names, places, characters, and incidents are either the product of the author's imagination or are used fictitiously, and any resemblance to any actual persons, living or dead, organizations, events, or locales is entirely coincidental.

ISBN 979-8-89922-134-7 (pbk)
ISBN 979-8-89922-151-4 (digital)

Printed in the United States of America

Dedication

To the challenges that made me stronger.

Content Warning

Warning: This book contains mature and sensitive content that some readers may find distressing. The narrative explores difficult themes including, but not limited to, drug addiction, alcoholism, the grieving process following the death of a sibling, the legal and emotional ramifications of a DWI arrest, struggles with anxiety, and a severe phobia concerning death and the afterlife. These topics are addressed within the context of the story and are not intended to provide a commentary on these issues. While the author has made every effort to handle these subjects with sensitivity, readers who are particularly susceptible to such material are advised to exercise caution.

Chapter 1

Miley

Have you ever woken up and thought, *What the actual fuck am I doing with my life?*

I'm thirty-one years old, recently divorced, and I hate my job with a burning passion. I absolutely despise walking through those doors every goddamn morning. My boss is an arrogant prick who I would love nothing more than to punch directly in the face. He's as pompous as they come. But I guess he can be with his award-winning streak as being one of the best defense attorneys in the country. His specialty, DWIs.

Yup, that's right. He defends those who choose to make the wrong decision.

People who literally put others' lives at risk. But that's not all he does. He defends all different types of criminals. He gives zero fucks. If you have the money, he will defend you.

And I work for him.

Yay for me.

I've been Jeff O'Connell's executive legal assistant for seven years. At first I tolerated it and pushed the ignorance of others to the back of my head. I didn't let it consume my life. I left work at work and didn't overthink it.

But now, now that I'm riding solo and am trying to busy myself by working extra hours, I loathe it. I don't want to assist with defending these dumbasses. They should get what they deserve.

But here I am, at 8:52 a.m., sitting in my car, staring at the front entrance, because I don't think I'm mentally capable of working at this firm anymore. It's killing me.

Well, maybe not killing me, but it's definitely not helping me. I refuse to live a life being unhappy. Which is why I asked my husband for a divorce eighteen months ago.

"MILEY!"

Jesus, Mary, and motherfucking Joseph. I look to my left outside my driver-side window and see my best friend, Colbie, standing there laughing. Colbie and I have gone to school together since kindergarten, besties ever since, and coincidentally, we work in the same building together on Broadway in downtown Albany. It's a historic area with a complex of government buildings, shoulder-to-shoulder storefronts, and the timeless charm of cobblestone pathways.

Colbie is a financial advisor on the eleventh floor at some hoity-toity institution, and I'm someone's bitch for a living.

I'm not bitter. I'm just saying.

That said, I don't like being startled, let alone first thing in the morning, and she purposely does that shit all the time.

"Asshole!" I scream through the glass while simultaneously rolling down my window.

"What cha doing?" Colbie says so cheerfully, it makes me again reconsider all my life choices.

"I'm debating if my salary is worth my misery."

Colbie dramatically rolls her eyes. "Your pity party is over. You've had months to dwell. I stood by your side when you ended your marriage, and I'll do it again if and when you tell your boss to go suck a duck."

She really is the best. She's been there for me since day dot. Her advice means everything, especially when others are always tiptoeing around me.

"I think today might be that day. I just want happiness. And this isn't cutting it anymore."

"No shit, Sherlock." She opens my door and takes my hand, practically dragging me out of my car. "You've been unhappy for so long"—she brings me in for a hug—"and I know you've solved one issue, but you need to solve the next."

Colbie is referring to two different things. The first being me ending my marriage of four years, and the second being my outlook on life, aka my severe anxiety about life as we know it.

I know that sounds absolutely insane, but let me try to break it down for you, even if it's just a little bit.

I need to live this one life that I've been granted with to its fullest. I won't accept anything less.

I have under one hundred years on this planet, and I'm going to enjoy every minute.

Why, might you ask?

Because I'm afraid to die.

I cannot grasp the concept of death.

I don't understand it.

I have so many fucking questions.

I need to know if heaven is real, or if the lights just turn out and you're done, to the black hole you go.

These are some of my serious questions that I need answers to.

Oh, and before you ask yourself what kind of religious shit am I into? Just know, I'm not a churchgoer. Not my thing, I'm good.

It's taken a long time and a lot of therapy to accept that there are no other options. I, at some point in my life, am going to die.

And because of that, I freak the fuck out. Full-blown panic attacks and everything.

My family and closest friends know this about me.

It started when I was five years old and continued until last year, when I finally sought help.

I now have to medicate myself in order to sleep at night.

But it's working for the most part, so that's a plus.

Once I grasped the fact that I only get this one life to live, I made it a priority to make myself as happy as I possibly could. First up was my marriage. I needed him to change. I needed him to be the person I married. I needed to feel loved, to feel wanted. But every night, I felt empty. I felt worthless. And I tried, I really, really tried, but he didn't and he wouldn't. He didn't care. It left me heartbroken, which ultimately led to me asking for a divorce.

I look at Colbie, and I know she's right. I'm the only one stopping myself from being happy at work. I need to move on. I did this once. I can do it again.

"I know, I'm going to talk to Jeff, I promise," I tell Colbie, half lying.

I've promised her this same thing multiple times. There's no way she believes me. Although she did almost shit herself when I told her that I asked Derek for a divorce.

We walk through the front door and into the open elevators where she presses the buttons for floors 7 and 11. The ride up is silent. She knows that I've met my max for today, and thankfully, she doesn't press the issue any further.

When the elevator stops on floor 7 and the doors slowly open, I know it's my time to depart.

Ugh. Fuck. My. Life.

"Love you. See you at noon for lunch?" I ask while giving her a hug goodbye.

"Yes. Text me if anything changes," she says as I exit the elevator, and it immediately begins to close.

"Will do." I half smile at her and continue toward my destination. Hell.

Approximately sixteen seconds later, I am greeted with the world's most annoying receptionist.

"Mr. O'Connell has two consults today," she says while practically shoving the files in my face.

"Thanks, Tracey—"

She doesn't let me finish my sentence. Typical.

"Your first is a college kid who got a DWI and has rich parents."

Oh, lovely. Can't wait.

"And the second?" I ask, even though it makes me cringe.

"A musician that let fame go to his head."

Okay, wow.

I thought I was blunt. Zero filter on this one over here.

"Was anyone hurt?" I interrupt.

"I'm just the receptionist, how would I know?" she responds fakely as she rounds her desk to answer the phone.

Ew. Bitch.

I take a deep breath so that I can gather myself and not lash out at the receptionist who's just doing her job.

"Thank you, Tracey."

She nods and adjusts her stupid-ass 2010 pencil skirt while greeting the caller on the other end of the receiver.

I head toward my office and am immediately summoned by Jeff. "Miley, when you're settled, I need you for a second."

Um, okay. On a typical day, you need me around thirty thousand seconds. Yes, I've done the math, but today, you just need me for one? Probably not. I call bullshit.

I set my shit down on my desk and head to his office. "What's up?"

He stares at me blankly. "Take a seat."

Alrighty then. This is weird. He typically barks his orders out or forwards me emails that I need to handle.

I make myself comfortable in one of the two chairs strategically placed in front of his desk and open my steno pad so that I can write down all his needs for today.

"I need you to sign this." He slides a document toward me.

"What is it?"

"It's a nondisclosure agreement," he responds quickly.

No shit.

"Why am I signing a nondisclosure agreement? I've worked here for years. This is a first."

"It's a requirement for our three o'clock consultation," he says firmly while typing away on his computer.

"I'm confused."

"Just sign the NDA, or I will find someone else to sit in on the consultation." He stands, taking off his suit jacket and hanging it on a hook near his entrance door.

I pinch my eyes together (Well, at least I try to. Thank god for Botox; those elevens aren't moving for another six to eight weeks) and stare down and skim the document. It appears to be pretty standard. The content basically says, "Fuck around and find out."

I look back up at Jeff as he sits back down at his desk and ask, "Did you sign one too?"

Being the top-notch douchebag that he is, he smirks and says, "Yup, signed it last night around eleven, so scribble on the paper so we can discuss."

Don't flip your switch, Miley. Take a deep breath. Don't react. You know he's an asshole. This is how he operates. Just sign the NDA, and let's get through this day.

I "scribble" on the paper and slide it back to him and smile. "Here you go."

He takes the document and says, "Greylan Asher was involved in an incident last night and is looking to retain us."

Why do I know that name?

Greylan

"Get up!" I hear someone yell from across the room, but I ignore them.

Why is my head pounding? Where am I? Who the hell is screaming?

"I said wake the fuck up!" the person says firmly, and I hear them walking toward me. I physically cannot lift my head from the pillow. It's painful to open my eyes. My mouth is so dry that I can't speak. I feel like death.

I slowly turn from my stomach and onto my back and slightly open one eye to see who is hovering over me like an asshole.

"Go shower. I left clothes in my bathroom for you," my manager, Ivan Stevens, says strictly.

I am so confused. What is happening right now?

I start to sit up and look around. I have absolutely no idea where I am. This isn't good.

"Where am I?" I mumble.

"At my parents' house." He looks super pissed. "You idiot."

THE ONE

Ivan has been my best friend since high school and is now my manager. I began singing in high school and continued throughout college. After I graduated, Ivan moved with me to Nashville and has been by my side ever since. It was a long journey, and to be honest, I never thought I was going to make it. I still feel like I got lucky. And I know if it wasn't for Ivan, I wouldn't be as fortunate as I am today.

"Why?" it's the only thing I am able to croak out.

"Jesus Christ, Greylan," he snaps. "You fucked up bad last night, and now we have to spend the entire day trying to fix it!"

Shit. I try to think. *What did I do yesterday?*

We arrived in New York around noon. I remember that. I played basketball outside of the arena with Ivan and some of the other guys on my tour before heading inside for a mic check around three o'clock. After that, a few of my buddies from college arrived since we are only less than an hour away from where we all went. A local college next to my hometown.

I played my sold-out show.

The same show I've played twenty-three other times in fourteen different states over the last three and a half months.

And then I went out with my boys.

I haven't been back to my hometown since my mother's funeral a few years back. I've never had a reason to. There's nothing left for me here anymore.

My dad passed away when I was an infant, and my only sibling, Jillian, has been gone now for almost a decade.

And then it hits me, and it hits me fast. Those vague memories from last night flash before my eyes, and my stomach completely drops.

"Fuck, man," I say as I attempt to get out of the bed. "What do I do?" I start to freak out a little bit. The only thing that's been able to calm me since my sister's death is music.

Ivan looks down at his watch. "Get in the shower quick. IV therapy will be here in twenty minutes, and once you can think straight, we will talk." And then he walks away.

I stumble toward the bathroom, take the fastest shower of my life, and try to replay everything in my head.

I walk into the kitchen and see a nurse setting up my IV. I can't say this is a first. I like to compare IV therapy to magic.

I take a seat and look toward Ivan. He responds with his eyes, which basically say, "Shut the fuck up, and don't say a goddamn word in front of this lady."

And that's what I do. I sit there in complete silence for forty-five minutes and continue to piece all the details from last night together.

After the nurse packs up and leaves, I look at Ivan. "What do I do?"

For a second, it looks like he might feel sorry for me, but then turns his back, and through clenched teeth, he slowly says, "I told you not to fucking go."

"Ivan, what do I do?"

"We're going to meet with my uncle Jeff," he says while texting someone on his phone. "And before you even ask, yes, I made him sign an NDA."

Chapter 2

Miley

"Who is Greylan Asher?" I ask while sitting back in his stiff leather guest chair.

"Seriously?" he says while typing away on his computer.

"I mean, the name sounds familiar, but I can't place it at this very second."

He turns his computer screen toward me and shows me a photo. "He's a rising pop country singer."

"Oh, that Greylan Asher," I deadpan. I definitely know the name, but I'm not sure if I know any of his music.

"Anyways," Jeff says, "I don't know much about the incident, but my nephew, Ivan, called me late last night asking for help."

"How does your nephew know him?" I ask because I'm genuinely curious.

"Irrelevant." He intertwines his fingers and places them over his gut while leaning back in his stupidly expensive chair, which I'm sure is much more comfortable than the one I'm sitting in.

What an asshole, am I right? Or am I right?

"This doesn't feel right. They made us sign a nondisclosure agreement. They probably killed someone."

"Probably not." He sits up and reaches for his phone. "I told Tracey to leave after lunch."

"Did she have to sign one?" I ask.

"No. This stays between us. All she knows is that we have a high–net worth musician coming in this afternoon, and I prefer it to stay that way." He sends a quick text, and when he is finished, he looks at me and says, "I'll need you to bring them up the back way."

I'm sorry, what did he just say?

"That's ridiculous," I say quickly.

"That's a requirement," he replies even faster.

I'm so annoyed right now that I don't even respond. I just stand up from my chair and walk directly out of his office.

This is absolutely insane.

And he's being dead serious.

I head to my office, shut the door, and hide behind my screen until it's time to go to lunch with Colbie.

I grab my bag, keys, and phone and head toward the exit, but as I'm walking out, Tracey stops me. "Mr. O'Connell wanted me to tell you that your client is coming early and to be back by two."

I think I literally just stare at her for a solid eight seconds. "Thanks."

I take the elevator down to the cafeteria on level B and head toward the corner table where I always sit with Colbie a couple times a week.

"My day has been so weird, and I'm so baffled that I'm practically speechless."

I plop down on my seat, sitting directly across from her where she looks at me, waiting for me to continue.

"I was just forced into signing a nondisclosure agreement before a potential client would come meet with us. We don't even know what the guy did. Oh, and I was ordered to bring him in using the back staircase. That's fucking weird, right?" I ramble. "And do you know what O'Douchebag said? He said, 'It's a requirement!' It's a fucking requirement that I escort some guy I don't even know to and from his vehicle and the firm."

She just stares at me.

"Make that make sense," I finish.

Colbie stands up and walks by me, taps the top of my head twice, and says, "I need a second to process all of that information. I'm going to grab a wrap. Be right back." She then walks away.

I follow behind her, grab a quesadilla with extra sour cream, and cash out.

THE ONE

On the way back to the table, she says, "I'm confused about the back door thing."

"Me too." I grab my stainless steel mug and go refill it. By the time I'm back, her wrap is almost completely gone.

I sit down and open my to-go container. "This entire scenario is confusing, but the crazy thing is, I'm actually looking forward to it. It's drawing me in. And that, to me, is alarming, considering I hate my job."

"It's very mysterious." She winks.

I scoop the end of my quesadilla into the sour cream, a glob of it clinging to the tortilla. "Hopefully he isn't a murderer," I mumble, my mouth full of cheesy goodness. If it's on the menu, I'll order it.

We finish lunch, and I head back upstairs to my office. I have approximately forty-eight minutes until they arrive.

My phone buzzes, and I slide open the text message.

> **Jeff**: I gave Ivan your number. He will text you when they are out back.
> **Miley**: Okay.

Thanks for asking me if that was okay, prick.

> **Jeff**: I will be in the conference room.

I don't respond. Instead, I Google our soon-to-be client.

> WikiBio: Greylan Asher is an emerging singer, songwriter, and musician from Gansevoort, New York, in the United States of America. Born on September 5, 1995, Greylan Asher is 29 years old as of October 2024. Details regarding his parents and siblings or their names, ages, and occupations are not available at the moment. Moreover, he has not shared anything regarding his early life with the public yet.

THE ONE

Okay, he's a super private person. Noted.

And he grew up around here. That's interesting.

I click on the Images tab in Google, and sweet baby Jesus, he is insanely good-looking. His dark almost black eyes look like they could pierce through your soul. His short textured hair accentuates his strong jawline and trimmed facial hair, which adds a touch of rugged sophistication.

I grab my phone and open my Instagram app and search his name. Right at the top with a blue check mark is his profile. Good lord, 2.7M followers. He's *famous* famous.

I scroll through more photos and videos and then switch to my YouTube app. I type in his name and play the first video that comes up.

> Empty whiskey bottle, sunrise
> peekin' through the blinds
> Another night I chased the shadows,
> leavin' good sense behind
> It used to be your laughter, that
> chased away the mornin' dew
> Now it's just the bottom of this
> glass, and a memory of you

Wow, that's dark.

Greylan is extremely talented, I will say that.

His music blends country, hip-hop, and pop elements, and his stage presence radiates an undeniable sense of "I know what I'm doing." It's very entertaining.

That said, I still feel a bit uneasy about him and his situation.

After watching a few more videos on YouTube, I grab my stupid steno pad and a pen, walk it over to the empty conference room, setting it down on the table where I typically sit, and then head toward the back staircase where I await for their arrival.

THE ONE

Greylan

I love my fans, but they don't need to know about my personal life before I became famous. If they knew, they'd talk about it. And if they talk about it, I'll sink. I'd probably drown.

It's not something I'm able to handle. Which is why I ask anyone who steps into my circle, even if it's just for a little bit, to sign a nondisclosure agreement.

Because my past still very much haunts my present and will likely haunt my future.

Never coming home mostly masks my broken heart, but occasionally, I'll have a severe panic attack.

And last night's incident definitely has me on the verge. Especially being so close to my hometown. Thankfully, Ivan knows this, which is why he asked his uncle to sign the agreement. He knows it's going to be a topic that needs to be talked about. He's seen me at my absolute worst. He stood by my side at my sister's funeral, and he was with me each and every night while I stayed with my mom when she was on hospice.

My mom was his second mom, and his mom is still mine. I honestly consider Ivan a brother to me. His family is all I have left.

"Thanks for asking him to sign the agreement. I appreciate that." I look over at him, and he acknowledges my statement with a nod.

"Where are your parents?" I haven't seen them in the couple hours that I've been here.

"Albany," he responds with a single word.

Shit. Mr. and Mrs. Stevens have always supported me. I knew they'd be there. Ivan probably didn't want to bother me with making plans with them because he knew my college friends were driving in. My college friends whom he absolutely hates.

"Do they know?" I ask him curiously.

"Do they know what, Greylan?" He seems pretty annoyed that I'm asking him questions when I'm sure he's the one who should be asking me the questions.

"What happened last night?"

"Do you even remember what happened last night?" he snaps.

"Yes." Well, at least I think I remember.

"I highly doubt that." He finally takes a seat at the table and says, "What the fuck were you thinking?"

"I wasn't thinking, Ivan." I put my head in my hands. "I was reacting."

"That's one way to put it. You're lucky I was close by." Ivan's parents' house is only minutes from the bar I was at.

"I know, thank you." If it weren't for him, I'd probably be in a jail cell right now.

"Let's get going. We have an hour drive." He stands and grabs I'm guessing his parents' car keys off the counter. "We can talk more in the car."

The car is silent. We don't talk. Each minute is a weighted pause. The slow, building tension, filling the space between us. We pull into a back parking lot shortly before two o'clock. Ivan grabs his phone to text someone. "Just letting him know that we are here," his eyes still on the screen. "His assistant is going to bring us in through the back so no one sees you."

I stay quiet, not wanting to complain that another person is going to be involved.

The back door opens, and out comes a woman with long dark hair and full lips wearing a fitted dress that accentuates her entire body.

We exit the vehicle as she approaches. "HI, Ivan. It's good to see you."

They know each other? I've never met her.

"Hey, Miley, thanks for meeting us out back. We appreciate it. This is my friend, Greylan. Greylan, this is Miley, my uncle Jeff's assistant."

Wow, this girl is naturally beautiful.

I extend my hand. "Nice to meet you, Miley."

"You as well." She heads for the door. "We're going to need to take the stairs up to the seventh floor. We don't have elevators in the back."

I'm so thankful for that IV therapy earlier. I'd be toast if I had to hike up seven floors being in the condition that I was in this morning.

Chapter 3

Miley

I am grateful for a lot of things in life, I truly am. I am grateful for my friends, for my family, and at this very moment, I'm so goddamn grateful that I washed my hair this morning. Washing my hair is a chore, and it only happens once every three days. Day one, it's spot-on, and on day two, it's usually still good to go. But on day three, it's very questionable; you never know what you're going to get. It is what it is. Sorry, not sorry.

But right now, I'm thanking my lucky stars that I put in the effort to do it because, good god, Greylan Asher is hotter than hell.

I greet him and Ivan at the back entrance, and I am instantly intimidated. Not because they're rude or anything like that, but because I have never in my life been this close to anyone famous or this good-looking.

We have to take the stairs up seven flights. I'm going to die. I should have practiced this a few times before they got here. I'm going to need to take at least two breaks at a minimum, and I definitely won't be able to hold any sort of conversation because I'm going to be so out of breath, I'll wheeze between words.

I open the door and hold it while they enter. The foyer isn't very big, but when they get inside, they stand off to the side so that, I'm assuming, I can lead the way.

Friggin' great. I'm in a sheath dress that lands an inch or two above my knees and three-inch heels. This is going to be a fail for sure, I can see it now.

I take the first few steps up and look behind me to see that they're following. "Three down, probably one hundred more to go." I laugh like an idiot. "I am going to count this as my cardio for today."

No response. Cool.

The first three flights of stairs were tolerable, but by the time I hit the fourth floor, I'm practically dying. My feet are throbbing, and I can barely breathe.

"You guys good?" I turn and ask.

Ivan is completely fine, zero complaints.

"I could use a thirty-second breather," Greylan says.

Ivan laughs at him, and I take advantage and try to catch my own breath as well.

I can feel the pulsing in my feet as I stand there. They're going to be so sore tomorrow.

"How are you walking up all these stairs in those heels?" Ivan asks.

"I'm barely surviving, actually," I think but accidentally say it out loud.

"Why don't you just take them off?" Greylan says.

Hmm. The floor is kind of gross, and I don't have socks on. But if I'm being honest, there's no way I can continue up these stairs with these heels on anymore. I'll trip, fall, and make a fool out of myself. I'd rather get dirty feet.

"Good idea." I smile, and then I kick those bad boys off and continue us up on our journey.

I focus the rest of the way up, taking long deep breaths in and slow breaths out while I continue to climb.

When we reach the top, I'm about to keel over. I place my heels on the ground and hold the wall with one hand while slipping my foot into each shoe and adjusting the back with my other hand.

I open the door for the two of them, and they enter and step off to the side, allowing me to come inside and lead the way.

We walk down the quiet hallway, and I hold the door open to the conference room where the king awaits his new potential client.

THE ONE

He stands at the head of the table and greets them both with a firm handshake and takes a seat. As always, I sit to the left of Jeff, and he holds his hand out to the right, showing Greylan and Ivan where to sit.

Jeff gives Ivan a folder and says, "Here are the signed nondisclosure agreements."

"Thank you," Ivan responds.

"I had Miley sign one as well as she will assist me with this case in the event you decide to retain me," Jeff says. "Shall we get started?"

Greylan

I'm not ready for this. I'm not ready to talk or open up to anyone other than Ivan, my best friend of fifteen years. But I need to. I don't have a choice. I'll be ruined if I don't. They are here to help me, and I need to accept that.

But for some reason, I don't want her to know.

"He's being charged with a DWI and possibly assault in the third," Ivan says out loud without any warning.

What the fuck, we couldn't ease into it?

I look over at Miley, and her demeanor instantly changes. She looks disgusted.

I'm so embarrassed.

I feel like a loser.

"I wasn't driving!" I shout, making it a point that I wasn't being reckless and dumb.

"Please elaborate," Attorney O'Connell says nonchalantly.

"I wasn't operating the vehicle. My phone died, and I was charging it, that's all. I didn't drive."

"Was the car running?" he asks.

"Yes, I had to turn it on in order to charge my phone to call Ivan."

"Was it your car? And where were you sitting, in the driver's seat?" he asks.

"It was my friend's car, and the door was open, and I was sitting half in, half out, waiting for the police to arrive."

"Why were the police arriving?" he asks while Miley takes notes.

"Because I had just been in a physical altercation with another individual inside the bar."

"Understood. We will come back to that. I'm assuming you were drinking if you were at a bar. Did you take a Breathalyzer or field sobriety test, and do you know if the bar has any cameras at their establishment?" he continues.

"We're unsure, but we hope so," Ivan interrupts.

"Yes, I was drinking, and yes, I took a Breathalyzer test at the station. But again, I wasn't driving the car," I tell him while watching Miley as she writes everything I say down.

"Surveillance will be key in this case. I can have the police report expedited should you retain my firm."

"Do you think this is something you could make disappear without publicity?" Ivan asks.

"How many people witnessed his arrest outside of the bar?"

"A handful at most," I say. "I don't think they have any knowledge about the DWI charge. They probably thought it had to do with the fight, which we would also need legal representation for."

"Tell me about the physical altercation that took place," he says while adjusting his positioning in his chair.

I take a deep breath. "I was at a bar in Saratoga with a few college friends, saw someone that I knew from years ago, and we got into a fight."

He looks at me and waits for me to say more.

"This guy was talking shit to me. I was instantly triggered. I attempted to walk away and leave, but he grabbed my arm and made another dumb comment, and I snapped."

"When you say you snapped, what exactly do you mean?" he questions me.

"I punched him in the face."

"And then he threw him up against a wall," Ivan adds.

Thanks, pal.

THE ONE

"So you were the primary aggressor?" He looks at me, and I guess I was, so I nod.

"When you said earlier that there's a possible assault charge, what did you mean?" he asks Ivan while making his own note on his legal pad, which was completely blank.

"At the time of the incident, the victim didn't press charges on him. When I got there, he told me he wouldn't if we paid him hush money," Ivan explains.

"The fuck I will," I interrupt

Attorney O'Connell takes a long deep breath and then says, "Okay, this will be two separate cases. I believe that I can get both wiped away with little to no publicity. We would require a twenty-five-thousand-dollar retainer, and you'd need to stay local while you await your arraignment date."

"Do we know when that is?" I ask.

"You'll get a letter from the court and be arraigned within the next two to three weeks," Miley answers.

"However, nothing is settled in an arraignment, so a hearing date would be set two to three weeks after that," Attorney O'Connell adds.

"He has twelve shows in the next six weeks. He can't stay local. He has a job to do!" Ivan moderately yells toward his uncle.

Attorney O'Connell ignores him and looks directly at me. "I suggest you reschedule your next few shows."

Fuck.

Chapter 4

Miley

The second Ivan said that Greylan was being charged with a DWI, my stomach flipped, and I felt instantly nauseous.

You could probably see the revulsion in my eyes at that very moment.

Thankfully, Greylan spoke up and said he wasn't actually driving the car. Which makes zero sense to me. How can he be charged with driving while intoxicated, but he wasn't actually driving the car?

And what provoked him to punch that guy in the face?

I have so many questions.

None of which I am going to ask because it's not my job to.

I'm paid to sit there and take notes. That's it.

I'm not sure why Jeff isn't asking more questions, but I'm sure he has a plan that he wants to execute, which he will disclose once he receives the ridiculously high retainer that he just asked for.

Twenty-five thousand dollars. Is he being serious?

I'm starting to think this whole thing involves paying off a small army to swing things in Greylan's favor.

And then he tells him he has to cancel four to six weeks of his tour, and he needs to stay local.

You can't just go and cancel a portion of a tour, can you?

He holds so many emotions on his face right now. I actually feel a bit sorry for him. He looks sad, mad, hurt, and defeated all at once.

I hope Jeff can pull this off for him.

"Nope, not happening," Greylan tells Jeff. "I'm not canceling and rescheduling my concerts to a later date."

Okay, this is about to get very uncomfortable.

"Can me and Greylan have a second alone to discuss?" Ivan interrupts.

Jeff nods and stands, and I do the same. "I'll be in my office, take all the time you need."

I follow Jeff out to the hallway and walk toward his office.

"Should I start to type up the notes?"

"No, go draft the retainer for him to sign."

I do as I'm told, and once finished, I walk it into Jeff's office so he can review it.

He glances through the standard language just as Ivan knocks on his office door.

"We're all set," he tells us.

"Are we moving forward?" Jeff asks his nephew.

"Yes. But we will have to come up with a plan to shift some of his tour dates. He'd like to perform his next two shows since the notice is so short."

"Okay. We will be back in a minute," he tells Ivan, and then looks to me. "The retainer looks good. Finalize and print and meet us back in the conference room."

I go back to my office and print the finalized retainer just as Jeff is exiting his office, and we walk back to the conference room together.

Ivan is texting on his phone when we enter, and Greylan is sitting back in his chair with his hands on the top of his head while he stares up at the ceiling.

We take our seats, and Jeff gives Ivan the retainer agreement. "I can take a check, card, or wire transfer."

Ivan reviews the agreement and gives it to Greylan to sign, and then pulls out his wallet and hands Jeff what I assume is Greylan's credit card. After the agreement is signed, Jeff hands the card to me. All he can see is dollar signs. I take the card, exit the conference room, walk back to my office, and enter the card number in our system and charge him twenty-five thousand dollars. Once the transaction is complete, I print out the receipt and head out of my office, but I am instantly startled by someone pacing the hallway nearby. It's Greylan, and he looks completely distraught.

"Hey, are you okay?" I ask.

He looks at me with his piercing black eyes, and the feeling of immediate attraction hits me like a rush of electricity throughout my entire body, and I instantly freeze.

"No, I'm not okay," he says while he continues to pace.

I don't know how to respond to him, so I go silent for a few seconds. I should probably just walk away, but instead I say, "I'm really sorry."

He stops pacing, and his eyes melt into my soul.

Holy hell, I am so fucking fucked.

"Let's go back," he says and starts back down the hallway toward the conference room.

"Would you like your receipt, or should I give it to Ivan?" I ask him like an idiot, and he just continues to walk. Alrighty then.

Greylan

There are numerous things in this life that I deserve, truly. But I will tell you this right now, I 100 percent do not think I deserve to be charged with a DWI. *Driving* while intoxicated. I wasn't driving the car. I had zero intentions on driving the car. Honestly, I'd never drink and drive. It's not who I am. And this might ruin my entire career and life. I have to cancel a portion of my tour, I'm going to have to lie to my fans, I'm going to have to stay in my hometown that torments me. It is going to physically pain me to have to stay here.

Staying here will bring back memories. Some good, but most are bad. It's a trigger for me. Even when I came back home to visit my mom when she was healthy and okay, it hurt. I still suffer the loss of my sister.

Next month is the tenth anniversary of Jillian's unexpected death. In a few days, it will be November, which means I will begin to shut down. I need to stay busy; I need to stay focused. I can't think about it, which is why Ivan booked me two concerts per week because he knows if I have time to sit and think, I won't be okay.

And you know what? I am so fucking sick of people saying, "It's been a decade, man. You need to move on." No, actually, I don't. Until they've lost a sibling, someone they've spent twenty years of life with is suddenly gone, they will never know the pain that's developed a permanent place in my body.

I feel so low and lost right now, the only thing keeping me upright is my best friend, who is actually being quite the asshole right now, and Miley. I don't know who she is or what it is about her, but I definitely don't want her to see me drown.

I head back toward the conference room and hold the door open so she can enter first. She seems stressed. Probably my fault.

"I'll pass on the receipt." I smirk at her.

A smile lights up her face, a masterpiece of curves and dimples, as she passes by and takes a seat.

"Where do we go from here?" I hear Ivan ask.

"We wait for the court date. He can tour until we know when it will be. I will reach out to the clerk of the court and ask that they send me the correspondence as well," Attorney O'Connell responds.

"And after we get that date, I have to stop touring?" I ask.

"Yes," he says. "That is something you and Ivan will have to work out on your own. Our time is just about up, so if you could provide me with your email address, I will send you a list of information we will need."

"You can just email it to me," Ivan interrupts.

"Our communications will need to be with Greylan directly as he is our client, but if he wishes that you be copied on all emails, we can do that." He slides his pad of paper over to me so that I can write down my email address. "Also, please write down your home address and phone number."

I write down the information and give it back to him.

"Thank you, Greylan. It was a pleasure to meet you. Keep an eye on your email, and we will be in touch very soon." He stands and reaches out to shake my hand. "Miley will see you out."

THE ONE

I shake his hand and thank him for his time, and we follow Miley to the back door. Going down will be much easier than the mountain we climbed to get here.

She walks us downstairs and straight to the car, and we thank her.

Ivan starts to back up, and I notice that Miley isn't walking toward the door, but is now walking the opposite direction. Weird.

"What is she doing?" I ask Ivan.

"Not sure." He pulls the car up next to her.

I roll down my window. "Where are you walking to?"

I catch her off guard, and she jumps a little. "To the front door."

"Why?"

She smiles. "I will keel over and die if I have to walk up seven flights of stairs again. I'm taking the elevator this time."

I laugh out loud. "Yeah, that was rough."

She shakes her head back and forth while looking down and, still smiling, tells us goodbye.

"Bye, Miley." I roll up my window, and Ivan drives away.

There's something about that girl that intrigues me.

"We can pretend you broke your leg and need surgery," Ivan says.

Jesus Christ.

Chapter 5

Miley

That interaction completely caught me off guard. I have no idea how to process anything that has just happened within the last couple of hours. And the worst part, I can't tell a soul because of the stupid agreement I signed.

Eh, well, my sister doesn't count, right? Because I'm not going to be able to hold this in much longer.

I make my way around the building to the front door and head toward the elevator that's going to transport me back to hell.

After I exit the elevator, I make my way to my office.

I am so close but so far away when I'm interrupted.

"Once you're settled, let's meet quickly to review what needs to be done in the Asher matter," Jeff says.

"Sounds good. I will be over in five."

I am about to pee my pants, so the bathroom is currently a necessity.

Once finished, I head to the king's castle and take a seat in the chair that's in front of the desk while he sits behind it at his throne, and then I take out my steno pad so I can write down everything he barks at me.

"Can you email Greylan and find out if he's interested in a $50,000 settlement with the guy he beat the shit out of?"

Um, is he asking me or telling me? I'm confused.

"Sure," I respond, because honestly, I have no choice. He is my boss, and I am paid to do what he tells me to do.

THE ONE

Do I hate it? I absolutely do.

I'm miserable working for him. Which is why every night when I get home, I search Indeed for a new job.

"Also, find out why the altercation erupted and ask him for a list of his upcoming tour dates, including travel."

Aye aye, Captain.

"Okay." I refrain from saying anything that will get me fired. "Should I ask him if he needs any assistance with a public statement as to why he is canceling a portion of his tour?"

"That's fine. It will cost him more money though."

Again, I am at a loss for words. I nod, head back to my office, close the door, and take a deep, deep breath. I reach for my phone and send a text to my sister. *Can I come over after work?*

There are certain things that I can talk to my best friend about that I can't talk to my sister about, and there's things that I can tell my core four because I love them, and they're my people. But with my deepest, darkest secrets, I go straight to my sister, and she holds them deep in her heart, never telling a soul. And I trust her with everything I have. Because she's my other half. My absolute favorite person in this whole entire world. My twin sister. And I love her so goddamn much, it's stupid.

> **Sutton**: Of course. Want me to come to your house instead? Fuckface is home, and I don't want to be near him.

She's referring to her husband whom she absolutely hates. I personally don't care for him either. But whatever advice I've given to her over the years, she ignores.

> **Miley**: Perfect. I'll be home by 6:30
> **Sutton**: I'll bring tacos!

I laugh out loud at that text. Because she will. She will come with a dozen of them.

THE ONE

I sit down and begin drafting the email to Greylan, asking him very invasive questions in a very professional way, and as I finish, Jeff is walking through my door, and I print him a copy to review.

Jeff skims my draft and approves it almost instantaneously. After working for him for years, I know exactly what he wants.

I fire off the email to Greylan, purposely not including Ivan. Although Jeff approved that we copy him on all correspondence, I will need the client to put that in writing before I do so, so that I am not liable for anything that is said. He is already making people sign nondisclosure agreements, imagine what would happen if someone said the wrong thing to the wrong person at the wrong time?

From: Miley Miller
Date: October 19, 2024 5:14 PM
Subject: Follow up
To: Greylan Asher

Dear Mr. Asher,

Thank you for choosing our firm to represent you in your recent legal matters. We understand that this is a difficult time, and we are committed to providing you with the highest quality legal representation.

To effectively strategize your defense, we would like to gather some additional information. First, we are interested in exploring the possibility of a settlement to resolve the assault case. Would you be open to discussing a potential settlement offer of $50,000? This could potentially lead to a resolution without the need for a lengthy legal process.

Second, we would like to learn more about the circumstances surrounding the incident. Could you please provide us with the name of the bar where the altercation occurred and the name of the individual who was allegedly assaulted?

THE ONE

Additionally, we would appreciate a detailed account of your recollection of the events leading up to and during the incident. Please share your perspective on what triggered the altercation and your understanding of the actions that took place.

Third, to ensure that we can effectively manage your schedule and accommodate any legal proceedings, we would be grateful if you could provide us with a copy of your upcoming work schedule, including any travel plans.

Finally, we anticipate that the public may inquire about potential rescheduling of your sold-out shows. Could you please share your thoughts on how you would like to address these inquiries? We can help draft a statement that effectively communicates your position and minimizes any negative impact on your public image.

If you have any questions or concerns, please let me know. We are here to assist you in any way we can.

Sincerely,
Miley Miller
Executive Legal Assistant
O'Connell Law Office, LLC

From: Greylan Asher
Date: October 19, 2024 5:47 PM
Subject: Re: Follow up
To: Miley Miller

Please call me Greylan.
And that was a very lengthy email, I need time to process it.

THE ONE

His response made me laugh, but he's right, I did send him a rather lengthy email, which he will need time to respond to. I decide to send him a quick summary of my original email and call it a night. I press send, shut off my computer, and head home.

> From: Miley Miller
> Date: October 19, 2024 6:08 PM
> Subject: Revised Letter
> To: Greylan Asher
>
> Greylan,
>
> Thank you for choosing our firm. To help us build your defense, please provide the following:
>
> - **Settlement:** Are you open to a $50,000 settlement?
> - **Incident Details:** Bar name, victim's name, and your account of the events.
> - **Schedule:** Please share your upcoming work schedule, including travel.
> - **Public Statement:** How would you like to address questions about show rescheduling?
>
> If you have any questions or concerns, please let me know. We are here to assist you in any way we can.
>
> Sincerely,
> Miley Miller
> Executive Legal Assistant
> O'Connell Law Office, LLC

When I get home from work at approximately 6:28 p.m., Sutton is already there waiting for me. I guess she really did need to get away from her spouse. She has a bag of tacos in one hand and a bottle of wine in the other.

"Tacos *and* wine? God, I love you." I reach in and give her a quick squeeze while we walk through the front door of my house.

I've been here for a year and a half, and I still haven't decorated. I have no desire to.

"Love you too," she says while sitting on a stool at the kitchen island.

I grab paper plates and napkins and give them to her so she can do her thing while I take care of beverages. I grab two wineglasses, add ice, and fill them almost to the rim.

Sutton lifts her eyebrow. "You good?"

"Super weird day. And I'm going to tell you all about it…as soon as you promise me you won't tell a goddamn soul."

"I really hope you didn't just say that," she deadpans.

"Just promise me, jeez."

"I promise." She rolls her eyes at me.

"We had a consult with a new client today, and he made us sign nondisclosure agreements because he's famous." God, that felt so goddamn good to say out loud. I chug half of my wineglass and feel as if I can finally breathe.

"Do I know the said famous individual?" she asks while taking a huge-ass bite out of her taco.

"I'm sure you know of him."

She finishes chewing, which takes longer than usual, considering she bit the taco completely in half. "Do tell," she mutters.

"Greylan Asher."

Greylan

After we left the attorney's office, we went back to Ivan's parents' house for dinner and then back to the hotel.

He's been very short and quiet toward me, but I deserve it. I just hope he gets over it sooner rather than later because I need him.

THE ONE

To keep myself busy, I check my email, and I read Miley's response to mine and smile. She literally dumbed her original email down for me. Which maybe I insinuated I needed, but what I really meant is that it's going to take me a little bit to respond because I need to think about what exactly I want to tell her.

I pull up my tour calendar and try to map out what I can do and what will need to be canceled. I have a show in Pennsylvania on Thursday and another on Saturday in Ohio. After that, I have a travel period where I can announce my postponement of the rest of my tour until after the holidays. If I'm doing my math correctly, that means I need to reschedule ten shows in seven different East Coast states.

I draft my email response and reread it multiple times. I know I'm being very short with answering the first two questions, so I try to make up for it with detailed responses to questions three and four.

I debate copying Ivan on my reply but choose not to. I like these one-on-one emails with Miley.

> From: Greylan Asher
> Date: October 19, 2024 9:16 PM
> Subject: Re: Follow up
> To: Miley Miller
>
> Settlement: I'm not giving that guy a dime.
>
> Incident Details: Porter's Pub. Rob White. Wrong place, wrong time.
>
> Schedule: Here's a *link* to all of our upcoming tour dates. We typically travel between each show. We have a 4 day break with no travel for Thanksgiving and a 12 day break with no travel for the holidays.
>
> Public Statement: Ivan is working on the statement but you have my full permission to email

him and ask him about it and offer assistance. If he thinks we do, that's perfectly okay with me.

-Greylan

After I respond to Miley, I shoot a text off to Ivan so we can try to figure this out. Talking to him in person isn't working, so I need to come up with another plan. He has to forgive me for what I've done. He's the closest I have left to family.

Greylan: Making sure we are on the same page. Playing Thursday and Saturday and then canceling/rescheduling the rest of the shows until Xmas?

Ivan: Yeah. 10 total. We need to come up with the excuse and then I will work out the rescheduling.

Greylan: Ok. Let's get through the weekend and announce something Sunday or Monday.

Ivan: Bus leaves at 10am tomorrow. I'll text you in the morning.

I guess that's the end of the conversation. I plug my phone in, jump in the shower, and get ready for bed while trying not to overthink anything and everything, if that makes any sense at all.

Chapter 6

Miley

I wake up to my alarm going off at six thirty in the morning, but instead of hitting the snooze button two or three times like I usually do because I dread going to work, I feel a sudden urge to get there.

Being able to talk to Sutton about everything last night took a small weight off my shoulders. Of course she knew who Greylan Asher was right away. She had so many of the same questions I have, and I promised I would keep her updated. She's now invested and will ask for updates daily.

I jump in the shower, tying my hair up in a tight bun so it doesn't get wet, quickly get ready, and then head out to work.

I purposely don't check my work email when I'm home, but it was very difficult not to open up the app to see if Greylan responded. Hopefully he understands my stupid sense of humor and isn't mad that I summed up my original email.

After I park, I head straight inside and to my office, thankfully dodging Tracey, and shut the door.

I'm so anxious to see if he replied. I want to defend someone who should be defended. I want to help him. I honestly don't think he deserves this. The DWI at least. He won't say much about the fight.

I open Outlook and turn into a ball of nerves when I see that he responded to me late last night. I click on his reply and quickly read it.

His response to a settlement was a hard no, but he did give me the name of the bar and the name of the person he was in a fight with. He also provided me with his tour schedule and gave me permission to reach out to Ivan with regard to a public statement.

I look up the information on the bar and print it out along with his tour schedule and take it to Jeff's office. His door is shut, so I knock, and he nods for me to come in.

"Do you have a second?"

"Yeah."

"Greylan responded. He's not interested in a settlement, and the incident occurred at Porter's Pub in Saratoga with a man named Rob White. He also sent his tour schedule." I hand him the information I printed out.

"Can you request the police report and contact the bar for surveillance?"

"No problem. Anything else?"

"Set up a call with me and the chief of police as soon as possible." He goes back to doing whatever he was doing before I came in.

I go back to my office and submit a FOIL request directly to the chief via email and ask if he is available for a call today.

I look up the number to the bar that Greylan was at, and they don't open until lunchtime so I head to the kitchen to make myself a cup of coffee.

"How was your secret client meeting yesterday?"

I look behind me to see Tracey standing there with her arms crossed.

"It was fine, but I cannot speak on it," I tell her.

"Oh, right. Silly me, I forgot," she says with a flake of attitude.

I smile and go back to making my coffee because I honestly can't deal with her right now.

"I just think it's weird that you're the only assistant in the firm that is assigned to work with only one attorney," she continues.

What the fuck is she insinuating?

"He's the managing partner, Tracey." I glare at her.

"Well, Trish, Lea, and Joyce all work collectively with the other six lawyers," she adds.

THE ONE

Do not snap, Miley. Do not respond. Just ignore her.
"And you get your own office. It's kind of odd, don't you think?"
This bitch.
"Are you asking me if I think it's odd that my predecessor, who worked exclusively with the managing partner, had a private office?"
She just stares at me like an asshole.
"No, Tracey, I don't think it's odd. My position is different from Trish, Lea, and Joyce. Now if you will excuse me, I have a job to do." I walk away so I don't completely explode.

Jeff has always worked one-on-one with his assistant/paralegal. His cases tend to be a bit more complex and come from either higher–net worth clients or from a referral of someone he knows.

Right now, I think Tracey is jealous and has a bit of FOMO going on, so I choose to ignore it and get on with my day.

When I get back to my office, I see that the chief's assistant responded to my email that I sent him. She states that he is available for a call at ten thirty this morning. I click on Jeff's calendar to make sure it is clear, which it is, thank god, and confirm that he is available and ask that he call his cell phone directly, providing the number. I am almost certain that Jeff doesn't want the chief of police calling the office line to discuss a client, especially considering we signed nondisclosure agreements.

After I hit send, I forward my email to Jeff and shoot him a quick text.

> **Miley**: The Chief is going to call your cell at 10:30. Your calendar is clear.

As always, Jeff responds almost immediately.

> **Jeff**: Thanks.

I roll my eyes, respond to several emails, Venmo my rent that's almost due, and by the time I'm done, it's almost time for Jeff's call with the police chief.

THE ONE

I decide to shoot him a quick text back to see if he needs anything else before his call.

> **Miley**: Do you need anything before your call?
>
> **Jeff**: Not on this. But can you reach out to Attorney Davis to see if his client accepted our settlement agreement in the Conway matter?
>
> **Miley**: Will do.

I email Davis's assistant and then impatiently wait for Jeff to brief me on his call with the chief, ignoring the other twelve emails that I need to tend to.

Greylan

Today sucks. I hate the small talk that is going on between me and Ivan. It's very weird, and I don't know how to fix it.

On top of that, I hate traveling. If I am not constantly doing something, anything at all, then my anxiety kicks in.

I keep checking my email to see if Miley has sent anything, but nope, nothing.

I decide to write some music to distract myself, which can sometimes go left if I'm not entirely focused.

Growing up, I was always drawn to music. I'd spend hours strumming my guitar and singing along to my favorite songs. When it came time to choose a college, I knew I wanted to pursue my passion. I enrolled at Skidmore College, just a few minutes from my hometown, where I studied music theory, composition, and performance.

After graduating, I felt a strong pull to Nashville, the heart of the country music industry. I packed my bags and headed south, determined to make a name for myself as a songwriter. The city was swarming with creative energy, and I quickly immersed myself in the local music scene. I started attending open mics, networking with other musicians, and honing my craft.

Eventually, my hard work began to pay off. I started getting noticed by industry professionals and was asked to write songs for other artists. My first big break came when one of my songs was recorded by a well-known country singer and became a hit. That success opened doors for me, and I soon found myself writing for a variety of artists across different genres.

Feeling inspired and confident, I decided to take the next step and pursue a solo career. I signed a record deal and began working on my debut album. It was a challenging but rewarding process, and I poured my heart and soul into every song. When the album was finally released, it exceeded all expectations. It topped the charts and propelled me to stardom.

Looking back, I'm incredibly grateful for the journey that led me to where I am today. It's been a wild ride filled with ups and downs, but I wouldn't trade it for the world.

The second I grab my guitar, my phone beeps, alerting me that I have a new email.

Very, very few people have my email address, so I know exactly who it is when I go hear the chirp.

>   From: Miley Miller
>   Date: October 20, 2024 11:27 AM
>   Subject: Re: Follow up
>   To: Greylan Asher
>
>   Dear Greylan,
>
>   I hope this email finds you well.
>
>   I'm writing to request your presence in the office early next week. We've made significant progress in our investigation into the recent incidents and have obtained the police report.

Additionally, we anticipate receiving the video surveillance footage soon.

I understand that you have shows this weekend, but if it's possible for you to return to Upstate New York on Monday or Tuesday, it would be greatly appreciated.

We're also awaiting a response from the District Attorney's office and need to provide you with a detailed update on our communications with the Chief of Police.

Please let me know if you're available to meet early next week.

Thank you for your prompt attention to this matter.

Sincerely,
Miley Miller
Executive Legal Assistant
O'Connell Law Office, LLC

My stomach flips when I read her email and am no longer focused on writing music. Instead, I head to the front of my tour bus and hand my phone over to Ivan so that he can read the email.

After he reads the email, he says, "Tell her you can be there on Monday" and then goes back to ignoring me.

My anxiety is so high right now, I physically don't know what to do. I can't function like this. Perform like this. Be managed like this. He's not helping my situation. I feel like he is making it worse. I just need a fucking friend right now, and he's being an asshole.

"That's all you have to say?" I ask.

He glances up from his phone and responds, "What else do you want me to say?"

THE ONE

I feel the urge to scream, to flip out, to get his attention. "I'm not playing your games anymore. I know I fucked up. But right now, I need you more as a friend and less as a manager." My hands are placed on the table strategically while I bend toward him.

He stares at me, and I stare back.

When he says nothing, I back up and say, "Fuck you."

I'm done for today.

Chapter 7

Miley

After Jeff finished his call with the chief, the police report was in my inbox within minutes. I was also able to talk to the owner of Porter's Pub, and it sounds like they are willing to hand over the surveillance video from outside, but we will likely need to subpoena them for the surveillance from inside. However, in order to get the judge to sign a subpoena, we would need to file a motion, and because charges haven't been pressed yet, we are at a standstill.

My phone vibrates, showing me I have a new message.

> **Jeff**: FOIL request for the body cam video as well.
> **Miley**: Should I send it directly to the Chief or his assistant?
> **Jeff**: His assistant. He's expecting it.
> **Miley**: Okay.

I email his assistant the FOIL request for the footage from the body camera the officer was wearing during the DWI arrest and head out for lunch.

I walk up State Street toward the Capitol and head straight for the food trucks. I would typically beeline it to the taco truck, but I'm eating the leftovers that Sutton brought over last night for dinner tonight.

Eenie meeny miney mo.

THE ONE

Do I want a gyro, salad, a burger, sub, or mac and cheese? Hmm. Salad it is.

The food trucks are only parked here for a few more weeks before they go into hibernation for the winter, so I usually come twice a week to enjoy their fare before they disappear. The lines are usually pretty long, but they move fast.

I zone out for a couple minutes while waiting for my turn to order, and when my eyes focus, they land right on the one person I never wanted to see again.

Because he hurt me, and he did it purposely, and then I divorced him.

Derek.

But why is he in Albany?

I turn my face forward in line and cross my fingers and toes that he doesn't see me.

My ex and I were college sweethearts. I loved him deeply; however, after we got married, his personality took a drastic turn. He became cruel and selfish, constantly belittling me. His emotional abuse drove a wedge between us, which caused even more issues. The pain of being around him was unbearable, so I packed my shit up, moved out, and filed for a divorce. And I haven't looked back since.

It's finally my turn to order, so I head up to the window. "Can I please have a Cobb salad with Russian dressing on the side?"

"Anything else?" the lady asks.

"No, thanks."

"Twelve even."

I hand her my credit card, and she cashes me out.

I grab my salad and then turn to leave when I'm stopped short because someone is literally in my bubble.

"Hi, Miley."

Nope. Not today. No, thank you. Goodbye.

I sidestep without saying a word and attempt to walk away, but he lightly grabs my upper arm.

"Get your goddamn hands off me right now," I tell him. And he does.

"Sorry, it's just so good to see you," he says.

THE ONE

"Why are you here?"

"What do you mean?" He responds.

"Why are you in Albany, Derek?" I snap.

"Because I'm meeting with a potential client, Miley." He says my name sarcastically, and it makes me want to knee him in the nuts.

"Then do what you came here for and leave me alone." And I walk away with my head held so high.

I walk back down State Street, faster than usual, and straight to my building.

I make it a point to not look back to see if he is watching me.

I get to my office, shut my door, and sit at my desk to eat lunch while scrolling through my phone.

That'll probably be the last time I make it to the food trucks before they leave for the winter thanks to him. I won't be showing my face there until the spring because I'll be too paranoid that he will corner me again.

I finish my food and get back to work. I open my email and freeze when I see that Greylan responded to my last email.

Why am I nervous again?

> From: Greylan Asher
> Date: October 20, 2024 12:54 PM
> Subject: Re: Follow up
> To: Miley Miller
>
> I'll be NY around 2pm on Monday.
> Let me know when I should come by.
>
> -Greylan

I head over to Jeff's office. "Greylan can be here on Monday in the afternoon. What time should I ask that he be here, and are you going to send Tracey home again?"

My ass isn't going to be able to handle hiking up all those stairs again while pretending to be their bodyguard.

"I think we should meet at a different location," he pauses briefly. "My place, Ivan's place, or his place. Let him decide."

THE ONE

I confirm that I will complete my duties and head back to my cave and email Greylan.

> From: Miley Miller
> Date: October 20, 2024 1:18 PM
> Subject: Re: Follow up
> To: Greylan Asher
>
> Given the sensitive nature of the topic and the potential for publicity, let's consider meeting somewhere more private.
>
> Attorney O'Connell suggested his home, your place or possibly Ivan's.
>
> You decide and then we can finalize arrangements.
>
> Sincerely,
> Miley Miller
> Executive Legal Assistant
> O'Connell Law Office, LLC

Greylan

After I responded to Miley's email about returning on Monday, I started writing a new song. I started with a simple riff on the guitar, experimented with different scales, and then added a melody.
Once I found my base, I started to jot down some lyrics.

> I'm searching for a light, to guide my way
> A love so pure, that will stay
> No judgment, no fear, just love and grace
> A sanctuary, a safe place

THE ONE

I was beginning to fit the lyrics to the melody, choosing chords that complement it, when Ivan walks over and says, "Sounds good, man."

I scribble a few more lyrics on my paper and ignore him.

I'm lost and alone, in this vast unknown

I continue to play and focus on the accuracy and timing, experimenting with different strumming patterns.

Seeking a heart, to call my own

I soften up on the strumming while singing the lyrics in my head and thinking about Miley. But why am I thinking about Miley? I don't write love songs…

Someone to love, without a trace of doubt
Someone to find me, when I'm lost and out

But I find myself writing a love song…

I switch from an A major to a C major and play it through once again.

"Try a D major," Ivan says.

I put my guitar down because now he is just annoying me, and I grab my phone to check my email.

Miley replied and said that she wanted us to meet somewhere more private and suggested some places, ultimately leaving me to decide.

Wait, where am I going to be staying while I'm back in New York?

And we still need to figure out how we are going to announce that I am canceling multiple tour dates.

I guess I can't continue to ignore him at this very moment, but I do plan on keeping it strictly business only because now I am just mad.

"Where am I staying on Monday when we get back to New York?" I ask.

THE ONE

"It's up to you. I can book you a hotel room, you can stay at my parents' house, or…" He pauses for a second. "You can go back to your own house."

I never sold my mother's house after she passed away. I don't have it in me. Too many memories and too much shit to go through. I've left it as is for years.

Don't get me wrong, it's been maintained. I have a weekly cleaner who comes in to take care of the inside of the house and a lawn care service that takes care of the outside.

At least I think they do. I pay them to do it. But honestly, I wouldn't know. Because I haven't gone back since my mom died.

And I haven't stepped foot in my sister's bedroom in a decade.

"I will take the hotel room for now."

Ivan nods, and I get up, leaving my music behind, and go into the bedroom at the back end of the bus and shut the door.

I grab my laptop and open my email to respond to Miley.

> From: Greylan Asher
> Date: October 20, 2024 3:19 PM
> Subject: Re: Follow up
> To: Miley Miller
>
> Preferably your place.
>
>   -Greylan

I hit send and reread the email I sent.
Shit.
Fuck.
Gah. That isn't what I meant. How do I rescind my email?
Goddamn it.
I respond again.

THE ONE

From: Greylan Asher
Date: October 20, 2024 3:22 PM
Subject: Re: Follow up
To: Miley Miller

I sent that too fast, sorry. Preferably Attorney O'Connell's house.

-Greylan

Jesus Christ. Now I look like an idiot.
And this is why I have a publicist.
I feel the bus stop, which means we are likely getting fuel. I look out the window and confirm.
I'm starving, but I don't want to go out to the main area for anything at all. Not for food, not for my guitar, and definitely not to socialize.
I lie down on my bed and turn on the television and attempt to find something to watch that actually interests me.
My phone dings, alerting me that I have a new email.
And a sensation of adrenaline and dopamine rips through me.

From: Miley Miller
Date: October 20, 2024 3:31 PM
Subject: Re: Follow up
To: Greylan Asher

That made me legit LOL.
Way to bring me up and then put me down, all in a matter of minutes.

I will finalize everything and send you the details tomorrow.

-Miley

Chapter 8

Miley

Greylan's email made me laugh so hard. The poor guy was probably freaking out after he sent me that email, so I decided to lighten the mood and joke around with him so he doesn't feel uncomfortable when he sees me on Monday.

I decide to head home after I reply because Jeff is in court, and quite frankly, I just don't want to be there anymore. Between dealing with Tracey's stupidity and seeing Derek, I'm tapped out for the day.

I don't say anything to anyone, I just leave.

That is the one thing Jeff doesn't care about. If my work is done and I am still reachable if needed, I can scoot out early every once in a while. Especially considering all the extra hours I've been putting in over the last few months.

After I am home, I can't stop thinking about the interactions I've had today, which just puts me in a terrible mood. And I've sworn off bad days. I don't want to spend my life mad or unhappy.

I grab my keys and head for the gym where I can run off my miserableness.

Ninety minutes later, I feel refreshed and erased the two toxic people who tried to insert themselves into my life today.

After I get home, I take a shower and then heat up my leftover tacos.

My phone rings. "Hello?"

"Tell me about your day," Sutton says.

THE ONE

I instantly know she is referring to Greylan. "It was good, how was your day?" I ask.

"As good as it could be, but enough about me. Did you talk to him?"

Yup. Knew it.

"We emailed a couple of times, but nothing crazy. He will be back on Monday."

"And...?" She wants me to continue.

"We got the police report and are working on getting the surveillance from the bar. I think they are going to give it to me, but the owner just needed to confirm with his partner. I will know more tomorrow."

"That's good. You will have to keep me posted," she says.

"I will. Are we all going to trivia tomorrow night?" I ask.

"Yes, I think so. I will send a text to confirm."

"Okay." I pause. "But, Sutton—"

"I know, Miley. I won't say a word." She interrupts me because she's a mind reader and knew exactly what I was going to say.

"I love you. See you tomorrow."

"Love you more." She hangs up, and I get a message almost immediately.

Group Name: Core Four

Sutton: Trivia tomorrow?
Miley: I'm in.
Peyton: Yup!!
Colbie: Fuck yeah.
Sutton: ♥

I can't stay focused. All I can think about is if Greylan responded to my email. I want to leave work at work. But I just need to know if he responded to me. I won't be able to sleep otherwise.

I click on my email app while holding my breath, waiting for it to load, and when I see that he responded only minutes after I replied, my heart races, and I become anxious.

THE ONE

What was I thinking of responding like that to him?

After freaking out for several seconds in my head, I take a deep breath and open the email.

> From: Greylan Asher
> Date: October 20, 2024 3:38 PM
> Subject: Re: Follow up
> To: Miley Miller
>
> I'm really sorry, my intentions weren't to bring you down. I just got ahead of myself.
>
> But if it's still a topic of conversation, I'd never turn you down.
>
> -Greylan

Wait, what?

Greylan

Miley never responded to my last email. Which, looking back, was highly inappropriate. I shouldn't have said that. But I also didn't want her to think that I was putting her down. She is drop-dead gorgeous, funny, smart, and witty. And the only thing I've been able to think about for the past two days.

After we arrived in Pennsylvania, I met up with my guitar player, Brody, for dinner and a couple beers. Brody is one of my closest friends as well. We met back in Nashville the first year I moved there and started playing together. He is incredibly gifted.

It's good to have him here. He has been mostly MIA this entire tour because his dad is pretty sick. He flies in the day before a show and typically flies out the following morning to go back home to be with him. It isn't looking good, and I wish there was something I could do to help him. I've told him multiple times to take the time off and not to come, but he insists.

He knows everything that is going on with me and the incident that occurred, but chooses not to ask questions and talk about it because he knows it will stress me out. I do the same for him, purposely never bringing up his dad's health. We have a great respect for each other, and I hope it continues to stay that way.

"I am going to cancel the rest of my tour after this weekend," I tell him.

"I heard."

He is the only person in my band who knows what is going on. And I intend for it to stay that way.

"If you could keep that between us, it would mean a lot."

"Always. What's your plan?"

I tell him that I am not sure and that I am just trying to get through these next couple of days and figure it out afterward.

He lets it rest there and then says, "I was going to tell you that I was going to take the next couple of months off to be with my dad."

I nod, unsure of what to say. I know he doesn't want to go into details. This is his chance to escape reality for the next seventy-two hours.

To help him relax, I decided to change the subject.

"I think I am interested in someone."

He stares at me. "Since when?"

"A couple days ago," I respond.

"Go on" is all he says.

"My attorney's assistant."

"You think or you know?" he asks.

"It's still too soon to tell. But she's normal, and I don't think she really knows who I am."

"Ah. Not some crazy psycho chick. That is definitely a plus."

I laugh because he's right.

I have yet to be in a relationship since I signed my record deal a couple years ago. It's too hard to tell who is genuine and who isn't. I don't have the time and energy for that right now.

We have another beer and shoot the shit, trying to forget about how messy our lives are right now, and then call it a night.

Chapter 9

Miley

I had absolutely no idea how to respond to Greylan's email last night when I read it. It caught me by surprise. I stand zero chance.

I get to work early and touch base with Jeff when he arrives.

"Greylan asked to meet at your house on Monday. I think four o'clock would work best because you have a deposition until two."

"That is fine with me. Let him know. Also, call the bar and see if you can pick up that surveillance today," he says.

I send Greylan a confirmation email and pray that it isn't awkward when I see him at the meeting. I will call the pub later because they aren't open right now.

> From: Miley Miller
> Date: October 21, 2024 9:09 AM
> Subject: Meeting Confirmation for Monday
> To: Greylan Asher
>
> Greylan,
>
> This is to confirm that our meeting has been scheduled for Monday, October 25, 2024 at 4:00 PM at Attorney O'Connell's home.
> **Address:** 108 Framing Way, Loudonville, NY

If you have any questions, please let me know.

> Sincerely,
> Miley Miller
> Executive Legal Assistant
> O'Connell Law Office, LLC

I text Colbie to see if she wants to have lunch today.

Miley: Lunch?
Colbie: For sure. 12?
Miley: Perfect.

The morning flies, by and I get a ton of work done. Feeling accomplished, I grab my phone and call the pub to see if I can come get the surveillance.

"Porter's Pub, please hold."

I'm put on hold almost immediately.

A minute later, the phone picks up again. "Can I help you?" a lady asks.

"Hi, yes. My name is Miley Miller. I'm looking to speak with Zack. Is he available?"

"One sec," she says.

The background is noisy. Probably busy with the lunch crowd.

"Hello?"

"Hi, Zack, this is Miley Miller. We spoke the other day about the video footage."

"Yes, hi."

"I was wondering if I could come get that video a little later today?" I ask.

He's silent for a few seconds but finally says, "Yes, bring a flash drive with you."

"Thank you. What time works best?"

"Any time after one thirty. Gotta run." He hangs up.

THE ONE

It's almost time for lunch, so I send Jeff a quick message and head to the lobby.

> **Miley**: Going to lunch and then straight to the pub to get the video. I should be back by 2:30.
> **Jeff**: Great.

I arrive first and sit down at our usual table and wait for Colbie. "I hate everyone today," she says as she walks over.

"Spill the beans."

"It's nothing. My colleagues are just useless sometimes. End rant. How's everything? How was the consultation with your secret mystery client? What's new?"

"You act like we don't see each other three to four times a week." I laugh. "Work has been busy. The secret client remains a secret, and hmm." I tap my chin, trying to think of something new that's occurred over the last forty-eight hours that I haven't seen Colbie. "Yesterday I walked up to the food trucks for lunch, and Derek was there. He walked up to me and touched my arm, and I told him to get his dirty and disgusting paws off me and to fuck off."

"You go girl!" She laughs. "But why was he in Albany?"

"He said he was meeting a client, but who knows? Will you pick me up before trivia? I've had a rough week. I need some drinks."

"How about we make Sutton drive?" she says, and I laugh.

Sutton isn't a big drinker and definitely not in public, so her driving makes sense.

> Group Name: Core Four
>
> **Colbie**: All in favor of Sutton driving us tonight, say aye.
> **Miley**: 👀
> **Peyton**: 🎯
> **Colbie**: 😬
> **Sutton**: You all suck.

53

THE ONE

We finish up our lunch, and she heads back to her office, and I head through the first floor lobby to my car so I can drive to Saratoga and get the video.

I thought about emailing Greylan and asking him if he wants to view it beforehand so it doesn't catch him off guard, but he has a concert tonight. I didn't want him seeing it to affect him, and I'm sure he is very busy with whatever musicians do before they perform.

I put on my sunglasses and start the car, then hit shuffle on my playlist. You never know what you're going to get with my music taste; it jumps from rap to rock and everything in between.

The drive to the pub is about forty-five minutes, but I don't mind. It's a beautiful day, and the scenery is stunning. Fall is in full swing—reds, oranges, and yellows painting the landscape. As I drive up north, I lose myself in the music, the vibrant colors of the changing leaves blurring past my windows.

I open the door to the front entrance and walk through. It appears to be a very relaxed hangout spot with a lot of televisions. It's much quieter than it was a couple hours ago, that's for sure. Just a few stragglers at the bar day drinking.

I walk over to the bar so that I can tell the bartender I am meeting with Zack.

She tosses a coaster my way and says, "What can I get you?"

"I'm fine, but I am looking for Zack. My name is Miley Miller, he is expecting me."

"I'll grab him," she says as she walks through the kitchen doors that are located behind the bar.

A minute later, he comes out.

"Ms. Miller." He extends his hand. "Thanks for driving up."

"Absolutely." I shake his hand.

"Do you want it queued up from when he first exits the bar?" he asks.

"Yes, that would be great. Thank you again." I hand him the flash drive.

"Just give me a couple minutes, and I will be right back out."

While I wait, I scroll through my Instagram feed, and then I go to open my DMs to watch the reels that some of my friends have messaged me over the last few days. After laughing to myself for several minutes at the stupid crap they sent, Zack finally comes back to the bar.

"Here you go." He hands me the flash drive.

"Again, thank you so much."

> **Miley**: I have the video from the bar. Heading back now.
> **Jeff**: The Chief just called and said that the body cam video is ready as well. Can you stop by the station and grab it?
> **Miley**: Yes.

At least I am still in Saratoga when he asks me to get it and not already back on the road.

I drive to the police station and pick up the footage from the civilian working the window in the vestibule.

That was painless, thank god.

Greylan

I spent the morning at a local radio station and then went to the arena for a sound check. Before every show I have, I usually play basketball with a few of the guys, but today, I'm just not feeling it, so I am just chilling on the bus.

Ivan comes in and sits in the chair next to mine. "I'm sorry for being an asshole." He pauses. "I think I'm just pissed off that your college 'friends' didn't have your back. They actually probably added fuel to the fire."

Ivan despises my college friends. He always has and always will. But they aren't terrible people, just reckless and immature.

"And like I said before, I know. I made a mistake," I respond.

"It could have been much worse."

"And it wasn't because they pulled me off him."

THE ONE

Ivan knows the built-up anger and animosity I have toward Rob. The hatred I have for him is something I'll never be able to explain.

"All right, I'm sorry, man. We will get you through this." He walks to the fridge and pulls out three Miller Lites just as Brody walks in.

"Thanks."

"I have been thinking about how we should announce that you need to cancel a few tour dates," Ivan tells us.

"I'm not pretending to break my leg." I take a swig from my beer, and Ivan and Brody both laugh.

"How about we just say that you're sick and that you need to cancel the rest of the 2024 dates."

"Then people are going to try to get all up in my business, and if they find out that I'm not sick, they will just call me a liar. I don't want to lie," I respond.

"Why don't you just keep it vague then?" Brody speaks up. "Tell them that due to unforeseen circumstances, you need to cancel and that you don't wish to speak on the issues that have risen."

"I guess that could work," I say.

"And then we just avoid the media entirely until this entire shit is done with," Ivan chimes in.

"All right, so it's settled?" I ask.

"Yeah. We keep it vague, and we don't speak on it after we make the announcement. I will work on the statement, and we can publish it on Sunday," Ivan confirms.

I nod and take a sip of my beer.

"One more round before we hit the stage?" Brody stands to go to the fridge.

"Yup," I say.

We finish our drinks, and then it's show time.

We go inside the arena and await our queue to take the stage.

After some liquid courage, I decide I'm going to email Miley again to ensure shit isn't uncomfortable on Monday.

Chapter 10

Miley

After work, I swing home to get changed quickly before Sutton gets here to drive us all to trivia. She grabs Peyton first, and on the way to the bar, we get Colbie.

When we arrive, the place is packed. We grab a table in the back, and Colbie signs us up for trivia while Peyton gets us drinks.

After a couple of rounds, they break so that they can tally up the score. I am pretty sure we dominated all the other teams. That's my cue to use the bathroom.

When I get there, there's a line outside the door, and I am stuck next to a group of drunk and annoying college girls.

"Can you take our picture?" a short blonde asks me.

I say sure just to shut them up and get them to stop talking. I snap their photo and hand the phone back just as one of the girls says, "Oh em gee, I freakin' love this song."

I listen for a second and realize it's one of Greylan's songs playing over the speakers.

"Best concert ever!" her friend says. "He is so hot, I'd definitely bang him."

I roll my eyes. *Good god. Settle down, girls. You're, like, twelve.* I try to tune them out while I try not to pee my pants. I realize then, Greylan never responded to my confirmation email. Not that he had to, but I wish he would so that it won't be awkward on Monday when I see him.

THE ONE

I open my email app to make sure that I actually sent him the confirmation, and waiting in my inbox is a response from him. I quickly open it.

> From: Greylan Asher
> Date: October 21, 2024 9:09 PM
> Subject: Re: Meeting Confirmation for Monday
> To: Miley Miller
>
> Confirmed.
>
> No response to my last email??

Dear lord, help me please. This is not real life right now.
What do I say?
How do I respond?
Multiple women exit the bathroom, and it's finally my turn, thank god. I go, wash my hands, and practically sprint back to my friends. I need to talk to someone about this. But this isn't the place to be discussing the very same person whose song is playing and everyone surrounding me is singing along.

Sutton gives me a look knowing exactly whose song it is, and I just shake my head and ignore her.

When it's done, the host comes on the microphone and announces the team with the highest score. It was very close, but we take home the bragging rights.

"Ready to head out?" I ask my girls.

Everyone is in agreement, and we walk to Sutton's car. She drops off Colbie first and then Peyton.

Once we are alone, I say, "I need to tell you something."

She looks over at me while driving and says, "Me too."

"You first," I say.

"I'm filing for a divorce."

Okay, well, I wasn't expecting that. But I really hope she is.

"You can stay with me," I tell her.

She smiles as she pulls into my driveway. "Thank you."

THE ONE

We get out of the car, and she pops her trunk and grabs a suitcase.

Oh, we are doing this already? Alrighty then.

We head inside, and she wheels her luggage into my room and tells me that she is sleeping in my bed with me, but it won't be for too long, just until she saves enough money for her own place. And I am completely okay with that. She can stay with me for as long as she wants. It'll probably actually help the severe anxiety I have at night. But her ass better stay on her side of the bed and not steal the blankets on me. Or breathe on me. Or snore. You know, all the things.

"So what happened?" I ask.

"Same shit. Nothing will ever change. He is a narcissist and therapy isn't working, so I'm done."

"Do you want to talk about it?" I stare at her, completely shocked.

"Nope. Not at this very moment. I'm fine, really. I actually feel relieved. Hopefully it will be a painless process."

She walks to my fridge and grabs two White Claws and sits on the couch and pats the seat next to her.

"Now, what did you have to tell me?"

"I don't know how to exactly explain the communications that Greylan and I have been having." I pause and grab my laptop off the end table next to me and open it. "So I'm just going to let you read them." I hand it to her and watch as she reads our email exchange.

"Holy fuck." Her eyes look like they are going to pop out of her head. "Holy fucking fuck, Miley."

"Do I respond?" I ask.

"Yes, you respond, you idiot." She is expressionless.

"But what if those emails don't mean what I think they mean?"

"There's only one way to find out."

She hits Reply on the email.

"Don't you dare!" I scream and reach for my computer, but she pulls it away and stands up.

"If you don't, I will."

"Okay, okay, okay, I will! I promise! Now give it to me."

"Right now. I want you to respond right now!" she orders.

"Fine. But if this gets me fired, you're going to have to find us both a new place to live."

"Yeah, yeah." She takes a sip from her White Claw while indenting the side of her can like a weirdo. She does this so she doesn't mix her drink up with anyone else's, and even though it's just the two of us, she still crushes the side.

"How do I respond?"

"Tell him you're down if he's down." She laughs.

"Oh my god, Sutton. No." I begin to type.

> From: Miley Miller
> Date: October 21, 2024 10:03 PM
> Subject: Re: Meeting Confirmation for Monday
> To: Greylan Asher
>
> I am interested in learning more about your perspective of said topic of conversation. Please elaborate.
>
> -Miley

Greylan

Tonight's show was fun. The crowd was energetic, and the band was on point. We get back to the bus a little after eleven, and I'm exhausted.

I go to my room at the back end of the bus and change out of my sweaty clothes and jump in a quick shower. When I am done, I flop on my bed and grab my phone. I was talking to Brody earlier and told him about the email I sent to Miley about how I'd never turn her down and how she never responded to me, and Monday is going to be super awkward now. He suggested that when I confirmed our meeting, I say something again. So I did. Right before I hit the stage so that I didn't pace around, waiting for her to respond.

THE ONE

When I unlock my phone, I can see that I have one email notification.

I am definitely nervous to open it and read what she wrote, if it's even Miley who emailed me.

I tap the app, and indeed, it's from her. I open it and read it, not once, not twice, but three friggin' times. Her response put the biggest grin on face.

She asked me to elaborate on my comment about never turning her down and that she's interested in learning my perspective on that specific topic.

I think I'm just going to be open and honest here and just say what I am thinking. Because she is all I can think about for some reason. She has my full attention.

I hit Reply, type out my message, and send it before second-guessing what I just wrote.

From: Greylan Asher
Date: October 21, 2024 11:41 PM
Subject: Re: Meeting Confirmation for Monday
To: Miley Miller

You caught my eye the moment I met you.
Goodnight, Mils.

And with that, even though my life is complete shit, I go to bed with a smile on my face.

*****

Friday was a long day of travel and songwriting. Thankfully, Brody stayed, and we—he, Ivan, and I—were able to kick it back and just hang out. It was something we all needed. A day to relax before the final show.

When I wake up Saturday, we grab breakfast, meet with a local radio station, and have a mic check at the arena. Afterward, me and the guys get lunch and play some basketball.

THE ONE

Miley didn't respond after my last message, but I also didn't keep the door open for her to do so. I checked my email about twelve times, hoping she'd say something, anything, but she never did.

At least she now knows that I have a thing for her.

Before we go on stage, I ask Ivan to rally the gang so that I can have a word with them. When my team meets me backstage, I tell them that tonight is going to be the last show of the year, and I need to cancel the next ten shows due to some personal stuff going on in my life. I don't elaborate, and they don't ask me too many questions. I have a great crew, and I know they'd have my back if I told them the truth, but that isn't something I want to do right now.

A little after nine o'clock, I walk on stage for the last time in 2024, and I give it my all for the next ninety minutes.

When I'm done, I'm spent. I take a long hot shower before locking myself in my room for the night.

Ivan sends me a draft of the statement he will be posting on my behalf tomorrow.

Dear Fans,

Due to unforeseen personal circumstances, I have made the difficult decision to cancel ten upcoming tour dates. I understand that this may be disappointing news, and I apologize for any inconvenience this may cause.

I will be taking a break from touring for the remainder of 2024 to address these personal matters. I am committed to rescheduling the canceled shows for a later date in 2025.

Please stay tuned for updates regarding rescheduled dates and ticket information.

Thank you for your understanding and continued support.

Greylan Asher

THE ONE

I approve it and go to bed. Tomorrow is going to be a long day of negative comments and traveling, but it's something I'm going to need to get through because the next day is Monday.

Chapter 11

Miley

Yesterday was a complete mental mess, and Greylan's email is still hanging over my head. I spent the day shopping with Peyton and Sutton, desperately trying to keep my mind off it. Colbie joined us later, and we ended up at a restaurant, laughing, and talking. But even then, it stayed at the back of my mind. So while Sunday promises the usual routine, Saturday was a day of avoidance and distraction, all thanks to a single bewildering email.

When I walk into the kitchen, Sutton is already out of bed and cooking us breakfast. She's definitely the better cook out of the two of us, so this new arrangement is definitely a huge win for me.

Sunday fun day typically consists of me cleaning, doing laundry, and then family dinner at my parents' house. I assume Sutton is going to tell our parents that she is filing for a divorce. She doesn't have a choice; they are going to ask where he is when he doesn't show up later.

"Morning," I say as I walk over to my Keurig.

"Good morning. Did you see Greylan's post on Instagram?" she asks.

I just look at her and grab my phone out of the front pocket of my huge hoodie. My sleep attire isn't attractive whatsoever. It consists of baggy sweatpants and oversized hoodies or T-shirts, depending on the weather.

I open Instagram, search his name, and click on his profile. He made the announcement within the last hour. It's a photo of a black

THE ONE

background with the message typed out in white font, telling his fans that due to some unforeseen circumstances, he's canceling the rest of his tour dates in 2024.

I immediately click on the comments and begin to read them. There are hundreds already, mostly positive, but all I can see are the negative ones.

There are rumors he parties too hard to perform...

So fucking glad I decided not to buy tix for this show haha

Who cares

I bet he's doing drugs and needs to go to rehab like the rest of them.

Maybe he should go back to writing music for others

That's not super sketch...

I feel instantly sick. These people literally follow him, so they're supposedly his fans, and they're being so negative. It makes me want to respond to each and every one of them and tell them to mind their own goddamn business. People shitting on him when they don't even know what he's dealing with. I am going to be following these comments all day.

I post one of my own.

To the haters: What kind of "fans" are you? Instead of speculating, maybe you should fuck off and mind your own goddamn business. Losers.

Sutton clears her throat. "Breakfast is ready."
"Did you read these comments?"
"Most of them. People are cruel. Don't feed into it."

THE ONE

Too late.

I stuff my phone back into my hoodie pocket and indulge.

These waffles are spot-on. I'm not sure why Sutton is a nurse for a living; she needs to be a chef.

"What's on your agenda for today?"

"Not much. I need to figure out the mutual bills me and Chris have and cancel the ones that are in my name," she responds.

"Do you need help?"

"Nope. It will be easy. But can you ask your boss if he knows any divorce lawyers?"

"Matrimonial attorneys," I correct her with a smile because nurses don't know legal terminology whatsoever.

"Whatever, same thing." She rolls her eyes.

"Can it wait until tomorrow, or should I text him now?"

"Tomorrow is fine. What are you doing before dinner with Mom and Dad?"

"Cleaning," I respond with a mouth full of waffles.

"I'll take care of the dishes."

"Do you want to talk about anything? I ask her.

"Not really. Like I said before, I'm really fine. More relieved. Did you feel that way when you left Derek?"

I sure did. It was like a thirty-pound weight was lifted off both my shoulders, and I could finally breathe again. "Yes. I felt instant relief."

"Do you think Mom and Dad are going to think we are a bunch of losers who can't stay married?" She laughs.

"No, they hated Chris and Derek. They know we can do so much better. We settled when we shouldn't have. They'll always have our backs," I tell her.

And it's true. Our parents are amazing. I wish one day I could have a marriage like theirs. It's so effortless. At least I think it is. They adore each other and laugh at each other. Whenever Derek thought he was being funny, it made me cringe and want to elbow him in the face.

"I'm going to tell them later."

"I figured, since he wouldn't be showing up to dinner."

"He won't. He got the picture" is all she says. I don't push her further.

I finish my breakfast and grab my plate and walk it over to the sink. "I'm going to chill for a little bit before I get my day started. Let me know if you need anything," I tell her, and then I go and plop my ass down on the couch and turn on the TV. I put the news on and watch it for about ten seconds before pulling my phone back out and checking the comments on Greylan's post.

I have 294 notifications when I open my Instagram app.

Holy shit. I've never in my life had that many notifications.

When I tap on the heart in the upper right-hand corner of the app, I have 288 likes on my comment on Greylan's post, five comments (all positive, thank god), and one new follower request.

greylanasher requested to follow you. 19m ago

Shut the front door. This isn't real life.

"Sutton!" I scream. "Come here!"

Greylan

Today absolutely sucks. I have so much love coming my way, but the few people who are hating on my announcement are killing me. I've been scrolling and reading all morning. I know I shouldn't, but I can't help myself. What else am I supposed to be doing on this bus? We've been traveling all day and still have hours to go. Ivan and I are the only two on the tour bus besides my driver, Ken. Brody flew back early this morning.

"Why didn't we just fly from Ohio to New York?" I ask Ivan.

"Because making Ken drive back to Tennessee solo is fucked up. Plus, we need to get shit from our houses for our prolonged stay in New York." He looks at me like I just asked the world's dumbest question.

"Sounds like you're trying to torture me."

He probably is. But why? I'm the one dealing with the backlash.

THE ONE

As I sit there, I think. I think about all the people involved in this mess I caused. And then realization hits me. Ivan is probably taking the brunt of everything. Fuck.

"Ivan…"

"Yeah?"

"What has the label said?" I ask and then hold my breath.

"It's under control. I did have to tell them something though."

"And what exactly did you tell them?"

"You're dealing with some serious personal shit."

"And that worked? They just dismissed it and let it be?"

"Not exactly." His leg is now bouncing up and down, and he appears to be nervous.

This is very much not like him. Ivan keeps it together, always.

"What aren't you telling me?" I ask.

"I have a call with the president tomorrow morning before our flight. He wants answers, and he is pissed."

I lean back and palm my face, taking a huge breath in and letting it out as I slide my palm down over my eyes and nose and past my chin. "Are we fucked?"

"I don't know yet. I am still trying to figure out exactly what to do and say. I need time."

Ivan is a very honest person. I know exactly what he is saying. He is telling me to leave him alone while he tries to figure out his next move.

"Do you need me to do anything?"

"No. Do not do or say anything, let me try to figure it out," he says, and I agree.

Ivan is in charge right now. I need to sit down and shut up. Understood.

I sit back in my chair and grab my phone and read more of the comments from my post until a comment from mileymiller14 catches my attention.

I click on her profile, but it is private, so I send her a follower request, not thinking twice of it, just as Brody sends me a text message.

THE ONE

Brody: He's gone.

No. No no no.
Please tell me he got to be there with him.
Please tell me he got to say goodbye.
Before I could respond, he sends another message.

Brody: Before he passed away this morning, he told me to tell you this: "there are always going to be people in your life that hate you for absolutely no reason, even more for you because you're famous. But take their negativity and build from it. Prove them wrong. Learn from your mistakes and push forward. Please don't ever fall backwards."

Another message comes in instantly.

Brody: The last thing my father told me before he closed his eyes and left was, "I love you, son. You made me proud. Publicly tell the world that I've left this life with everything I had left in me and that I am so grateful that I had you with me every second of the way due to the generosity and support of your music family.

I literally have no idea what to respond or say, so I say only what is on my mind.

Greylan: I love you, man.

Ivan sits next to me and shows me his phone. It's a post from two minutes ago from Brody's Instagram page. The first photo is a classic rock 'n' roll moment: a young Brody, wide-eyed with admiration, watching his dad shred the guitar with Rivers Luck. Fast-forward a few years, and the second photo shows Brody holding his own on stage while his dad cheers him on from the sidelines. The caption reads,

> It is with profound sorrow that I share the news of my father's passing. He fought valiantly. We ask for privacy as we mourn our loss. I extend my sincere gratitude to my music family for their generosity and support.

"He wanted everyone to reconsider their initial conclusions," Ivan says.
"We need to stay in Tennessee."
"We will be with Brody and be at the services, I promise. Nothing has been arranged yet, but either way, you and I will both be there. However, right now"—he shows me his phone again, and it's a message from Brody to Ivan that says he will keep us informed with all the arrangements and to stay the course—"we stick to our initial plan, and we do not confirm nor deny anything to anyone at any time. Am I clear?" he says strictly.

Did Brody's dad know he was about to die and ask that his death take the blame for my canceled tour dates? Because it sure sounds like he did.

Chapter 12

Miley

After I received Greylan's follower request, I slowly died. I accepted it immediately, and instead of cleaning like I was supposed to, I found myself scrolling through every photo I have ever posted to make sure there wasn't anything too embarrassing on my page.

"Should we post a recent twin selfie so that he knows there are two of you?" Sutton laughs.

"No." I shut her down.

"Come on. It can be a test. We can see if he likes it or not."

"Are you going to let me look better than you in it?"

Sutton really is the prettier twin. I'm just smarter, funnier, and much more laid-back.

"We look exactly the same, dummy."

I roll my eyes. "Fine. But I'm not posting it if it comes out bad," I tell her.

We go near the window where the lighting is good and snap a few selfies that, surprisingly, come out really good.

Sutton grabs my phone. "Post this one."

"What should the caption read?" I ask.

"Double trouble."

"No."

"Twice as nice."

"You're an idiot."

"Single as a Pringle?" She laughs out loud.

"Jesus Christ, Sutton. No."

I grab my phone back from her and type "Sunday fun day with the Twinner" and post it. I throw my phone on the charger in my bedroom and tell myself that I'm not going to check it until all my laundry is cleaned and put away.

After the last shirt is hung up, I run to my phone, keeping my promise not to touch it, and check to see if he liked my photo. I get super bummed when I see that I have twenty likes, but he is not one of them.

Oh well, it's only been two hours. I am sure he will see it and like it at some point.

Sutton and I head to our parents' house for dinner, and she tells them that she's filing for a divorce. They were both very supportive and offered that she come back home, which she denied instantly.

Back home, I call it an early night while she dives into a romance novel on the couch. Before sleep completely claims me, I scroll through Instagram, a last-ditch effort to see if Greylan acknowledged my post—still nothing. Fifty-five likes, a personal record, yet nothing compared to the thousands he gets. I don't know why I even let myself entertain the thought that someone like Greylan Asher would be interested in someone like me.

*****

The next morning, anxiety claws at me, forcing me to work almost forty minutes early. The day unfolds, a blur of tasks, compounded by the looming meeting with Greylan at Jeff's house. Jeff's home office is a familiar setting; this isn't his first client meeting here. I gather the flash drives with the videos, the police report, bar information, and everything else I need and leave the office at three, the weight of the meeting heavy in my hands.

Greylan

Ivan said that the meeting with the president of my label went better than expected, and they came to their own conclusion about

THE ONE

why I was canceling ten of my tour dates. They believe it is due to my lead guitarist losing his father, and Ivan didn't correct them. He stayed the course. He didn't deny nor confirm anything.

My flight landed in New York at noon, and I asked Ivan to rent me my own car for a few days so that I don't need to depend on him for anything. After I got my rental, I checked into my hotel in downtown Albany and told Ivan I would meet him at his uncle's place at four o'clock.

To say I am nervous about this meeting is an understatement. My anxiety might be at the highest level it has ever been. Between finding out the status of my case, seeing Miley, Brody's dad's death, and the negativity I'm still receiving, I'm just about burnt out.

I try to relax for a little while when I get to my room, but I can't calm myself down. I try to find a distraction, something, anything at all, when I remember that I sent Miley a follower request on Instagram. I check to see if she accepted it, and indeed, she did. I click on her page, and the first photo I see is of her and—hold up, she's a twin? Miley has an identical twin. Wow. I didn't see that one coming. I think I can tell them apart though. Miley has long hair that is parted slightly off-centered but not completely on the side, and her sister's hair is shorter and parted straight in the middle.

I spend a good hour going through each and every one of her photos, and wow, that girl is absolutely gorgeous. Most of her photos are of her and her friends or her family or just her and her sister. She has one solo selfie from two years ago when she did a before and after of a haircut, but that's it.

There is also a post from two years ago with multiple photos of Miley and her grandmother who passed away. I swipe through the photos, and the last one is of Miley and her grandmother, and Miley is in a wedding dress.

Wait, is Miley married?

I didn't see a ring on her finger.

I close the app, the bright screen fading to black, and the image of her in that wedding dress lingers in my mind, a stark contrast to the professional meeting I'm about to attend. I shake my head, trying to clear the image, and focus on the task at hand. It's time to go.

*****

I pull up to Attorney O'Connell's house at 3:53 p.m., and Ivan is in his car waiting for me. I get out, and we walk up to the entryway together.

"You good?" he asks as he rings the doorbell.

"No. Are you?"

Miley opens the door, and I freeze. I almost forgot how beautiful she is in person.

"Come on in." She opens the door wider for us to enter.

As soon as we walk in, Ivan's aunt Annie practically tackles him to the floor, which makes Miley laugh. "Jeff's office is just down the hall," she says as she begins to walk toward our destination.

She's wearing tight black pants with pointed heels and a fitted blouse that is tucked in. Her long black hair is tied back and flows down her back, and I cannot stop staring at her.

We enter Attorney O'Connell's office, but he isn't there.

"Weird, not sure where he went," she says. She looks embarrassed.

I take a seat in one of the empty chairs just as he pops in and tells us that he will be back in a minute, he just needs to take a quick call.

Miley takes a seat and opens her notebook, skimming her notes in awkward silence.

"So, you have a twin sister?" I ask.

She looks up and smiles. "I'm prettier, smarter, and funnier."

I laugh. "I concur."

She goes back to reading her notes, but I'm not done talking to her. I'm going to take advantage of this one-on-one time with her.

"Does it make you uncomfortable that I requested to follow you on Instagram?"

She pauses, still looking at her notebook. "Not really."

"Then why are you trying to hide behind your notes right now?" I ask.

She shuts her book and looks up. "I'm not."

"Does it make you uncomfortable that I told you that you interest me?"

"No."

"Why did you comment on my post about canceling my tour for the rest of the year?"

"What is this, twenty-one questions?" she asks.

"It can be."

"I commented because people were being disrespectful toward someone they don't even know, and it pissed me off. Do you want me to delete it?"

"No. I like that you stuck up for me." I grin.

"Any other questions before our meeting starts?" she asks.

"Actually, yeah. One more."

"Shoot."

"Are you married, Mils?"

She stares at me for a second, and then finally says, "Not anymore," just as Ivan and Attorney O'Connell walk through the door.

Chapter 13

Miley

I think the only photo I have left on social media from my wedding day is one that is clustered in with several others that I posted a couple years ago after my grandmother passed away. Which means Greylan most definitely stalked my Instagram.

"Good to see you, Greylan," Jeff says while shaking his hand and taking a seat.

"I'd like to brief you on our postponement of Greylan's tour before we get started with the legal jargon you're about to hit us with," Ivan interrupts.

"Of course," Jeff responds.

"We publicly announced yesterday that we are canceling ten shows and plan to reschedule them at a later date in 2025. The label caught wind, and rightfully so, they were pissed."

"Our plan was to announce the cancellation and refuse comment thereafter, which is still intact," Greylan chimes in.

"Did you speak with the label?" Jeff asks.

"Yes. This morning," Ivan says, "but everything is good right now. They drew their own conclusion as to why we needed to cancel the tour for the remainder of the year."

"And what was their conclusion?"

"Our lead guitarist's father passed away yesterday. They think that's why we canceled multiple tour dates," Ivan replies.

"I realize I should have done my homework and should know this, but who is your lead guitar player?" Jeff asks honestly.

THE ONE

"Brody Rivers." Greylan answers.

"His father was Richie from Rivers Luck?"

"Yes."

"Oh, wow. Great band. Huge loss. Sorry," he tells the two of them.

They tell him thanks and reassure us that everything is going fine with the label and that they do not intend to comment on anything.

"Do we have an arraignment date yet?" Greylan asks Jeff. "Because I cannot miss the services for Brody's dad. He is one of my best friends, and I need to be there."

If Brody is one of Greylan's best friends, that means that he likely knew his dad pretty well and is really suffering a loss of his own right now.

"Your arraignment date is on Thursday, which is why we needed you back today," Jeff tells him.

I didn't even know that. What the hell.

"Do we need to prepare for that?" Ivan asks.

"No. We just need to show up, plead not guilty, and then they will schedule the hearing. But your presence is mandatory," he tells Greylan.

"Do we know when the hearing is going to be?" he responds.

"Unfortunately, no. I was able to expedite the arraignment after speaking with the chief of police, but once you're arraigned, we will be at a standstill. The judge will schedule the hearing at the court's convenience."

Greylan looks nervous and anxious. I know he doesn't know what to do or say, so he allows Ivan to do most of the talking.

"What's the plan?" Ivan asks.

"We are going to plead not guilty. I have the surveillance from outside of the bar and also the body cam video from the officer who arrested you." He looks at Greylan. "These videos won't be played at the arraignment, but we will submit them as exhibits for our pending hearing."

"Are there any concerns pertaining to the footage?" Greylan asks.

"Miley, can you set up the videos for us to review?"

Oh, we are going to watch them right here, right now?

I wish I had watched them beforehand, but once I retrieved them, I brought them straight to Jeff like a dumbass.

This is going to be a first for all of us, I think.

"Will do." I stand up to go and get the first video ready.

Greylan

When Miley pulls up the video on the large mounted monitor that's on the office wall, I start to internally panic. I only remember flashbacks after the altercation. I remember I was so heated that I went outside to call Ivan and noticed my phone was dead, and I asked my friend Jensen for his keys so I could go charge my phone. I didn't think anything of it.

I hold my breath when Miley clicks the play button from the wireless mouse next to her notebook.

When the video starts, you can see the door slam open, and I walk out fast, holding my hand and bending over. Jensen and Liam, my old college buddies, are right behind me, making sure I'm okay.

I look over toward Ivan to see his reaction when it's confirmed that the two of them didn't feed the fuel. His expression is blank.

The video continues, and you can clearly see me pull out my phone from my left pocket and then realize that it's dead. I ask Jensen for his keys so I can go to the car and wait for the cops just as Craig's stupid ass comes stumbling out the door with a beer in his hand and almost face-plants.

"YOU JUST FUCKED THAT MOTHERFUCKER UP!" he yells.

This is so embarrassing to watch.

I turn my back to him and walk toward Jensen's car without saying a word. We tolerate Craig, but he most definitely never grew up. He thinks he's twenty-one, and I'm pretty sure he still lives in his parents' basement.

I read the room, and they are all glued to the screen, including Miley. She looks like she is holding her breath.

THE ONE

I look back at the screen, and I am now opening the car door, sitting half on the driver seat, half off, one leg still planted on the pavement where the car is parked.

You can see me move a wire in the car, obviously the charger, plug in my phone, and place it in the cup holder. I then adjust my body, turning it completely so that I'm seated sideways on the seat and both feet are outside of the car. The door is still open. I am talking to Jensen in the video, and Liam is trying to get Craig to sit on the bench outside. Shortly after, it appears that I am on my phone talking to likely Ivan when the cruiser pulls up.

"Miley, can you pause the video?" Attorney O'Connell asks, and she does. "From what I can see, you do not have any intention to operate the vehicle."

"I would never drive a car after drinking."

"I think that this video is great for your case. You never put two feet inside the car, and you never shut the door. This will definitely work to our advantage."

Miley presses play on the video again, and you can see the officer walk over to me and asks me a few questions. You can't hear what is being said because of the distance between the surveillance camera and where we were standing. A few minutes later, the officer walks into the bar, and we just stay there and wait.

"Do you want me to fast-forward until the officer comes back out?" Miley asks.

"Yes," Attorney O'Connell responds.

She fast-forwards the video until headlights pull up.

"Play it," Attorney O'Connell says out loud.

Miley does, and you see Ivan walking toward me as I stand there waiting, and he looks livid. He yells at me in the video, and then it looks like he and Jensen exchange some words.

Soon after, the officer exits the pub and walks over to me, Jensen, and Ivan. The officer then turns me around and cuffs me. Ivan is losing his shit the entire time.

"Do you remember what he said to you right there?" Attorney O'Connell asks.

"No."

THE ONE

"He was reading him his Miranda rights," Ivan interrupts.

"Miley, can you switch the video to the body cam footage?"

The video begins right when the officer exits his vehicle and walks toward us and says, "What's going on? Which one of you guys were involved in the fight inside the bar?"

I admit that it was me.

He then asks, "Why is there a problem?"

And I respond, "I was at the bar ordering a drink when some jackass I knew from high school kept talking shit to me, and when I was walking away, he grabbed my arm, pulling it back, making me drop my beer, and out of self-defense, I turned around and punched him in the face."

"Who was the other person involved?"

"Rob White."

"You said he grabbed your arm from behind when you were walking away, and you punched him?"

"Yes, sir."

"When did this begin?"

"About ten minutes ago."

"Okay. I am just going to get a statement from the other party inside, and I will be right back. Hang tight," he says and walks into the bar.

The video is still playing on the screen.

Is it going to show the interaction between Rob White and the officer and what his side of the story was?

My stomach bottoms out all the way to the floor.

I can't breathe.

I can't watch this.

What if he says something about my sister? I can't handle this.

I am about to have a full-blown panic attack.

"Can you please pause it?"

Chapter 14

Miley

I press pause on the video and look at Greylan as he stands from his chair. His eyes widened, their pupils dilating like saucers as he stares at the mounted monitor. He doesn't look okay. His face is pale, and his jaw is clenched tightly.

"You good?" Ivan asks him.

"I need a second. Please excuse me," Greylan says as he exits Jeff's home office.

Jeff looks very confused and asks Ivan what is wrong with Greylan, but Ivan isn't sure and tells us he is going to just check on him quickly and leaves as well.

Something is off right now. Like they are hiding something. I think they are nervous to hear whatever the victim is about to say to the officer that was recorded on the body cam. I knew we shouldn't have hit them with this, and they should have reviewed it prior to meeting with us.

"Do you think they are hiding something?" I ask Jeff.

"Possibly with the altercation, but right now, my only focus is on the DWI charge, and these videos are gold for us."

"Maybe we should ask him if he wants to view them privately before we all sit and watch them together?" I suggest.

"We don't have time for that."

Heartless as ever.

"Should I check on them?" I ask just as Ivan walks back into the home office.

"Everything okay?" Jeff asks Ivan.

He sits back down in his chair. "He needs a few minutes, but can I talk to you privately?"

I feel like the two of them look at me simultaneously. I can take the hint.

"Would anyone like a drink?" I ask, standing from my chair.

"Some water for everyone would be great, Miley."

I open the office door just as I hear the front door shut.

Did Greylan leave?

I head to the kitchen to grab four bottles of water when I notice Greylan sitting on the front porch.

Leave him alone, Miley.
Don't go outside.
You can't control every situation.

I disregard the angel on my right and head toward the front door, open it, and walk out.

Greylan is sitting on a chair with his hands in his head and doesn't even turn when I open the door.

I sit in the chair next to him for a solid sixty seconds before asking, "Are you okay?"

He slowly lifts his head up, turning it slightly to the side, looking me dead in the eyes, and tells me, "Not at all."

Greylan's posture is slumped, his shoulders dropping and his head bowed. His eyes are filled with a sense of resignation, and the expression he wears on his face is straight sadness. His overall demeanor conveys a sense of hopelessness.

"Do you want me to leave you alone?"

"No."

"Do you want to talk about it?"

"No."

I'm confused. I don't know how to help him unless he opens up. And that is the only thing right now that I want to do right now. I want to help.

I watch him for a moment and notice that he is trying to calm his body down with a breathing technique. I can tell, I've done this a thousand times.

I stand up, without thinking, and walk in front of his body, squatting down so that we are eye level.

He looks up.

"Greylan, what is wrong?"

He stares at me, looking lost and completely out of it, and then looks down at the ground. "I can't describe the way I am feeling, and I can't talk about it either," he says while taking a long drag of air in through his nose and slowly letting it out through his mouth.

I can relate to this. I've built my entire life around trying to avoid this exact feeling. The severity could possibly be what Greylan is experiencing right now.

I again speak without thinking. "Does it feel like you're being trapped in a whirlwind of intense fear?"

He looks up. "Yeah."

"Is your heart racing?"

He nods.

I pause for a second so he doesn't think I am trying to be his shrink.

I place my hands on the top of his knee caps, and his eyes immediately melt into my entire soul. I give them a quick squeeze and tell him, "I think you're having an anxiety attack."

He nods, but that's it.

When he doesn't respond, I stand from my position to leave him alone.

"Don't go."

And I don't. I just sit back down in the chair next to him and stay present.

We sit there in silence for a good five minutes when he finally says, "How did you know exactly how I am feeling?"

I pause, wishing I had some time to come up with a response, but I don't.

When people think of anxiety, they think about someone who can't handle big crowds or stressful situations. And I always thought that too, until I was diagnosed with anxiety last year. When my doctor told me I had a phobia/panic disorder, I laughed. Maybe because I didn't understand the definition of it. Having an intense fear of a specific situation. My disorder left me with intense symptoms of restlessness, irritability, and sleep disturbances.

The only time I didn't have anxiety is when I was at work, when I was preoccupied, or when I was drinking alcohol. And I used all three options to try and stop it. Until one night, almost two years ago, I had a panic attack so bad that I almost drove myself to the hospital in the middle of the night. A panic that attacked my body with an intense surge of fear. Within seconds, I was sweating, I couldn't breathe, and my entire body turned hot, and I began to tingle everywhere. I literally felt like I was going to die. And I never, ever wanted to feel something like that ever again.

I told Sutton about it, and she told me I needed to make an appointment and tell my doctor. She would even go with me, so I finally agreed and went.

I now have to take medication before I lie down in my bed at night. Because that's where I thought about it most. *What happens when I die?* When my brain was unwinding from the day but couldn't fully shut down. But now that I took that big leap to seek help, I'm doing pretty damn good, I must say.

"I've lived with anxiety my entire life and have had several attacks." I pause, looking him in the eyes. "It's incredibly overwhelming and frightening."

"What helps you get through yours?" he asks.

That's a good question. I've tried everything to subside the evilness that lingers every night, trying to scare me when I lay my head down to go to sleep. Medicating myself is the only thing that has helped. But I think I should keep that to myself and respond as I would before I started seeing my therapist.

"Not being alone usually helps me. And once the panic is gone, talking about what caused it has helped too. I've called my sister on multiple occasions. What usually helps you?" I ask him.

"Avoiding being back near my hometown."

Okay, I am following. Being here is a trigger for him. And the guy he punched in the face might be connected to the struggles he's been facing.

"Have you tried talking to someone about it? I'm sure your family would listen and support whatever it is you're going through."

Greylan stares blankly at the trees ahead and responds, "Let's get back inside."

Greylan

The instant Miley's touch met my knees, an electric current surged through me. My panic started to melt away, and I could feel my heart slowing down. The fear began to fade and was replaced by a sense of calm and peace. It was like nothing I have ever felt before. In that moment, I knew I had found something truly special.

I head back inside and hold the door open for Miley. She doesn't say anything as she enters. She just heads back into the office and sits back down next to Attorney O'Connell.

"Sorry about that. I just needed a minute," I tell him.

"Ivan briefed me on your relationship with the victim. We do not need to review the footage of his conversation with the officer in a group. However, we will need to know what was said seeing as the officer exited the bar after speaking with him and immediately placed you under arrest."

"I would be okay with you asking me questions via email after you review their conversation, but this isn't something I am able to watch right now."

"Understood. Let's do this. Miley, please email Greylan and Ivan the video for their review. Once I review it in depth, Miley will email you with any questions I have. How does that sound?"

"Good," I tell him.

"She will get that over to you shortly. Let's wrap it up for today, and we can meet back up tomorrow to finalize everything before the arraignment," Attorney O'Connell says.

"What time?" Ivan asks.

"Miley will look over my schedule and email you soon." Attorney O'Connell stands, and I follow. He shakes my hand. "Thank you for coming in. Miley will see you out, and we will be in touch tonight."

THE ONE

As we walk out, Ivan is stopped by his aunt again. He looks at me, and I tell him that I am going to head out and that I will text him later.

Miley follows me to the door and opens it. I don't say anything to her, but only because I don't know what to say, so I just leave. I head down the stairs and hear her shut the door just as I hit the pavement.

"Greylan."

I pause, still facing forward.

"If you ever need someone to talk to, just let me know."

I look back and give her a weak smile. "Thank you, Mils."

I go to my rental and head back to my hotel room.

As soon as I get to my room, my phone alerts me that I have a new email.

> From: Miley Miller
> Date: October 25, 2024 5:37 PM
> Subject: Meeting with Attorney O'Connell
> To: Greylan Asher
> Cc: Ivan Stevens
> 📎 attachment
>
> Greylan,
>
> I wanted to let you know that Attorney O'Connell is available to meet with you tomorrow morning at 9 AM at his home office.
>
> I've also attached the footage from the officer's body camera for your review.
>
> Please let me know if 9 AM doesn't work for you.
>
> Sincerely,
> Miley Miller
> Executive Legal Assistant
> O'Connell Law Office, LLC

THE ONE

I open the attachment, press play on the video, and it starts from the beginning.

I replay our interaction over and over again. Who is this guy? And why did he give me a DWI? Does he know Rob?

The video keeps playing, and I can feel the panic begin to rise. I can't handle this.

The officer walks inside toward a group of three men and asks which one of them was involved in a physical altercation. Rob slightly raises his hand, stepping forward.

I physically can't breathe.

"Can we talk somewhere a little more quiet?" The officer asks him.

My heart begins to race. It's beating so fast in my caving chest, I feel like I'm about to die.

They walk into the bathroom hall together.

"What happened?" The officer asks Rob.

"I told him I loved his sis—"

I hit the side button on my phone so fucking fast, shutting it down, and then I begin to drown.

I try to breathe, but I can't. I try every method that I've learned. With long slow pulls in through my nose and a slow breath out, I think about the things that help get Miley through an attack.

Not being alone. Talking about it.

I grab my phone, open it, and find my Instagram app. I tap it and search for Miley's profile and click on Message.

Greylan Asher: I can't watch the video

Miley immediately responds.

Miley Miller: Are you okay, Greylan?

I go ahead and tell her the truth because at this point, I have absolutely nothing to lose. My head is already under the water.

Greylan Asher: No.

THE ONE

>Miley Miller: Where are you?

When I don't respond right away, she sends another message.

>Miley Miller: ?????
>Greylan Asher: Renaissance on State
>Miley Miller: I'll be there in 5. Room number?
>Greylan Asher: 414

Chapter 15

Miley

After I left Jeff's house, I went back to the office to tie up some loose ends. The second he told me that he wasn't okay, I started packing up my stuff. Thankfully, his hotel is only minutes away.

I grab my phone and purse and leave the office. I keep my car parked in the lot and walk up State Street to the Renaissance Hotel. I head straight to the elevators and press the number 4 while I try to catch my breath. I didn't necessarily run here, but I did walk up that hill rather quickly. I find room 414 and knock on the door. I'm nervous, but I try not to think about that.

It takes him a moment to open the door, but when he finally does, I walk into him and wrap my arms tightly around his waist, resting the side of my head on his chest, and hug him.

He lets go of the door, causing it to shut. I feel his arms, warm and strong, encircle me, and I feel a surge of something I can't quite name. Something I've never experienced in my entire life. It's not just the warmth from his body or the comfort from his presence. It's a strange tingling sensation that's spreading through me.

I close my eyes and melt into him. The scent of pine needles and damp earth fill my senses, and I realize, in that very moment, that I'd never felt so at peace.

We stay like this for several minutes, and I savor it.

After a while, I can hear his rapid heartbeat slowly decrease, and his breathing begins to even out.

"Thank you," he says.

I simultaneously loosen my grip and turn my head so that I am looking straight into his dark eyes. "Are you okay, Greylan?"

"I am now."

I smile and bow my head so that my forehead is on his chest. "That's because I give the best hugs."

He pulls me in tighter and rests his chin on the top of my head. "Stay for a little bit."

"That's probably a bad idea," I say, speaking into his chest.

"Dinner."

I shake my head no.

Greylan steps back. "Have dinner with me and talk."

He's following my method on how to reduce the strength of an anxiety attack. I can't tell him no. That would be terrible.

"Okay."

He smiles at me, and oh my fucking god, I melt. I'm practically a puddle.

He walks farther into the very spacious hotel room and takes a seat on the couch. "What shall it be?" he asks.

Being the greedy asshole that I am and leaving zero room for negotiating, I tell him, "Tacos."

"Sounds good," he says.

"I'm just going to text my sister real quick to let her know that I will be home later than usual."

He acknowledges my statement and orders the food on his phone while I text Sutton.

> **Miley**: Hey, I am going to be home later than usual. FYI
> **Sutton**: Why?
> **Miley**: I'm with Greylan... I will tell you later. Bye.

I know that she's not going to accept that response and will have something else to say. I smirk when I see the three dots moving as she types out her response.

"What's so funny?" Greylan asks.

"Nothing."
I look back down at my phone and literally laugh out loud.

> **Sutton**: get it, girl
> **Sutton**: 🔥

I look up, and Greylan has the biggest smirk on his face, staring at me.

God, this man is fucking perfect. Ten out of ten, without a doubt.

"Beef or chicken?" he asks.

"Both."

"All set, twenty minutes." He tosses his phone on the end table. "Do you want something to drink?"

"Water is good, thank you," I say, walking over to the couch and taking a seat.

Greylan hands me a bottle of water and sits next to me. "Seriously, Miley. Thank you for coming here and helping me."

I give him a concerned smile. "Do you want to talk about it?"

"I'm not sure yet."

I can tell he's thinking about it, so I just patiently wait.

"What causes your anxiety?" he asks.

Oh. Okay. Maybe he wants to learn more about my anxiety in hopes that it'll open him up to speak about his.

For a very long time, I couldn't talk about it. But now I'm mostly okay. My only concern now is that someone might think that I am actually full-blown crazy.

"I have a deep-seated fear of death."

I pause for a second to gauge his reaction. It's hard to read, so I just wrap it up quickly so we can move on about me and talk more about him.

"It sounds crazy, I know. But it's been like this since I was a child. I have to take medicine in order to sleep at night," I say, hoping to end the conversation.

"Your feelings are absolutely valid. No one can understand your emotions like you can because they're not in your head."

"Thanks."

"Have you always had to take medication?" he asks.

"No, I actually didn't get treatment until last year. I had an attack so bad that I almost drove myself to the hospital. I knew at that moment that I needed help. And I now have a kick-ass therapist."

"Do you still have them? The attacks."

"No, not so much anymore. I've had a lot of therapy, and I also had to make some pretty big adjustments to my life. I'm mostly okay now."

"What do you mean?" he asks.

"You can't just take a pill and magically be fine. It takes a lot of work to face a fear so massive that it causes a panic attack."

"Was one of your life-altering decisions to get a divorce?"

Nope. This is not something I want to discuss with him, not right now at least. I dodge the question and clear my throat. "Your turn. Why does being back home give you anxiety?"

He leans his head back on the top of the couch and stares at the ceiling. He's thinking, I can tell. After a minute, he turns his head to look at me, and I can physically see the pain in his glossy eyes. He hurts so bad.

"Because it's where my sister was killed."

Greylan

Talking to Miley is easy but also very hard. I know she is going to have a lot of questions now that she knows my sister died. Questions that I'm not sure I'm ready to answer. Because it brings back memories. And remembering hurts.

I'll forever feel the loss, and it will never be okay.

Miley looks at me, really looks at me. "I can't imagine what you're feeling, losing a sibling, the pain that's taken a permanent place in your heart. I'm really sorry, Greylan."

Miley is genuine. She doesn't pity me. She literally dropped what she was doing to come save me. She's real, she's honest. And it makes me want to open up more.

THE ONE

"The guy I punched at the bar, he dated her."

Just as she's about to ask me another question, my phone chimes. Saved by the bell. It's a text from DoorDash letting me know our food is outside of my hotel room door.

"Food is here."

I grab it and walk over to the small table in the room, and we dig in.

"So good," she says with her mouth full, and I just smile at her.

This girl is something.

She doesn't care that I'm famous.

She doesn't care if she talks with her mouth full.

She has zero filter.

And she's making me really happy.

"What's your favorite food?" I ask.

"Are we playing twenty-one questions again? Because you must give to receive." She smirks.

I laugh. "Okay, let's play. What's your question?"

"What's your favorite food?"

I shake my head. "You're a question stealer."

"Fine," she laughs. "I'll answer first. I love me a chicken quesadilla."

"Steak," I tell her while biting into my beef taco.

"Next question?" she asks.

"You can ask one now," I respond with my mouth full.

She thinks for a second. "What inspired you to become a singer-songwriter?"

I've been asked that question a lot over the last several years, and my answer is always the same. "Nothing in particular. I just really like music and enjoy singing. People started to tell me I was good at it, so I kept going."

"Do you have a favorite song?"

"That's two questions. But no, I don't have a favorite song. I love each and every song I write. If I don't love it, I won't record it or sing it...if that makes any sense. My turn. What's your favorite song?"

"Easy. Everlast, 'What It's Like.'"

THE ONE

I nod, agreeing, because it's actually a great song.

"What was your sister's name?"

I finish chewing. Not expecting her to ask that.

"Jillian."

"Jillian," she repeats. "Beautiful name."

"What's your sister's name?" I ask.

She smiles. "Sutton."

"Do you live together?"

"Yes. She is going through a divorce and bunking with me at the moment. Where do you live?"

"Nashville. Where do you live?"

"Guilderland," she replies, finishing her first taco and grabbing another.

Miley fills me in on more about herself and her twin, including the nitty-gritty details of her sister's divorce. We also chat about her childhood and family. They sound incredibly close and happy, which I absolutely love. It makes this ache in my chest for my own family grow stronger. A sudden urge hits me to finish the video, but I know I can't do it alone.

"Will you watch it with me?"

"The video?" she questions.

"Yeah."

"Of course."

We finish our food, and I sit back on the couch, patting the spot next to me. Once she sits down, I reach over to the light on the end table and shut it off.

"What're you doing?" she asks.

"I'd rather watch it in the dark since I'm probably going to spiral."

When she doesn't say anything, I unlock my phone and open up my email, clicking on the video again.

"Did you watch it yet?" I ask her.

"No."

It starts to play from the beginning, and we watch in silence on the small screen in my hand. Once my interaction with the officer is done, I begin to sweat and can feel my heart speed up.

THE ONE

Miley inches her body closer to mine so that we are touching. "Do you want me to hold the phone?"

I hand it to her and wipe my sweaty palms on my jeans while trying to breathe at the same time.

Miley adjusts herself, propping her feet up, almost hugging her knees. She places the phone up on them, balancing it, and leans into me more.

I leave my hands on my lap as the video continues to play, and I try to focus on my breathing. I can see Miley watching me in the dark, but it doesn't make me feel uncomfortable. It's actually making me feel better that she's here with me.

The officer is now walking toward the hallway with Rob, and I can feel my panic begin to rise.

"What happened?" the officer asks Rob.

I close my eyes. I can't watch it anymore.

"I told him I loved his sister, and then he punched me in the face and threw me into a wall."

I physically can't breathe. My body is shaking. My heart is pounding so hard that I can hear it.

"What happened prior to you telling him that?"

"We exchanged words, but I can't remember exactly what was said."

"What happened after you 'exchanged words' with each other?"

"He punched me in the face."

"So you didn't provoke him by grabbing his arm, causing him to spill his drink?" the officer questions him, and it catches me off guard.

"Nope."

"You sure?" the officer asks. "Or can you not remember? Your eyes look very red and glossy. Are you using again?"

Rob laughs in his face. "I remember what I said."

And I remember too, clear as day. I know exactly what is going to come out of his mouth, and I can feel myself spiraling. I want to grab the phone and throw it.

Miley reaches her hand up and touches the back of my neck.

THE ONE

"I told that motherfucker that she was going to die sooner or later," Rob says to the officer.

And I drown.

"Please turn it off," I choke out, and Miley shuts it off and places it next to her on the couch.

She doesn't say anything, and neither do I. We just sit there in the dark as I have my panic attack.

After a while, I feel her head fall to my shoulder, and her fingers move up and down my neck, massaging it.

I rest my hand on her thigh, pulling her closer, and she brings her right hand up to my chest, placing it directly over my heart.

And that's how we stay.

Attached.

Chapter 16

Miley

When I open my eyes, they focus on the lit television across the room. My head is on Greylan's lap, and his arm is resting on my hip. I must have fallen asleep. I slowly lift myself off him and check the time on my phone. It's 1:27 in the morning. I have thirteen missed calls and six text messages from Sutton.

I look over, and Greylan is sound asleep, his head leaning back on the couch, slightly tilted to the side.

I quietly grab my things and tiptoe out of his room, hoping I don't wake him. I walk to the elevator and quickly respond to Sutton.

<u>Miley</u>: I feel asleep!!!
<u>Miley</u>: OMW!
<u>Miley</u>: Sorry!!!!!!!

The elevator stops on the first floor, and I exit, heading toward the doors to walk back to my car. As soon as I am open to leave, someone calls my name. "Miley."

I look back, and Greylan is standing there, half asleep.

"Where are you going?" he asks.

"I have to go home. Sorry, I fell asleep. I'll see you in a couple hours."

"Where is your car parked?"

"At the office. I walked here."

He walks forward, pulling his hoodie over his head and opening the door for me.

"What're you doing?" I ask.

"Walking you to your car."

"You don't need to do that, I'll be fine. It's just down the hill."

"You are not walking in downtown Albany alone at one thirty in the morning."

"Fine. But I'm driving you back here so you're not walking alone at one thirty in the morning."

Thank god the walk is somewhat quick because it is really cold out, and all I have on is a long-sleeved blouse and pants.

"Which one is your car?" he asks.

There are only two cars left in the parking lot this late at night, and one is probably the night security guard.

"The black S4."

Greylan walks over to it and opens the driver-side door for me. I tell him thanks as I get in, and then he shuts it, walking over to the passenger side.

I blast the heat and start to back out when I notice Greylan staring at me.

"You could have just stayed the night instead of trying to sneak out."

"Coulda. But Sutton was minutes away from driving here, and she would've knocked the door down."

I head up State Street and pass the hotel on the opposite side of the street. "I am just going to turn around and let you out right in front," I tell him as I do a U-turn at the top of the hill. I throw my four-ways on and illegally park in front so that he can get out.

"Thank you again, Miley. I'll see you in a little bit." He smiles and gets out and heads back into the hotel lobby.

Once I see that he is in, I drive home.

When I get inside, I head straight to my room to let Sutton know I am home so she isn't worried anymore. She didn't respond to my messages, so she's either pissed or passed out.

"Hey, I'm back. Sorry, I fell asleep." I whisper, but she doesn't respond.

THE ONE

I grab sweatpants and a hoodie and change quickly and then go brush my teeth. Once I am done, I slip into bed in an attempt to fall back to sleep.

"Let's not do that again. I was worried," Sutton says half asleep.

"I'm sorry."

"You're lucky I can track your phone. I knew where you were when you initially messaged me and saw that you were still there," she continues. "Next time I will show up, so don't test me."

I know she isn't messing around. She really will show up. I am actually surprised she didn't.

"I know, sorry."

"I want the details in the morning. Love you, night."

"Good night, I love you."

I shut my eyes, and all I can think about is Greylan.

Greylan

Miley was right. Not being alone definitely helps. I fought through my panic for about twenty minutes, and she stayed by my side the entire time. Once she fell asleep, I thought that maybe I should wake her but decided not to. I wanted her to stay. I wanted her to be with me.

I watched television for a little while and must have fallen asleep too. When I heard the hotel door click shut, I knew she left. I grabbed my key card, slipped on my shoes, and headed down the stairs after her.

I have to be at my attorney's house by nine, and it's about a fifteen-minute drive without traffic. I jump in a quick shower and get ready. I throw on jeans, a hoodie, and a hat and head to my car at eight thirty.

I get there ten minutes early and send Ivan a text letting him know.

Greylan: Here. ETA?
Ivan: Few mins

THE ONE

I debate waiting for him, but the second I see Miley's Audi pull up, I get out and walk to the front door, meeting here.

"You have a nice car," I tell her.

"Thank you." She knocks on the door, and Attorney O'Connell answers it while talking to someone on his cell phone. He nods for us to come inside.

We walk in, and he tells us that he is just finishing up a call and he will be in shortly.

Miley unpacks her laptop and notebook then takes off her jacket and hangs it on the rack near the door. "Do you want water or anything?" she asks.

"No, I'm all set."

"We never finished the video."

"I know. And no one emailed me any questions."

She thinks for a moment. "Just tell him you reviewed most of it and see if he has any questions."

I tell her okay just as Ivan and his uncle enter.

"Good morning," he says, taking a seat. "Did you have a chance to review the footage?"

"I watched most of it." I look over to Ivan, and he has a concerned look on his face. He called me a couple times last night, but I kept sending it to voice mail. Not because I didn't want to talk to him, but because Miley was asleep on my lap.

"I got tied up last night, so I didn't get to review it. Miley, can you queue it up please?"

I freeze. I definitely don't want to watch this again. "If you don't mind, I'd rather not watch it again. Do you mind if I step out?"

"That's fine. Miley, can you see Greylan to the kitchen? Maybe get some coffee? I will come get you once Ivan and I are finished," he says.

Miley queues up the footage for Attorney O'Connell, and we both go out to the kitchen.

"Dodged that bullet," I tell Miley as I sit at the island.

She smiles. "Do you want coffee?"

"Yes, please. Just a splash of cream."

THE ONE

She goes into the cabinet and pulls out two coffee cups and fills them with the pot of coffee that is already made. She adds creamer to mine and walks it over to me and then proceeds to make hers with a fuckton of cream and sugar.

"Would you like some coffee with that cream?" I laugh.

"Play nice."

"Oh, I wish you'd let me play nice." I wink, and she practically spits her coffee all over the place.

"Jesus, Greylan. Tell me how you really feel." She pauses then quickly adds, "Actually, don't. Don't tell me."

I bark out a laugh just as Ivan comes into the kitchen.

"How much of this video did you watch?" he asks.

"Until he told the officer what he said to me at the bar."

"My uncle needs you to come back in."

We all go back in, and the video is paused at my arrest. I take a seat and look over at Ivan. I really do not want to watch this right now.

"Miley, can you rewind the video for me? I can't figure it out."

Miley begins to rewind it.

"All right, stop right there."

The video stops at where Miley and I left off last night.

"Did you watch this part, Greylan?" Attorney O'Connell asks me.

"No. This is where I stopped the video last night. I had a hard time watching it and didn't want to continue. Sorry."

"I think watching this part is important, and I think we have something bigger on our hands than we initially thought," he says. "Miley, play it."

The video plays and the officer says, "It sounds like you instigated him."

Rob is swaying in the video, likely drunk and high. He slurs, "You need to arrest him for hitting me."

"I didn't see him hit you. Right now, it's 'he said, she said.'" The officer writes something in his small book then continues, "I will have to see if the bar has any surveillance."

THE ONE

Rob yells at the officer, and the officer tells him he will write up the report and that he will be in touch. Rob then appears to get angry at that response and yells, "You're not going to arrest that asshole for hitting me?"

The officer ignores him and then starts to walk away when Rob says, "Wasn't he just outside in the driver seat of a running vehicle? I'm pretty sure that's illegal, isn't it, Officer? I'd hate for your chief to get the surveillance from outside of the bar and for you to lose your job because you're not doing it correctly."

And the officer freezes.

"Pause it, Miley," Attorney O'Connell says.

Chapter 17

Miley

Jeff is very confident that he can wipe away Greylan's DWI, especially with the videos we now have. After our meeting is wrapped up, I head into the office, and Jeff calls the district attorney to see what can be done...but the answer is nothing. Nothing can be done until after the arraignment. And we still don't know if this Rob guy intends to press charges on Greylan or if he is just looking for a free handout, but either way, if charged, it's likely only going to be a violation.

When I walk into the office, Tracey holds a finger up to me, essentially asking me to stop for a second while she speaks to someone on the phone. "She just walked in, I will transfer you now," she says and places the call on hold. "You have a call on line 2," she quickly says before answering another call.

Great. Not even a rundown on who it is or what they want.

I go to my office, set my shit down, and answer the call waiting for me. "This is Miley."

"Hey."

And with that one word, I know right away who is on the other end of the phone.

"Hey."

"Sorry to bother you. I just have two quick questions."

"Okay, ask away. I am all ears."

"Do you think I should be good to fly out Friday morning and stay the weekend in Nashville to attend the services for Brody's dad? I could be back by Monday."

"That should be fine. Second question?"

"Will you have dinner with me?"

I freeze. This isn't a good idea.

If I continue to hang out with him, I am going to catch feelings, and I can't let that happen. We are two different people living two completely different lives in two different states. It would never work, and I would end up getting hurt.

"That's not a good idea."

"For you maybe."

"I'm sorry. I can't, Greylan."

He is silent for a moment. "Can I at least have your number?"

"Like my cell phone?"

"Um, yeah?" he asks as if it's a question to a question.

"Why?" My response flies right out of my mouth.

"Because I am interested, Miley."

I am at a loss for words. Greylan Asher can legitimately have any female in this entire world, and he's interested in me? And he wants my number? And to take me to dinner? I don't understand.

I look at the number on the caller ID and write it down, knowing he's likely calling me from his cell phone. I decide to abruptly end the call, and maybe I will text him later after I have time to process everything coming out of his mouth.

"Sorry, Jeff is pacing. I gotta go." I hang up, not giving him an opportunity to respond.

The phone feels hot in my hand, the weight of his words pressing down on me. I need to distract myself, to push the image of him, his voice, his impossible interest, out of my mind, even for a little while.

After my call with Greylan, I make my way down to the basement to grab lunch with Colbie. It's so hard not to talk to her about him, so I make it a point to ask her random questions about shit that I could give zero fucks about. Questions about stocks and investments and other various things that I've never, ever mentioned in our two and a half decades of friendship. Thankfully she goes along with it.

My afternoon flies by, and before I know it, it's a little after five o'clock. I decide to scoot out early and head home, knowing I am going to get an earful from Sutton.

THE ONE

When I get there, she is cooking dinner and jamming out to music.

"What's for dinner?" I ask, startling her.

"Chicken parm. Alexa, off!" she yells at the device, but it still doesn't shut off. "ALEXA, OFF!"

I laugh. "You don't need to scream at it."

"Shut up. Tell me everything and start from the beginning."

Okay, she isn't messing around. Do tell or die. Understood.

"We had a meeting yesterday, and during it, we played the surveillance video from the incident along with the body camera video that the officer was wearing. Greylan couldn't watch it anymore and had a panic attack at Jeff's house. I helped him through it and told him the methods I have used in the past, not being alone and talking about my issues…and then we all went our separate ways, and I emailed him the video he was unable to watch, as instructed, and then he reached out. So I went to his hotel and helped him through another attack, but then fell asleep."

"You're lying out of your asshole. I said tell me everything."

Yup. She's definitely not fucking around.

"When I got to his hotel room, he was practically hyperventilating. I walked in and, without thinking, wrapped my arms around his body, attempting to calm him down. We stayed like that for a while, and once he was calm, he asked me to stay for dinner. He ordered tacos—"

"Bonus brownie points right there," she interrupts.

"Anyhoo, we ate the tacos, and then he asked if I'd finish watching the video with him, and I agreed. If you tell anyone this, I will fucking—"

"Shut up and keep going."

"So the guy he punched was his sister's boyfriend."

"Oh shit. Is she mad?" she asks.

"She's dead."

Sutton says nothing.

"This guy poked the bear, and Greylan punched him in the face. I don't know the history and Greylan didn't want to talk about it, but from what I've gathered, this guy might have something to do with his sister's death."

"Wow. Okay. So then what happened?"

"Nothing. He asked me to finish watching the video with him, I agreed, and after we watched it, he had another panic attack, and I held him through it, and in the process, we both fell asleep."

"And that's all that happened?" she questions.

"Yeah. I woke up in the middle of the night and left."

"Please tell me you didn't just duck out without saying anything."

"I tried, but then he woke up. And then this morning, we had a second meeting."

"How'd that go?"

"Well, it ended with him asking me to dinner, me telling him no, and then him asking me for my number."

"Stop it!" she says while plating our food. "And then what?"

"Ugh, I freaked out and pretended Jeff needed me."

"For the love of God, please tell me you gave him your number!"

"Eh."

"Jesus, fuck."

"I took his number from the caller ID and saved it to my contacts…if that's any consolation."

"You are seriously mental. Give me your phone."

"For what?" I ask, but she helps herself, snatching it from off the counter, and it unlocks immediately when she shows her face to the screen. Stupid twin shit.

"Because you're a dumbass."

Miley: My number, as requested.

Greylan

I'm not sure that I've ever been turned down before. I definitely haven't been since being in the spotlight, I know that for sure, so Miley's hard no is catching me off guard.

"Has the label reached out to you regarding anything else?" I ask Ivan during dinner.

"No, they are giving us space. I know Reed will be at the funeral though, so be prepared for that."

"Can I talk to you about something?"

"Anything," he responds.

"When you were with Laurel, how did you know that you really liked her and that it wasn't just some crush?"

"You're joking, right?"

"No."

He blinks, opens his mouth, and then shuts it. "I don't know. I just knew. But fuck that bitch, please don't ever say her name in front of me again."

Alrighty then. It's still a sore subject for him. Noted.

"Why are you asking?"

I scratch my head. "I can't stop thinking about Miley."

"I'm sorry, what?"

"Miley. Miley Miller. I want her."

"No. It'll never work. Leave her alone."

Why wouldn't it? At the very least, why couldn't we at least try to make it work? She is absolutely beautiful and down-to-earth. She calms me down and makes me smile, and I just want her. I need her.

"I can't. There's something about her."

He rolls his eyes at me and takes a sip from his beer just as I get an incoming text message.

Unknown: My number, as requested.

I smile, my fingers flying across the screen.

Greylan: What are you doing?

"Is that her?" Ivan asks just as we pay the bill at the hotel restaurant.

"Yeah. I'm going to head up for the night. I'll call you in the morning." I take the elevator upstairs, and he goes outside to his car. He's staying at his parents' house until we figure out what we are going to do next week. Something I don't even want to begin to think about.

> **Miley**: Having dinner with Sutton. What are you doing?
> **Greylan**: Just had dinner with Ivan. Since you turned me down...

I unlock my hotel door, kick off my shoes, and impatiently wait for her response.

> **Miley**: LOL

She laughs but I'm being serious.

> **Miley**: What did you have for dinner?

She's trying to change the subject.

> **Greylan**: Steak. What did you have for dinner?
> **Miley**: Chicken parm.

I stand from my spot on the floor and untuck my shirt before texting her back.

> **Greylan**: If you could have dinner with one person (living or dead), who would it be?
> **Miley**: Are we playing 21 questions again?
> **Greylan**: We can...

I set my phone down and undress, tossing my clothes near my suitcase, thinking of what to text her next.

> **Miley**: Okay, fine. But if you ask the question, you have to answer it, too.

THE ONE

Oh, this is going to be good. Let's go.

> **Greylan**: The only person I want to have dinner with right now is you.
> **Miley**: You're very persistent. I'd choose Bradley Cooper.
> **Greylan**: Harsh.
> **Miley**: Favorite movie?
> **Greylan**: Die Hard. Your turn.
> **Miley**: Silver Linings Playbook

I smile to myself and text her back.

> **Greylan**: If you could go on a vacation to anywhere, where would you go?
> **Miley**: Easy. Hawaii. You?
> **Greylan**: Hawaii
> **Miley**: You're just saying that.
> **Greylan**: I'm not. I really do want to go to Hawaii.

There's a long wait before the next text. Gray dots dance along the screen before they disappear and reappear.

> **Miley**: Oh, no! There's a spider in the house. What's the move?

I literally laugh out loud at her question. She is so random sometimes.

> **Greylan**: You have the opportunity to ask me any question in the world and you want to know what I would do if I saw a spider?
> **Miley**: I think it's a very important question…
> **Greylan**: I'd get a paper towel, grab it and flush it. What would you do?

> **Miley**: Scream like a little bitch and call for help.

I bark out an even louder laugh and picture her on top of a refrigerator with her cell phone in hand, ready to call 911.

> **Greylan**: Describe yourself in three words.
> **Miley**: That isn't a question.
> **Greylan**: Play along.

I set my phone down for a second and take a deep breath.

> **Miley**: Fine. Honest, Reliable, and Thoughtful. Your turn.

My phone beeps with a text, and my reply is instant.

> **Greylan**: Beautiful, smart, and funny
> **Miley**: Did you just describe yourself as beautiful?

I chuckle and text her back.

> **Greylan**: I was describing you, Mils.
> **Miley**: Oh. I think you were supposed to describe yourself.
> **Greylan**: Okay… Driven. Flexible. Creative. You're up next.

I close my eyes, holding my phone to my chest, waiting for her response.

> **Miley**: Talented, sexy and confident.

Oh, okay. I'll take that.

THE ONE

> **Greylan**: Did you just call me sexy?
> **Miley**: Maybe, maybe not.
> **Greylan**: I'll take that as a yes. You get the next question.
> **Miley**: What's your biggest pet peeve?
> **Greylan**: When someone is constantly on their phone. You?

I fucking hate when someone is always staring at their phone.

> **Miley**: Being late / people arriving late.
> **Greylan**: My turn. Why did you get divorced?

There's a delay. Dots forming and then disappearing.

> **Miley**: Long story short, he was a douchebag. I'm getting tired. Lack of sleep last night.
> **Greylan**: Sweet dreams, Miley. You still owe me 16 answers.
> **Miley**: We can pick it back up tomorrow. Goodnight, Greylan.

Chapter 18

Miley

Trying to sleep last night after texting with Greylan was impossible. I tossed and turned all night, unable to get him out of my head. When I finally did fall asleep, I had a dream that I had the best sex of my entire life with him. And when I tell you that I woke up heated, I am not joking. I was throbbing. I haven't been intimate in well over two years, so I am definitely overdue. The worst part, not being able to do anything about it because Sutton was in my bed.

I go back to my office after grabbing my third cup of coffee of the day, and Jeff stops me.

"Can you send Ivan and Greylan the details for tomorrow's arraignment? We need to be there by ten. I need you to come with us."

What? I've never gone to an arraignment with him before. Why now?

"Why do I need to be there?" I question.

"Because you're tight with the clerk. I need you to see if he can be arraigned last so that there's no one else in the chambers when he sees the judge."

"Can't I just call her and request that he go last?"

"No. Then they will look into the name. I need you to put her on the spot. We will plan to get there twenty minutes early, and then you can work your magic."

I am so tired, I can't even think straight. I just tell him okay and go back to my office and send the email to Greylan and Ivan.

THE ONE

From: Miley Miller
Date: October 27, 2024 2:16 PM
Subject: Court Tomorrow
To: Greylan Asher
Cc: Ivan Stevens

Greylan,

    We will need to leave the office at 9 AM to head to Saratoga for your court appearance.
    Please don't come into the office; we can meet in the parking lot and follow each other up. We will be requesting that you are arraigned last so that we can speak with the judge privately in chambers.
    Attorney O'Connell will handle all the talking; you just need to be present. Please wear a suit for the appearance.
    If you have any questions, let me know.

Sincerely,
Miley Miller
Executive Legal Assistant
O'Connell Law Office, LLC

A few minutes after I send the email, I get a text. Speaking of the devil.

Greylan: Why wouldn't we just drive together?

I don't even know how to answer that question, so I respond honestly.

Miley: I'm just taking orders from the boss. Want me to ask him?
Greylan: No. Are you going to be there tomorrow?

THE ONE

Miley: My presence is mandated.
Greylan: I just talked to Ivan. He's already going to be up there so he will just meet us at the municipal center.
Miley: Okay. I will let Jeff know.
Greylan: Sounds good

*****

Instead of going straight home after work, I head to the mall to get some new clothes to wear tomorrow. I want to look good and feel good. Sutton's working the night shift at the hospital, so there is no need for me to rush home.

I find a cute pair of tan high-waisted pants that form perfectly to my body, and I match it with a white silky blouse and nude pointed heels.

When I get home, I take a long hot shower and task myself with washing my hair. Since Sutton isn't here, I eat an edible and grab a White Claw, knowing that I won't be judged in my own home while trying to enjoy myself.

I start blow-drying my hair just as my phone chirps.

Greylan: If you could have any superpower, what would you pick?

I respond right away.

Miley: Seriously?
Greylan: Yup. You owe me more answers.
Miley: I'd want to fly. What would you pick?
Greylan: Telepathy
Miley: I just Googled "21 questions" and you are getting the first question that popped up... What's the weirdest dream you've ever had?

THE ONE

My phone starts ringing, a strange sound that I don't typically hear. I look down, and I have an incoming FaceTime call from Greylan.

I die.

I look like a fucking wet dog right now.

This is not happening.

There's absolutely no way in hell that I'm answer— I drop my phone, and it connects the call. *Fuck.* I quickly scramble to cover the screen.

"I'm fresh out of the shower. I am not turning my screen on."

"I once had a dream that I was naked on stage, playing the guitar with my boner."

Sweet baby motherfucking Jesus. This is *not* real life.

I'm so high from my edible that I laugh uncontrollably for at least thirty seconds straight. I'm always unfiltered, but right now, there is no stopping what is going to come out of my mouth.

"Did you at least finish on stage?" I laugh even fucking harder. I am so full of giggles, I don't know what to do. I just need to shut up, try to get unhigh.

His laugh consumes me. It's so genuine and full-bodied. Loud. Much louder than I am capable of.

"I woke up before that happened. Now tell me yours."

For the love of God, I am not sober enough for this.

"I had a dream last night that we had sex."

I slap my hand over my mouth as soon as it slips out. Holy fuck. I didn't just say that. Please tell me I didn't.

"How was it?" he asks.

Yes. Yes, I did just tell him that. Lord help me right now.

"A solid eight and a half."

"Not bad. I'll take it. You gonna turn your camera on at all?"

"Nope. Sure as shit am not."

He laughs again, hard and heavy.

"You're up," I tell him.

"After a long workday, what do you usually do?"

I take some time to think about his question because everything I do is more recent; it's nothing that I've done in the last decade.

THE ONE

"I usually go to the gym after work and then get ready for the next day. I sometimes hang out with my friends. Other days I just binge read or clean. What do you do?" I ask.

"When my day is done, I'm usually so exhausted that I pass out. But in my spare time, I write music, play basketball, and hang out with my friends."

"How many songs do you have?"

Without skipping a beat, he responds, "Forty-four. My turn. Does talking to me make you uncomfortable?"

"No, talking to you makes me confused," I tell him honestly.

"Why?"

"Because you could talk to anyone in the world, and you're talking to me."

"I don't want to talk to anyone else. I like talking to you."

"Okay."

"Okay?"

"Yeah. I'll give you one more question, and then I have to blow-dry my hair."

"Will you have dinner with me tomorrow night?"

What's tomorrow? Thursday? I try to think about what I have going on.

Trivia.

"I already have plans with some friends, but you can join us if you want. Ivan too. Thursday night trivia."

"I will take what I can get."

Greylan

The morning light filters through my blinds, a gentle nudge into consciousness. I drag myself out of bed, the lingering echo of last night's phone call still buzzing in my head. I need to focus. I grab my navy blue suit and corgi shoes from the closet and throw them on my bed before jumping in the shower.

THE ONE

I talked to Ivan last night after I hung up with Miley and tried to convince him to go to trivia with Miley and her friends tonight, but I'm not sure he is having it. I still have some persuading to do.

On to my next challenge, driving with Miley to court. I know driving back to Saratoga might give me a bit of anxiety, but if she's with me, I will be distracted.

I check the time, and it's close to nine. I leave the hotel and walk to the firm. I see Miley and Attorney O'Connell exiting the building just as I approach.

A little white lie never hurt anybody...

"Can I catch a ride with you? My rental won't start."

The two of them look at each other, and then Attorney O'Connell says, "I have a hearing in Montgomery this afternoon, so I am headed straight there after your arraignment, but you can ride with Miley."

Score.

That's just what I wanted to hear.

He gets into his brand-new Mercedes EQS and takes off, leaving me alone with Miley, who, I must say, is looking fine as hell.

"I find it really hard to believe that your rental wouldn't start," she says, walking to her Audi, shaking her head.

I follow behind her, placing a hand on her lower back, opening the driver-side door.

"It worked though, didn't it?"

She rolls her eyes, and I take her car keys from her hand.

"What're you doing?"

"Driving." I smile at her.

"You're not driving my car, Greylan. I am perfectly capable."

I ignore her while walking her over to the passenger-side door. "Wanna know a fun fact?" I ask.

"No," she responds sarcastically.

"I have the same car at home."

She sits, and I close the door, making my way back to the driver's side.

"What is actually happening right now?" she asks as I start her car.

I laugh.

She looks nervous as hell. And it intrigues me.

Because she is nervous about me, Greylan Asher, the person, not the celebrity. And I honestly don't think that that has even clicked in that beautiful brain of hers.

Actually, I know it hasn't. She legitimately asked me to go to trivia on a Thursday night in public. Forgetting that I am famous… forgetting that people are going to harass me all night long.

And I think that's what I like most about Miley, she's super smart…but also clueless about who I really am.

"I needed a ride to Saratoga, and we're both headed there, that's all."

She gives me the side-eye as I back out her blacked-out Audi S4.

After several minutes of silence, she turns on one of her playlists and hums along a rendition of "Fast Car."

"Are any of my songs part of your favorites?"

"No, sorry. I actually don't know many of your songs."

And there it is.

"Don't be sorry, it's all good."

"Are you going to come to trivia tonight?"

"I am still waiting on Ivan's approval," I tell her, and she looks at me sideways, and then after a few seconds, it finally clicks.

"Oh. Are you allowed to be in public when you're famous?"

I nearly choke on my own saliva.

"It's more about how much I was to be disturbed. It should be okay though. Ivan will say yes."

I hope he says yes. As my manager, I kinda need to do what he says…to an extent.

She is pretty quiet after I mention the fact that people might interrupt me all night once they realize that I'm near them, but then says, "Do you need my friends to sign an NDA in order for you to hang out with them?"

"Depends. How much do they know about me already?"

Her face goes pale.

"Colbie, my best friend, knows I have a secret client, and Peyton, Sutton's best friend, doesn't know a thing." She smiles.

"And Sutton?" I'm sure she knows everything. They live together, they're very close, and they're twins.

"I'm sorry, Greylan...she's my safe harbor. My ride or die. The one person I know, without a shadow of a doubt, who would walk through fire for me—and I'd do the same for her. We've been through too much together. She knows every single messy, embarrassing, and terrifying secret I've ever had. Entrusting her with something like this is second nature. It's...instinct."

"I figured." I laugh to lighten the mood. I'm not mad about it at all. "They don't have to sign anything."

"Are you sure?"

"I'm sure." I pull into the lot and park the car a few spots down from Ivan's.

"Jeff wants you to stay in the car. I need to go in and convince the clerk to reorder those being arraigned and somehow get yours to be last."

"How are you going to do that?"

"Not a clue. I know the clerk, but I don't know if she'd pull any strings for me."

"Okay. I will come sit with Ivan, and then you can text me when you want us to go inside."

"Yes. Or I will come out."

I open my car door and go straight to the passenger side, opening it for her.

"Such a gent," she says sarcastically.

I just smile as she walks into the courthouse, then I go sit in Ivan's car.

"Hey."

I get straight to the point. "I need to spend more time with that girl. Just say yes to trivia. Maybe she has a hot friend for your miserable ass. But her twin is off-limits. Don't even think about it."

"I think this entire scenario is fucked up. But I know you're not going to let it go, so fine, whatever, we can go—but I'm bringing my shit with me and staying in your room tonight. We have an early flight to catch."

Chapter 19

Miley

I head inside the courthouse and through security toward the chambers where the clerk is checking all of this week's criminals.

"Hey, Jen."

"Hi, Miley. How are you? What brings you in today?" she asks.

"Just helping out Attorney O'Connell. He has three court appearances in three different counties today. I am on standby until he comes running in here."

"Oh wow, sounds like a shit day for you." She laughs. "Anything I can do to help?"

Score.

"Actually, yes. He is the attorney of record for the Asher matter. Any chance you can put them last?"

I cross my fingers and toes, praying she can make some changes in the schedule.

"Not a problem." She scribbles something down on the paper in front of her and smiles.

"Thank you so much, I owe you one."

"No, you don't. I am happy to help. If you need anything else, holler."

Wow, that was easy.

I step into the hallway and text Jeff.

> **Miley**: All set. Greylan is last.
> **Jeff**: Great. Thanks. What did you tell her?

> **Miley**: That you have three appearances in three different counties and asked if your client can be arraigned last.
> **Jeff**: Nice work. When the room is almost cleared out, let me know and we will head inside.
> **Miley**: Okay. Greylan is with Ivan in the car.
> **Jeff**: Thanks. I am parked next to them.

Oh, great. That's real nice.

I walk back over to Jen after the line dies down. "How many people are being arraigned today?"

"Only twelve. Shouldn't take too long."

"Thank you again," I say.

I go inside the courtroom, take a seat in the back, and send a text to Greylan.

> **Miley**: You're last. I will text Jeff when it's time to come inside and he will get you.
> **Greylan**: Thank you, Miley.
> **Greylan**: Ivan said yes to trivia tonight.
> **Miley**: Really?
> **Greylan**: Really.
> **Miley**: Gotta go. Court is starting.

I slowly freak out in my head. I don't know what I was thinking inviting him to a local bar in Albany that's usually crowded to play trivia. This is going to be interesting. Am I supposed to tell Colbie and Peyton that he is coming? That he is the secret client I haven't been able to talk about? I am starting to sweat thinking about it. I sent a text to Sutton.

> **Miley**: SUTTON!!
> **Sutton**: MILEY!!!
> **Miley**: I am having an emergency.
> **Sutton**: What did you do now?

Miley: I invited Greylan to trivia tonight... and he said yes! I'm freaking out.
Sutton: Shut
Sutton: The
Sutton: Fuck
Sutton: Up
Miley: You're not helping my situation
Sutton: Sorry, now I'm freaking out. I get to meet Greylan Asher. Holy shit.
Miley: STOPPPPPPP IT
Miley: What do I do?
Sutton: What do you mean what do you do?
Miley: Colbie and Peyton will be there. Do I tell them?
Sutton: Idk. Probably I guess. Do we all have to sign NDA's? HAHAHAHA
Miley: No. Just don't ask about the legal shit he's going through.
Sutton: Done and done.
Miley: I will send a group text and see where it goes...

Group Name: Core Four

Miley: Trivia tonight?
Sutton: Down
Colbie: Yes. I will meet you there. Gotta work late.
Peyton: Sorry, I can't. Working a double. Meant to text you earlier. Have fun!
Sutton: Again? Seriously?
Colbie: Booooo!
Peyton: I know, I know. I'm sorry!

THE ONE

Miley: We will miss you!

Miley: We can drive over together and meet Ivan and Greylan?
Sutton: Sounds good. See you later. Love you bye
Miley: Love you more.

I've been sitting on this bench for over an hour and am starting to get annoyed. If I paid more attention, I would know how many people have been arraigned, but in reality, I am clueless.

I do a quick head count of those who remain, and I see eight people left, some accompanied by family or an attorney and some by themselves. If I'm guessing correctly, there are only four more people until Greylan is up, so I decide to send Jeff a text.

Miley: You should start to head in. The chamber doors are open. I think there are three more people ahead of Greylan.
Jeff: en route.

I start to get nervous. This judge is being hard on everyone. I really hope that this is a quick and painless process for him. I feel extremely uncomfortable being here. Jeff has asked me to do some random things over the years, but I've never once had to sit in during an arraignment. Trial, yes. Never ever an arraignment.

Several minutes pass, and I am now beginning to freak out.

Where the heck are they?

There are only four people left in this courtroom, and one of those people is me. I text Jeff.

Miley: ETA? It's getting close.

Jeff: Hovering in the hall. Be in after this next person is finished.

Phew.

The three of them walk in, taking a seat next to me, just as the second-to-last person is being arraigned.

THE CLERK:	Criminal cause for arraignment. Counsel, please state your appearances.
MR. O'CONNELL:	Jeffrey O'Connell for Greylan Asher. Good morning, Your Honor.
THE JUDGE:	Good morning. Sir, just tell me your full name.
MR. ASHER:	Greylan Paul Asher.
THE COURT:	Thank you. This is an arraignment for you, Mr. Asher, for pending DUI charges.
THE COURT:	Mr. O'Connell, have you discussed the charges set forth in the indictment with your client?
MR. O'CONNELL:	Yes, I have.
THE COURT:	Does your client wish to enter a plea at this time as to the charges in the indictment?
MR. O'CONNELL:	Yes. He will plead not guilty.
THE COURT:	Okay. It is on the record. We will schedule a future court date for the preliminary hearing.
CLERK OF THE COURT:	Are there any dates that you are not available?
MR. O'CONNELL:	No, Your Honor.

THE COURT:	Okay. We will get that on the schedule and be in touch.
MR. O'CONNELL:	Thank you, Your Honor.
MR. ASHER:	Thank you.

Greylan

Today was a complete waste of time. Literally nothing happened. I have no idea why I actually even had to be there. I spoke my name, and that was it. And now I'm annoyed because I had to cancel tour dates for this.

We all exit the chambers together and head outside where we have a brief conversation with Attorney O'Connell before leaving for his next appearance.

"Ivan needs me to go back with him," I say to her right in front of Ivan as we walk toward their cars.

"What's the plan for later?" he asks both me and Miley.

I look to her for an answer because I am clueless.

"I am going to head home after work, and then I will drive back with my sister around seven and head to Trixies on Pearl. My friend, Colbie, is going to meet us there. My other friend, Peyton, can't come tonight."

"Okay. What time should we meet you there?" I ask.

"Trivia starts at eight. We get there around seven thirty. You can meet us around then."

"Is it walking distance from the hotel?"

"Yes. It's super close. Just head down State Street and take a left on Pearl, and it's two blocks down on your right."

"Sounds good," I smirk. "I will text you when we are on the way."

"Okay." She smiles as she gets into her car, and I wait for her to back up and drive away before I sit in Ivan's…rental? Or is it his parents' car?

"Whose car is this?"

"Noah's."

Noah is Ivan's brother. He is a couple years older than us.

"How is Noah? I haven't talked to him in way too long." I feel bad. We all used to be very close in high school and college. I miss that dude.

"He's great. He will be finished with his fellowship in May. We need to throw him a huge party."

"Hell yeah. I'm really proud of him."

And I am. I can't believe that he went to college for thirteen years and is about to be a surgeon. Insane. Couldn't be happier for him.

"Me too. He's home. You will see him later." He pauses. "Oh, we are going to have to drive back to Albany and grab your rental and then follow me to bring him his car back since we are going straight to the airport in the morning."

"All right."

"And we have to have dinner with my parents, and then we can go to trivia."

"Okay."

Ivan's phone rings through the car speakers. "Hello."

"Ivan, it's Reed."

"Hey, Reed. What's up?"

"I know Greylan is taking some time off, but the CMAs reached out and asked if he is still performing next month. He is up for three awards."

"No shit, when was that released?" Ivan asks.

"This morning."

"Nice. I will check it out." He looks at me, nodding his head up and down, and I give him a nod, basically saying, "Hell yeah."

"You want to ask him and give me a call back?" Reed questions Ivan.

"He'll still do it. Him and I had already talked it over together."

"Great. I will send you the details."

"Thanks, man." He hangs up. "Look up what awards you were just nominated for."

"Okay."

Holy. Shit.

THE ONE

Artist of the Year
Song of the Year
Album of the Year

"Artist of the year, song of the year, and album of the year."

"That's fucking awesome, man. Congrats!" He seems genuinely happy for me.

"I couldn't have done it without you."

And I really couldn't have. Ivan has been through hell and back with me, never once leaving my side. He's one of the best, most down-to-earth guys, and I am lucky enough that I get to call him my best friend.

"What song is nominated?"

Great question. I click on the article, and…are they serious right now?

"Actually two." I'm completely shocked. Never in a thousand years would I think that I'd (a) be going to the Country Music Awards, (b) perform at the Country Music Awards, and (c) be nominated for three different awards, one award nominating me twice. I am baffled. "'Memory of You' and 'A Helluva Lot.'"

We drive back to the Renaissance to grab my rental, and I follow Ivan back up north. I call Brody on the way to check in. It rings twice before he answers.

"Hello?"

"Hey, just checking in with you. I'll be home in the morning."

"I'm doing all right. The planning sucked though."

"I wish I was there. I'm sorry."

We talk for a while on the phone, and he said that he would play at the CMAs. I didn't even ask him. I wasn't going to ask him for another couple weeks. He needs time to grieve. But he came right out and said it; he said he wanted to play and that he would be there—and that definitely makes me happy.

"What're you guys all doing tonight?" I'm assuming he is with his entire family, which is fairly large. He has four siblings who are all married and some have kids and whatnot. Plus his dad's old band mates and very close friends.

"Going through photos with everyone."

"I will have food delivered for everyone. You're at your mom's house, right?"

"Yeah. That would be great. Thank you."

"No problem. We land around ten thirty in the morning, and then we will be over. Love you, brother."

"You too." He hangs up as I'm making my way up Ivan's parents' driveway.

When we get inside, his mom, Betsey, gives me a huge hug, and Kirk gives me a slap on the back. His parents are really great.

"Smells good," I tell Betsey.

"Meatloaf and mashed potatoes," she says with a big smile on her face.

Tonight is going to be a good night.

We all sit down for dinner just as Noah comes in, just waking up. He probably worked all night.

"Holy shit, look what the cat dragged in," Noah says, and I stand up to give him a handshake/back slap.

"How are you, man? Congrats on everything. You're at the homestretch."

"Thank fucking god," he says.

"*Mouth!*" Betsey interrupts.

We all laugh.

We all eat.

We catch up on each other's lives.

And then we say goodbye and drive back to Albany.

When we get there, I jump in another quick shower and pack up my stuff for tomorrow. Ivan's chillin' on the pullout bed.

"You ready? It's almost seven thirty."

"Yeah. Let me text her quickly to make sure she is there."

Greylan: About to head over.

She responds almost immediately.

THE ONE

Miley: We are at the far back table (left corner) where no one will see you.
Greylan: Thanks. Be there shortly.

I throw on my Carhartt and trucker hat, trying to disguise myself as best as I can. "Leggo."

Ivan rolls off the bed and grabs his shoes. "Don't make me regret this."

We leave the hotel and make our way to Trixies on Pearl. The streets are moderately crowded, but nothing terrible.

"So how much do you like this girl?" Ivan asks.

"A lot."

I do. I like her a lot, a lot. This intense feeling I'm having toward her is blowing my mind. I'm not sure I could stop this desire even if I wanted to.

"You should tell her that."

"I plan on doing just that tonight," I say confidently.

Ivan enters the bar, and I follow behind him. "Back left corner."

"You lead," he tells me, and I do.

I walk through the crowded bar area to the back and see her in the corner with her twin sister. When I see her and she turns seeing me and we lock eyes, my stomach fucking drops so fast. It drops so fast, I feel like I'm on a roller coaster, and we are doing 60 mph down the first descent.

I grab the chair next to her and pull it out and then sit, looking right at her. "Hey."

Chapter 20

Miley

My heart is seriously pounding out of my chest so hard right now. I can't believe he showed up. He came out in public just to hang out with me. I can't grasp what I am physically feeling in my body right now. It's absolute chaos.

"Hey." My smile is probably so big right now.

I look over at Sutton, and she's just staring me down wide-eyed.

"Oh, Greylan, this is Sutton. Sutton, this is Greylan, and this is Ivan." I point to the two of them, and she waves stupidly at Greylan.

"Nice to meet you," he says while reaching out to shake her hand.

"Hi. I'm going to grab a drink. Does anyone want anything?" Ivan asks.

"I'll have a beer," Greylan tells him.

I give Sutton "the look" that says, "Go fuck off for a second," and luckily, she takes the hint right away. "I'll come with. White Claw, Miley?"

"Yes, please."

They both go to the bar, leaving me and Greylan all alone in the back.

He slides closer and looks me in the eye. "Are you nervous?"

"Maybe," I say honestly.

"Why?"

Why am I nervous? I think. *I don't know. Maybe because you're a famous musician that's choosing to hang out with me, who has shown interest in me?*

THE ONE

Maybe he just wants to have sex while he is staying in New York for an extended period of time. Maybe I shouldn't overthink this entire thing, and I should just grab it, run with it. Have fun. Maybe I should flirt back and see where it goes. What do I have to lose?

"Because I find you incredibly sexy, and it intimidates me," I say hesitantly.

Okay. There. I said it.

His hand falls to my inner thigh, and he leans in very close and whispers, "Dream about me last night?"

Christ, my face heats under his gaze.

"Because I had a dream about you." He gives my leg a small squeeze, and my stomach fills with a thousand butterflies.

Keep it together, Miley. You got this.

I shift slightly in my chair, but not enough for him to pull his hand away, and I smirk, asking the very same question he asked me after I told him about my dream. "How was it?"

Greylan instantly barks out a laugh, genuine and full-bodied.

"You get a ten, Mils."

He's smart not giving me an eight and a half like I gave him. But I was only joking. His performance in my dream exceeded my expectations and was undoubtedly a solid ten. I woke up throbbing, so that must say something.

"Holy fuck!" I hear someone say.

I look up and see Colbie standing there, staring at us.

When did she walk in, and why does she look a little mad?

"Did you forget to tell me something?" she asks just as Ivan and Sutton walk up with our drinks.

Crap. I did forget to tell her. I really meant to give her a heads-up. I didn't want to catch her off guard like this. I know how she can be.

"Colbie, this is Grey—"

She cuts me off as I try to introduce the two of them. "I know who it is. What the fuck, Miley. Why didn't you tell me?"

Okay, this is about to get super uncomfortable.

I stand up. "Let's go grab you a drink. Be right back, guys." I take her hand and drag her to the bar. "Chill out. I was going to tell you, honestly. I forgot, and it all happened so fast. Please don't be mad right now."

"Is he your secret client?"

"Yes, but I really can't talk about that, so please don't ask me any questions regarding his case."

"Fine, but you better fucking tell me everything else that is happening between the two of you because from what I just witnessed, this is not just two friends 'hanging out.'"

"I will. I pinky promise. But can we please just talk about it later? I don't need your awkward moodiness right now."

"Whatever," she says, grabbing her drink and heading back to the table just as trivia begins.

"All right, all right, all right, welcome to Thirsty Thursday Trivia. I'm your host, Double Des. We have twelve groups playing tonight. We will have three rounds with ten questions in each round. Tonight's trivia topic is music. Ya'll ready?"

Colbie claims the pen and paper, as per her usual, and says, "If we don't win tonight with you two on our team, we're gonna have some serious fucking problems."

Alrighty then. Still in a bad mood. Great.

She chugs her drink just as a waitress is walking by, and she orders everyone another round.

"First question, which country singer is known for songs like 'Jolene' and '9 to 5'?"

"Easy," Sutton says. "Dolly Parton."

We all agree, and Colbie writes it down.

"Which artist holds the record for the most number one hits on the Billboard Hot 100 chart?"

"The Beatles," Ivan says right away.

"He didn't say band, he said artist," Sutton tells him while looking offended that he actually said the Beatles.

"What's your guess?" I ask Greylan.

"Um, Madonna?"

"Anyone else have a guess?" Colbie asks.

We all shake our heads no.

THE ONE

"Madonna it is." She writes down our answer and then scribbles out our team name on the top of the paper and writes "Core Not Four" like an asshole.

"Which song by Queen was voted as the best song in a 2002 Guinness World Records poll?"

The waitress comes back with our drinks, and Sutton slides the one Colbie ordered over to me since she's driving.

"Not a clue," Colbie says. "Boys?"

"'Bohemian Rhapsody?'" Greylan seems a little unsure but Ivan confirms.

"Yeah, definitely 'Bohemian Rhapsody.'"

"Which artist's 2014 album *1989* marked a full transition from country to pop music?"

Colbie is already writing the answer down before the question is fully read out loud.

The alcohol is hitting me, and I can't concentrate on anything. I'm just watching everyone else around me, slightly stressed out that Colbie is in a mood and still very nervous that Greylan is sitting next to me.

"What was the name of Johnny Cash's band?" DJ Des asks the crowd.

We all look at each other, thinking hard.

"It's at the tip of my tongue." Ivan says.

"Isn't it just Johnny Cash?" I ask, and both Colbie and Sutton both nod their heads, agreeing with me.

"The Tennessee Three," Greylan chimes in as he takes a sip from his beer.

Colbie writes down his answer, questioning it in her head the entire time, not certain it's correct.

The host asks the next five questions, and we all finish our drinks in the process. Greylan and Ivan are holding the team down. Well, at least I hope they are.

At the end of round one, we turn our cards in and wait for the results.

"All right, ready for the answers?" The host is back on the mic. He reads each question and then tells the crowd the answer. Our answer to question number one is correct, which we already knew.

THE ONE

"Question number two: which artist holds the record for the most number one hits on the Billboard Hot 100 chart?" He pauses. "The answer: the Beatles."

We all stare Sutton down because Ivan answered it correctly when the question was asked.

"You said artist, not band!" Colbie yells, and everyone looks back at our table.

We get the next eight questions right and end up winning the round. Thank god. I'd never live that down.

I grab my phone and Google "Which artist holds the record for the most number one hits on the Billboard Hot 100 chart?" And yup, it reads as follows: "#1 - The Beatles, #2 - Madonna." These guys really do know a thing or two about music.

There's about ten minutes until the second round of trivia, so I use the opportunity to go to the bathroom. "I'm going to the bathroom really quick. Be right back." I stand and walk down the short hallway to the bathroom where there is thankfully only one other person ahead of me in line.

I do my thing, and when I'm finished, I walk out and see Greylan walking toward me, likely going to the bathroom as well.

I'm feeling the buzz for sure…and when that happens, my confidence level tends to go higher, resulting in an unfiltered Miley. Everyone's favorite person.

"Hey." I give him a perfect wink as I go to walk by, but he walks into me instead, gripping my hips with his large hands as he backs me into the wall.

He leans forward, stopping when his mouth is next to my ear, and whispers, "You are absolutely beautiful, and I very much want you."

As he moves back, I bring my hands up to his chest and slide them up around his neck and smile. "Maybe once you're back from Nashville."

"Oh my god! It is him! It's Greylan Asher!" someone practically yells out loud.

We both look over and see a group of girls all giggly and shit.

It makes me want to punch them in the face. Like back the fucking fuck up, can't you see he is with someone right now? You imbeciles.

"Do you wanna go someplace else?" I ask.

"Definitely."

Greylan

I've been interrupted numerous times in my life by fans and paparazzi, but I think that may have been one of the worst timings. I was going to tell her how she makes me feel. I was going to kiss her.

We walk back to our table just as round two is getting ready to start.

"Do you guys want to go somewhere else? I've been spotted."

"Yeah, sure." Sutton stands, grabbing her jacket from off the back of her chair, and Ivan does the same.

Colbie pounds the rest of her drink. "Where to?"

"Do you want to try that new bar down the street?" Miley asks.

"Sounds good."

We walk a couple blocks to our new destination, and when we get there, there is a cover band playing, and I must admit, they sound pretty good. Luckily, it isn't very crowded here, and we are able to grab a table right away.

"I'll grab drinks from the bar. What does everyone want?" Ivan asks.

"Two White Claws for me," Colbie says, adding, "Sutton, I need a ride home."

"Okay," she laughs. "Ivan, can you get me a Sprite?"

"Sure. Miley?"

"I'll have a White Claw as well, only one though. Please and thank you."

I think she might be getting drunk, but it's hard to tell because she definitely holds her own.

Ivan goes to the bar and leaves me with the ladies.

"So, my company is merging, and I might lose my job," Colbie announces.

Okay, well, that came out of nowhere. And definitely explains her mood.

"What? Why?" Miley asks.

I suddenly feel uncomfortable being around for this conversation.

"I don't know. They won't tell us anything else. They told us that the merge will happen in January and that they anticipate multiple layoffs."

"They'd be dumb to let you go, and you know that," Sutton says. "Stay positive."

Trying to engage in the conversation, I ask, "What do you do?"

"I work in wealth management. I am a financial analyst."

"Impressive," I tell her honestly. Because I truly think anyone who understands stocks and money management is smart as hell. I wish I understood it.

"How do we cheer you up?" Miley asks.

"White Claws."

Perfect timing as Ivan hands her two of them.

We all have a good time with several laughs and a couple more drinks, minus Sutton, who is driving.

Miley's laugh is contagious. Sutton's too. They both sound very similar when they speak, but their laughs are slightly different, which is probably because of their different personalities and how they choose to project it.

"I want to sing karaoke," Colbie says.

"That's a band, not karaoke, and no, you're not convincing them that you know how to play the guitar and asking them to go on stage...again," Sutton tells her, and Miley uncontrollably laughs.

"That happened once. Go ahead, chastise me."

From an outsider looking in, Miley and Colbie like to have a good time, and Sutton appears to be their babysitter, which is okay with me. It's good to know that someone is looking after them.

"Will you teach me to play the guitar, Greylan? So I can get Mama Miller's permission the next time I want to go on a stage?"

Colbie is actually funny now that her bad mood has worn off.

"For sure."

"Oh my god. Will you please go on stage and sing a song? I bet they'd let you," Sutton asks.

"I might die if you do that," Miley mutters to herself, but we can all hear her.

Hmm. Interesting. I sit back and listen to their conversation play out.

"Why? You don't even know any of his songs," Colbie interrupts.

Confirmed again. Miley doesn't really know who I am.

But maybe if I do sing, I have a chance at winning her over.

"If I do go up there, we'd have to leave right after."

They all stare back at me like I have two heads, in complete shock.

"And I'm not singing any of my songs. That would be weird," I add.

"Are you fucking with me right now?" Sutton questions.

Nope.

"Ivan, can you go find out if they cover any of the songs I cover?"

Ivan heads over to the band that is taking a quick break and starts talking to one of the members while Colbie orders a round of shots, which Sutton hesitantly agrees to take as well.

After a couple minutes, Ivan comes back to the table. "'Purple Rain.' They will introduce you after the next song."

All right, we're doing this.

I grab one of the shots and hold it up. "Here's to you, Miley… hopefully you don't die while I'm up there." I wink at her.

We all hit glasses and toss our shots back.

"Cheers!"

I slide my chair back and stand, grabbing my half-empty beer, and make my way toward the back of the stage.

The intro of "Purple Rain" begins, and I am suddenly nervous. I'm typically unfazed when it comes to performing, but right now, I'm almost scared. Scared to sing in front of Miley.

I hold my pint glass with my fingers around the opening at the top and place my other hand inside my pocket. I hear the band's vocalist yell, "Give it up for Greylan Asher!" I step up onto the stage, raising my drink to the crowd, and walk to the microphone where I slightly look down toward the ground, tapping my foot while listening to the beat, waiting for my cue to start. I close my eyes and sing the first verse, "I never meant to cause you any sorrow." The crowd goes fucking nuts. I smile as I open my eyes and take it all in for a second before I look out to the crowd and sing, "I never meant to cause you any pain." I step back and slightly rock my body to the beat, absolutely loving the feel of it, and when it's my cue, I find Miley and stare directly at her and tell her, "I only wanted, one time, to see you laughing."

The beat picks up, and my voice gets slightly deeper with a faint growl. "I only want to see you laughing, in the purple rain."

The band joins in, and collectively we sing the chorus. "Purple rain, purple rain."

The look on Miley's face is everything, everything I've ever needed and more, and it makes me fucking cheese in front of everyone. I shake my head and sing it again, "Purple rain, purple rain." I rock back for a beat and sing it to the crowd. "Purple rain, purple rain." And I conclude the chorus by telling Miley, "I only want to see you bathing, in the purple rain."

And when I get off stage, Miley walks directly up to me and kisses me in front of the entire bar, not giving a damn about who is watching us.

Chapter 21

Miley

The second my lips touched his, everything changed. My want, my desire, my need for him, it accelerated. It was like nothing I've ever felt before. Pure euphoria. And when he kissed me back, hard and deep, everyone surrounding us went wild, cheering and chanting.

Greylan breaks away, hopefully because he knows he's about to be bombarded, and grabs my hand, leading us out of the bar.

When we step out into the cold night, Ivan, Sutton, and Colbie are in complete disbelief, staring at us, very confused.

I look down at our connected hands and back to them and pull away. "I'm so sorry, I don't know what I was thinking…I—"

"I think we are going to give you guys a moment alone. We will meet you at Sutton's car in a few minutes," Colbie interrupts.

"I'll walk you guys over and then head back to the hotel," Ivan tells them.

After they leave, I look to Greylan. "I'm so sorry, that was very unprofess—"

Greylan grabs my face and kisses me. He kisses me with intensity, like he's begging for more but also savoring every moment. And I take it all in, every fucking ounce.

His mouth slows, and then he lets out a sigh as he draws back and rests his forehead on mine. "We should probably go. I'll walk you over. Is Sutton parked in your office lot?"

"Yes."

THE ONE

We begin the walk to my firm's parking lot when I begin to shiver from the cold.

Greylan notices and leans in, wrapping an arm around me. "Are you okay?"

"I'm more than okay."

"I have an early flight, but when I come back on Sunday, can I see you?" He smirks.

I smile at him and tell him yes just as we approach Sutton's car. "Good night, Greylan."

"Good night, Mils."

I get into the passenger side, and my sister and best friend stare me down. Down, down. Way down.

"Holy fuck!" Sutton basically screams.

"You have a lot of shit to catch me up on. Give me all the deets or die." Colbie is not playing around.

I just shake my head back and forth and squeal. How is this my life right now? I try not to freak out, but I am so giddy, it's stupid.

"I don't even know where to start," I begin. "He's been at the firm a lot lately, and one thing led to another. He made a few comments slash passes, which led into flirting. He asked me to dinner, but I already had plans with you guys, so I said no, but then felt bad, so I invited him and that's it. He took the dive in when Ivan and Sutton were at the bar, and that's when you walked in. And then when I went to the bathroom and saw him in the hallway, he made the first move."

"Are you going to hang out with him tomorrow?" Sutton asks.

"No, he's flying back home for a funeral. His friend's father just passed away."

"What else do we know about him? I tried Googling him but couldn't find shit," she adds.

"His sister died, and he has very bad anxiety being back in his hometown. I don't know anything about his parents though. We haven't gotten that far."

"How did she die?" Colbie asks.

"I'm not sure. He won't talk about it, and I didn't want to pry."

"What's her name?" she continues.

THE ONE

"Jillian, why?"

"Looking up her obituary."

"Jesus Christ, Colbie. Stop it," Sutton says.

"Too late. And we both know you were going to do the same shit when you get home and aren't driving a car."

"I feel like this is an invasion of privacy," I mumble, half asleep with my head resting on the window.

> Jillian Asher, age 18, of Gansevoort passed away on Friday, November 28, 2014, as the result of injuries sustained in an automobile accident.
>
> She was the daughter of Rochelle Davis Asher of Gansevoort and the late James Asher, who passed away when she was only four months old. Jillian was a recent graduate of Saratoga Springs High School and was attending Adirondack Community College.
>
> Survivors in addition to her mother are her brother Greylan of Gansevoort, her uncle Robert (Bethany) Davis of Tampa, Florida, and her best friend, Abele Jones of Saratoga. The family will receive friends at the funeral home on Monday, November 24th, from 4 to 6:30 pm prior to the service.

"Well, that didn't tell us much," Colbie says like an asshole. "But now we have mama duke's name. Let's look her up!"

"This is wrong," I mumble.

We stop at a red light and Sutton searches "Purple Rain" on Apple Music and hits play just as the light turns green. "Sorry, guys, I need to listen to this on repeat the entire drive home."

"His mom is dead too," Colbie says.

Well, I think that's what she says. The music is pretty loud, and everything is a little foggy.

"What?" Sutton asks while turning down the music.

"His mom, she died too...a few years back. And both obituaries have minimal immediate family listed." She stops talking for a second and then says, "I'm pretty sure Greylan doesn't have any family left."

The weight of her words settles in the car, a heavy silence broken only by the hum of the tires on the asphalt. The image of him alone flickers in my mind, and the feeling of sympathy tightens in my chest. I turn away from the window, the city lights blurring into streaks, and try to shake off the feeling. *This changes nothing*, I tell myself, but the thought feels hollow, lost in the echoing emptiness of Colbie's disclosure.

Greylan

My alarm went off at five in the morning so that we could make it to the airport by six, but I snoozed it a few times, so now we are on borrowed time. I drop off the rental, and we pass through TSA precheck rather quickly, just in time to catch our flight. Thankfully everyone else is on board, and we are in first class, so I'm able to dodge any fans. Realistically though, no one is actually looking. As soon as their ass hit the seat, I'm sure they all passed out because it's early as hell.

"I'm going back to bed." I tell Ivan then throw in my AirPods.

Last night was amazing. I can't believe she kissed me. It's the only thing I can think about, and it stays that way until I fall asleep.

When I feel the plane's tires hit the runway, I'm instantly awake. My phone vibrates a few times in my pocket as I gain service. I usually pay for the Wi-Fi, but I didn't want to be bothered during my nap, so I just let it go.

When I check it, I have six messages. Five messages are from a group text between me, Ivan, and Brody. Brody tells us he will be at his mom's house all day and to come by whenever, Ivan telling him the time we should get there and asking if there is anything we need to bring or grab on the way, Brody telling him no, and Ivan telling him okay.

THE ONE

And then there's a sixth message waiting for me from the girl who has my full-blown attention: Miley Miller.

> **Miley**: I don't know what else to say other than I am so sorry for being a drunk fool and throwing myself at you last night.

Is she regretting it? Is she regretting everything that happened last night? Everything that's been happening over the last couple of weeks?

> **Greylan**: I'm going to pretend you didn't say that. Because it sounds like you're having some regrets, which I definitely am not.

I put my phone back in my pocket and follow Ivan off the plane. I need to focus on helping Brody right now. I will touch base with her in a little while.

We walk to the parking garage where Ivan left his truck, and I jump into the passenger side of it, turning on the heated seats because, damn, it's cold.

"Wanna grab breakfast quick?" he asks.

"Sure. But I don't feel like being seen in public, so can we just hit up a drive-through?"

"Hardee's?"

"Perfect."

"So what's the deal with you and Miley?"

"I don't know, man. But I really like her."

"I can tell. She's really chill. And her sister—"

I cut him off right away. "Don't even say it. She's going through a divorce right now, leave her alone."

"Is smoking hot," he finishes his sentence while smirking.

Douche.

"Anyways, I'm just about ready to beg her to have dinner with me. I'm going to ask her again tonight."

"Okay. Let me know if you need me to make any reservations. But speaking of next week, what's your plan? Do you want me to get you the hotel again, or do you want to go to your house or stay with my parents?"

"I don't know yet. I will let you know by Sunday."

The thought of asking Miley to dinner again hangs in the air, a small hopeful spark within the heavy atmosphere we're about to walk into. I try to push down the anxiety that starts to creep in when I think about Brody's family and the weight of their grief. I take a deep breath, bracing myself for the inevitable wave of sadness.

When we arrive at Brody's mom's house, it's surprisingly okay. Everyone is all right. And that helps me breathe a little easier.

I go straight to his mom and give her the best goddamn hug I think I've given anyone ever. My heart hurts for her. She just lost the love of her life, the man she was married to for thirty years.

"Greylan, honey, it's so good to see you!"

Ivan and Brody jump in, group hugging Mama Rivers, and she laughs.

After we break apart, I give Brody a man hug, and we all head to the living room where some of his dad's former bandmates are gathered along with his siblings, their families, and several other family members.

There's a lot of laughing, a lot of crying, and a lot of reminiscing. We go through the photos that they picked out and make picture boards to display at the service, but looking at them brings back so many of my own childhood memories that I had with my sister and my family. My family that I miss so much, it hurts.

I sit back and watch the way Brody interacts with his mother and sisters, how grateful they are to have had time with Richie before his passing, and I think that it's finally time for me to take a step forward in my life. To be grateful that I once had Jillian and my mom in my life. I don't want to dwell on the what-ifs anymore. I want to try to love again. And I want to be loved again.

After dinner, Ivan drops me off at my place, and he goes to his. The services are tomorrow, and I already know it's going to be a long day.

THE ONE

I start the shower as soon as I get home and feel myself harden immediately, knowing that I am finally alone, finally able to give myself a release after everything that happened last night.

I grip myself tightly and close my eyes as I wait for the shower to heat up. Just thinking about her drives me insane. No one has ever affected me the way that she has.

I step inside, and instead of washing, I let the hot water run over me as I close my eyes. My hand moves, finding its own rhythm, the tension building within me.

Fuck, that feels good.

I prop myself against the shower wall with my other hand while the water hits my back, and I pump myself harder, my mind wandering to last night. To me pinning Miley against the wall. To the way her body felt in my hands. I stroke even faster, the need for release rising quickly.

The look on her face when we were in the hallway…

"Fuck," I grunt as all the pleasure pulses at the base.

The smile on her face when I started to sing on stage…

The sway of her hips as she watched me perform…

And the way I felt when her lips pressed against mine.

"Ahh, shit," I mutter as my cock swells in my hand, and then I come so hard and so fast all over the shower wall, unable to control it. I take in every last second of pleasure until I fall against the tile with both hands.

Holy shit.

I'm not sure if I've ever done that. I don't think I've ever came just thinking about a woman, not thinking about her naked, just thinking…about her.

God, I need to see her again.

I finish my shower and towel off before changing into sweats and a T-shirt. I grab my phone to text Miley and see that she responded to my message from earlier this morning.

Miley: I'm just not sure it's a good idea…

Chapter 22

Miley

Greylan still hasn't responded to my message from this morning. I am so embarrassed that I threw myself at him last night, something I shouldn't have ever done.

When I get home from work, Sutton is getting ready to leave for work. It's going to be a quiet night for me. I need Gatorade, a good book, and my bed more than anything right now.

"You look like shit," she says.

"Thanks, I still feel like shit. Why'd you let me drink that much last night?"

"You were fine. Couldn't even tell you were drunk."

I set it down on the counter and grab a drink from the fridge just as my phone vibrates.

"Your boo just texted you."

I try to play it cool and not show any type of reaction in front of her because I have no idea what he would respond after I told him that we basically shouldn't hang out anymore.

"Aren't you going to be late for work?" I ask.

She looks at the clock on the stove and quickly finishes making herself a sandwich. "I'll be home in the morning. Love you." She grabs her keys and slides them into her scrubs and heads for the door.

"Love you too." I hurry to grab my phone from the counter and read his message.

Greylan: Have dinner with me on Monday.

THE ONE

Is he really going to ignore the last message I sent him? I could lose my job if Jeff ever found out that I was hanging out with a client.

I pause my fingers over the keyboard. My heart itches. I don't know what to do or say. Maybe getting involved with a client is actually what I need. Maybe it will give me the ambition to actually go out and find a new job. A job that I will enjoy going to, a job that I love.

Miley: I could lose my job, Greylan.

He's quick on the trigger, the dots appearing right before his text message comes through.

Greylan: Ivan knows not to say a word.

I'm between a rock and a hard place right now.

Do I want to say yes? Hell yeah, I do. I am so unbelievably drawn to this man, it's stupid. But it's all so…complicated.

For starters, he's fucking famous and lives in a different state.

I set my phone down on the coffee table and head for the shower, giving myself time to think. Weighing the pros and cons.

I take my time, running every scenario through my head, and by the time I'm ready to get out, the water starts to turn cold.

I throw on a hoodie and sweatpants and reheat yesterday's leftovers that are in the fridge. By the time I get back to my phone, there's another message waiting for me.

Greylan: What will it take?

I must admit, he is very persistent. I'm not sure he's not taking no for an answer.

Miley: What do you mean?
Greylan: I'm finally happy… & I'm not ready for that to end. So what will it take for you to have dinner with me?

Wow. Okay. I literally have no idea what to say to that.

> **Miley**: I don't know.
> **Miley**: But why haven't you been happy?
> **Greylan**: Is that what you need? For me to open up?

Yes, actually. I'd love to know what is going on in that beautiful head of yours.

> **Miley**: Maybe.
> **Greylan**: Since you've been around, I've been able to sleep and dream. My sister's death isn't haunting me. You distract me. In a good way.

I'm just going to ask the question that I've wanted to ask for a while now.

> **Miley**: How did your sister die?
> **Greylan**: She was in a car accident.

Dots start, then stop. Start. Then stop.
Christ, Greylan.
And finally…

> **Greylan**: And she was an addict. That guy at the bar was her dealer/boyfriend. She hit a pole going 45 mph when she was high and was on life support for a week before my mom pulled the plug.

Oh my god. I wasn't expecting that.
I take a deep breath in just as my phone rings.
Greylan.
"Hello?"

"I haven't felt anything since my sister died. I've been numb for almost a decade." He pauses for a second. "But when I met you, I felt this sudden zap of life inside me. And it's not something I'm willing to walk away from. So just give me a chance…please?"

Greylan

I tell Miley everything.

I tell her my biggest regret in life was not being able to save my sister. That I've always felt like I failed her. Like there was more that I could have done to help her. And I'm not sure I've ever truly forgiven myself for that. But I think I'm ready to.

Growing up, Jillian and I were inseparable. It was always just me and her. Our mom worked two jobs just to make ends meet, and when she wasn't working, she was drinking herself to sleep. She didn't pay much attention to us but always made sure we had everything we needed. No questions asked.

Once we both got a bit older, our priorities shifted. I focused a lot on music, and her focus was more on her social status. I didn't think much of it until she overdosed her junior year of high school… and when that happened, I became angry. Angry because she befriended the wrong crowd. Angry because she became a follower. And angry because she became distant. Very distant. She chose heroin over everything. Over everyone.

I started to become a father figure, and she didn't like it. Our mother couldn't be bothered with anything ever, so she was zero help.

The night my sister was in the accident, she called me asking for money, slurring her words. I immediately told her no, but could hear that she was in the car driving, so I told her I was going to call the police if she didn't pull over right away. She hung up on me, and thirteen minutes later, my mom called. They said my sister was dead on the scene, but the EMT was able to get her heart going, and she was transported to Saratoga Hospital. I haven't been the same ever since.

But I'm getting there, slowly but surely. This is big for me... being able to talk about my upbringing and Jillian's death. And after doing so, I'm okay. I feel all right.

"You never have to stop loving her, Greylan. You know that, right?"

"I know."

"Are you okay right now?" she asks. After witnessing two panic attacks, I understand why.

"Surprisingly, yes."

"Can I ask you another question?"

"You can ask me anything you want, Miley."

And she can. I will answer anything she wants to know. Because I trust her and because I want to. It feels good to be able to open myself up to someone. Someone who won't judge me or pity me.

"What happened to your mom and dad?"

I knew that question was going to come next. And if I'm being honest, I honestly don't know what happened to my dad.

"My dad died when I was a baby. My mom wouldn't talk about it, but my aunt told me it was from a heart attack in his sleep. My mom died a few years ago from liver failure."

My mom and I weren't exactly close, but it still hurt watching her die. I knew she was an alcoholic since I learned what that meant in primary school. She mostly held it together though. She was a functional alcoholic. She worked from sunrise to sunset, and once she was home for the night, she drank herself into a coma. But after Jillian died, she got worse, drinking any chance she got, and her heavy alcohol use led to chronic pancreatitis.

I think she wanted to die. And I only say that because before she died, she was hospitalized due to her disease. I was in the hospital room with her when the doctor said, "If you continue this lifestyle, you're going to die." The next day, she signed herself out of the hospital against medical advice, and on her way home, stopped at the liquor store for a bottle of vodka. A few months later, she came deathly ill and was hospitalized again. Her liver was failing, and the doctor gave her only a couple months to live. She was put on hospice and died a few weeks later.

"Before she died, she told me that she was proud of me and that I would be okay. I never believed her until now. I think I am going to be okay. Even though I have no one left," I add.

"You have me."

I smile. "Do I?"

"Yes, I think you do."

"Does that mean you're going to let me make you your favorite food on Monday, and you'll hang out with me?"

If that doesn't win her over, I don't know what will. But at this point, I need to pull out all the cards. I need her and I want her… and I won't fucking stop until I have her.

She laughs. "That sounds a lot like you inviting yourself over to my house."

I think in my head for a hot second and say it before I can stop myself. "That or you can come to my house in Gansevoort."

"You have a house here?" she questions immediately.

I guess I neglected to tell her that.

"I do."

My heart starts to race thinking about going there. I try to calm myself.

I'm okay, I'll be okay. Miley will be there.

"Sutton is on a double Monday, so you're more than welcome here," she says just as I'm about to freak out.

"Sounds perfect. I have some cleaning up to do there since I'll be back for a while."

"It's a d—" She corrects herself immediately. "Great!"

I chuckle to myself and shake my head.

"I'm going to lay down. Tomorrow is going to be a long day. Can I call you after the services?"

"Of course. Good night, Greylan."

"Good night, Mils."

Chapter 23

Miley

"Okay, give me all the details." Sutton barges into my room, and I glance at the clock. It's a little after seven thirty in the morning.

"It's a Saturday morning, are you kidding me right now? Go away."

She strips out of her scrubs and jumps into the bed. "Nope."

I turn away, needing at least two more hours of sleep, but she tries to spoon me.

"What are you wearing tonight?" she asks.

"What's tonight?"

"The Halloween Masquerade Gala."

"Halloween is tomorrow," I mumble, half asleep.

"Jesus Christ, Miley. You told me you'd come with me tonight. You promised."

I roll over, trying to wake myself up a little bit. I know we talked about it, but I don't recall committing to going, but fine, I will do whatever she wants me to do…as long as I can go back to sleep for a couple more hours.

"Okay, I am. Chill. I'm still half asleep. I'll wear whatever you want me to wear. Now can I go back to bed?"

"Fine."

*****

"I'm not wearing that."

"You said, and I quote, 'I'll wear whatever you want me to wear,' end quote."

She is so friggin' annoying sometimes, I can't take it. I grab the stupid dress she wants me to wear along with the mask for the gala and head to the bathroom to change.

"I look ridiculous!" I yell through the door.

"It's a Halloween fundraiser for sick kids. It will make them happy. Now hurry up."

I look like a fucking peacock. I have a fitted teal dress on with a feathered mask that's itchy and uncomfortable. But I'm just going to zip my lips and try to get through this night because that's what good sisters do.

I walk out of the bathroom, and Sutton is in a beautiful pink dress with a matching lace mask, looking hotter than hell.

"So you get to dress up as Barbie, and you have me looking like a fucking bird."

She spits out her water everywhere. "You have no one to impress tonight…I do."

"Oh yeah? Who?"

"The thirty doctors that are going to be there. I'm single, remember?"

"Um, so am I."

"The fuck you are." She throws a rag over her spit water that's all over the floor and wipes it up with the toe of her pointed heel. Gross. "Let's go, we are going to be late."

"Who's driving?" I ask.

"Me."

Phew. At least I can indulge if I'm going to be walking around as a big bird.

The ride is a bit uncomfortable, the ridiculous feathered mask is digging into my cheek, and I can barely sit in this tight-ass dress. I take a deep breath, trying to mentally prepare myself for the onslaught of doctors and the inevitable small talk. A silent promise to myself to grab a strong drink the moment we arrive forms in my mind. Sutton parks her car in the lot, and we head toward the entrance.

"Is that a red carpet, Sutton?"

"It sure is."

"If you think I'm taking a picture on it, you're absolutely insane."

I attempt to walk the other direction, but she grabs me. "Yes, you are."

"For fuck's sake!"

Thirty seconds later, we are posing in front of the backdrop for the photographer.

"Can you please take one with my phone too?" She hands him her phone.

"I hate you," I mumble through my teeth while faking a smile.

Once we get inside, Sutton heads toward a table to find where we are sitting.

Sutton Miller & Guest

"You wasted no time going back to your maiden name," I say as I grab a glass of champagne from the server walking around.

"I never legally changed my last name." She smirks.

Sutton was married for under a year. And I am almost certain that everyone knew it wasn't going to last…even her. I think she is smart for not changing it. Because shit, going back and forth with having different last names is dumb. I'm not sure that I'd ever change mine again. It's too much work. And then having to reverse it is even harder.

"What table are we at?"

"Nine."

We make our way over and take our seats as more guests arrive. Sutton looks through the photos that we took outside and posts one to Instagram. I'm not being cocky or anything, but I look decent in feathers, so I approve.

"Share it to your story," she says.

"No."

She gives me a dirty look. "Why not?"

"Because you already posted it. We have the same mutual friends."

THE ONE

"No, Chris deleted me. And I look good. So share it."

Heavy eye roll.

"You're annoying." I take my phone out of my clutch and share it on my Instagram. "Done, now let's go grab some apps and a drink."

*****

Sutton was awarded tonight with the Health Nurse of the Year Award, which she says she didn't know about, but I think she had an inkling. I couldn't be more proud. But it did make for a busy night with a lot of photos.

"Hey, I am going to run to the bathroom quickly. I'll be right back," I whisper to her as she has a conversation with the medical director at Saratoga Hospital.

After I go to the bathroom and wash my hands, I step aside, letting others pass, and grab my phone from my clutch. It's a little after eleven, and I have one missed call and two text messages. All from Greylan.

Crap. We were supposed to talk tonight, and I've been so distracted trying to keep Sutton happy that I forgot.

> **Greylan**: Today sucked. Heading home soon. Call you in an hour or so?
>
> **Greylan**: Looks like you're out. Call when you're home.

That was an hour ago.

Shit.

I text him back quickly.

> **Miley**: Sorry!!! I forgot that I had to go to this fundraiser with Sutton and lost track of time. I hope we are leaving soon. Can I call you when I get home?
>
> **Miley**: Side note, Sutton was awarded nurse of the year!!! Super proud.

THE ONE

Greylan responds right away.

> **Greylan**: Yeah. You can call whenever. That's really big for Sutton. Tell her congrats!

I head back to where Sutton is to see if she is ready to leave. I had a couple drinks tonight and am getting tired, and all I want to do is talk to Greylan. I know he had a rough day, which means his anxiety is likely high, and I just need to make sure he's okay.

"Hey, are you just about ready?" I ask just as she finished up her conversation.

"Yeah, let's give 'em a good ol' Irish goodbye." She laughs and beelines it for the door with her plaque in one hand and her keys in the other.

Once we are outside, I rip the itchy feathers from my face and give her the biggest hug. "I am so proud of you. I hope you know that."

"I do. Thank you."

We climb into her Range Rover because like me, she loves herself a nice car. I shiver. "Howwww doooo I turnnnn on myy heated seatt."

She pressed twelve buttons while reversing, and I feel instant warmth on my ass and back. Thank god.

"Do you care if I call Greylan while we drive home?"

"What's in it for me?"

"Nothing," I say bluntly. "Now just shush it and drive it."

I call him, but he doesn't answer, so I send him a text.

> **Miley**: Almost home. I should be up for another hour or so.

"I forgot that Greylan told me to tell you congrats, and if I haven't said it again and again, I'm super proud of you. You're amazing. I know you love helping kids and that that award means nothing to you, but it should. You're a rock star, and I envy you."

"Thank you, I love you."

"Love you more," I tell her just as my phone rings, and we pull into my driveway.

"Shh!" I give her the evil eye. "Hey."

"Hey," he responds softly.

Oh shit. He doesn't sound okay. I scoot out of the car and make my way inside.

"Are you okay?"

"Yeah, I'm all right, just tired."

"We don't have—"

He interrupts. "I want to."

"Me too." I smirk, shutting Sutton out of my bedroom. I strip out of the weighted dress and throw on sweats and a hoodie, stumbling, half buzzed. "What are you up to?"

"Packing. Ivan and I are flying back tomorrow. What are you doing?"

"Nothing anymore. About to get into bed and be done with today," I tell him.

"Same. It was a rough one today."

"Do you want to talk about it?"

"No, not really. I'm honestly fine. Just exhausted. I need a vacation."

I hop into my bed just as Sutton walks in, and I signal for her to not say a friggin' word. "Ditto."

Greylan pauses for a second. He sounds a bit hesitant, and then says, "Question for you."

"Shoot."

"Will you come to the CMAs with me?"

I nearly choke on my own saliva.

"Like the Country Music Awards?" I manage to ask.

He chuckles. "Yes."

"I'm not sure I'm sober enough for this conversation right now. Can we discuss it tomorrow?"

"Yeah, we have a few days before I need to let them know if I'm bringing a guest."

And when he says that, I start sweating instantly. I don't fit in with his people. I'm not going to be able to pull this off. What the fuck am I going to wear? I try changing the subject.

"So what time are you thinking for dinner on Monday?"

"When do you get out of work?"

I put my phone on speaker. "One sec." I open my calendar to see what we have going on in the office on Monday. Not much, thankfully. "I should be able to leave by five, five thirty."

"How does six work?"

"Perfect." I smile to myself.

Greylan

Yesterday was a long day, but thankfully, it was mostly okay. Many people attended the services for Brody's father and showed their support to his family. It was nice to see. Sad but nice.

Ivan: Here

I grab my luggage, lock up the house, and make my way to Ivan's car just as he pops his trunk open for me.

"Doesn't look like you packed much," Ivan says, and he's right, I didn't. I don't know how long I'll be in New York, and I could always buy more clothes if I need them.

"It's plenty."

"You never asked me to book you a room."

Right, shit. I completely forgot.

"I'll just stay with you tonight, and we can figure it out later. Did you at least get me a car?" I ask.

"Yeah."

*****

By the time our flight lands, it's almost dinnertime. We grab my rental and start driving to Ivan's parents.

"Before we head to your parents' house, can we swing by my house?"

Ivan just stares at me from the passenger seat and doesn't respond.

"It's fine. I'm fine. I just want to go inside and see how much stuff I need to start going through while I'm back here. It will take ten minutes, tops," I tell him.

"If you say so."

I still remember these roads like the back of my hand. I take the main road for miles and then turn onto my childhood street, driving all the way to the dead end and pulling into the long gravel driveway that leads to my house. The place I haven't been back to for years.

It's a small three-bedroom house with a lot of land surrounding it. Very quiet and peaceful.

I park the rental, open the door, and get out. I take it all in for a second, looking around. The landscaping and upkeep look great, thanks to the company I've hired over the years.

"You good?" Ivan asks.

I nod as I make my way up the front step and punch in the code on the door to unlock it. I had the locks changed and a security system put in after my mom passed away. Not that there is much left here. My mom's house has always been mostly empty. She never kept a thing. Except for what's in my sister's room, which has gone untouched since the day she died.

I walk in, and it still smells exactly the same, except with a hint of cleaning products. It's immaculate inside. There are a few totes in each room with stuff in them that I need to go through. I open a kitchen cabinet, and the dishes are still inside, the drawers still have silverware, but the counter is clear and so is the kitchen table. I peek inside a small tote that is in the corner of the room to see what was packed up. It has some mail and paperwork inside, likely all trash, a few cookbooks, and old magnets. This room will be easy to go through. The same with the living room. The only things left are the furniture and two totes in the corner of the room, which likely have photos in them. I'll keep them closed for the time being.

THE ONE

The bathroom is empty, and so is the laundry room. I walk upstairs to where the three bedrooms are and poke my head into my mom's room. It's mostly empty. The only things left are her bed, which is made, a dresser, and several totes that are piled up.

I walk into my room, and it's exactly the same as when I left it.

"Doesn't look like you have much to do here," Ivan says.

"Yeah, should be easy."

"What's your plan for the house?"

I'm not exactly sure what I want to do just yet, but I know I don't want to sell it.

"I don't know, maybe I'll rent it out or something."

I head back downstairs, not attempting to look in Jillian's room.

"I can help you if you need me to."

"Thanks. Let's go, I'm starving."

When we get to Ivan's parents' house, dinner is just about ready. It's just the four of us because Noah is working. We talk about the services but get interrupted every few minutes by the doorbell. I keep forgetting it's Halloween today and how busy this neighborhood gets. His family loves it though. When we are finished eating, they go out on the front porch to pass out candy, and I take the spare bedroom upstairs.

> **Miley**: Happy Halloween. I hope you had a good flight.

I think this is the first time Miley ever initiated a text message, and it makes me happy, really happy.

> **Greylan**: It was painless. How was your day?

She responds right away.

> **Miley**: It was good. Had dinner with my mom, dad and sister and passed out candy to the trick-or-treaters 🎃

THE ONE

I want to know more about her and her family.

> **Greylan**: Is Sutton your only sibling?
> **Miley**: Yup. I think we were too much work so my parents were done with kids after we were born.
> **Greylan**: LOL. What do your parents do?
> **Miley**: They're both retired now but my mom, Kelly, was a 3rd grade teacher and my dad, Phil, was an accountant.
> **Greylan**: Fun fact. I almost went to college for education.
> **Miley**: I could see that.
> **Greylan**: Tell me something I don't know about you.
> **Miley**: I hate my job.
> **Greylan**: I already knew that. Try again.

There's a delay before the next text. Gray dots dance along the screen before they disappear and reappear.

Chapter 24

Miley

I stare down at my phone, reading his question over and over again. I know he has asked about my divorce a few times, and this might be a tactic to learn about it. I take a deep breath, knowing that what I am about to send is going to lead to a discussion about what happened between me and Derek, but given the fact that he's been so open and honest to me, I want to do the same.

I hit send before I have a chance to overthink it.

>**Miley**: I haven't been with anyone since my ex-husband who I met in college.

How's that for honesty?

I haven't had sex in well over two years. And Derek and I were together for ten years. A decade of mediocre sex. Imagine that.

>**Greylan**: And how long ago was that?

Is he asking me the last time I had sex or how long have I been divorced? I take a wild guess.

>**Miley**: I haven't been with anyone in a couple years.

THE ONE

I leave it at that, making sure not to ask him the same question because I most definitely don't want to know the answer. It's none of my business, and it makes me sick to my stomach just thinking about it.

> **Greylan**: What led to your decision to get divorced?

This is difficult for me to talk about because he was unfaithful to me on multiple occasions. I'm afraid people will think I wasn't a good-enough wife or that I wasn't able to satisfy him.

> **Miley**: After we got married, he became cruel and selfish, constantly belittling me. He made me feel worthless. His emotional abuse drove a wedge between us which caused even more issues. Despite my efforts, he didn't change and eventually cheated.

That was the worst day of my life. The pain I endured was excruciating. I felt my heart split in half when he stabbed me in the back. But I learned something that day. I learned that no matter how much you might love someone or how much you want to make it work…sometimes it just doesn't. Sometimes it's not meant to be. Sometimes it's time to move on.

But I should have left sooner, and that's my fault. The second he made me feel worthless is when I should have walked out the door.

I will never let anyone walk all over me again.

Know your worth, set your boundaries, and never let anyone disrespect either of those things.

My phone rings, and it's Greylan FaceTiming me.

As soon as the video connects, he says, "There are people in this world who can't feel big unless they make others feel small, and he sounds like one of them. I'm really sorry he did that to you, Miley."

"It's okay. I've moved far past it."

"If it's any consolation, I think you're worth it."

THE ONE

I smile. "Thank you."

"What are you up to for the rest of the night?" he asks.

"Dodging trick-or-treaters and watching a scary movie with Sutton when she gets out of the shower. What are you doing?"

"I'm working on a new song."

"Can I hear it?" I immediately ask, wanting to hear him sing again.

He stands up, sets his phone against something, fixing the angle a couple times, and then he grabs his guitar. "It's not finished and still needs a lot of work." He sits on the edge of the bed and starts tuning it.

"I have zero musical abilities, but I can try to help." I'm not even sure why I just said that. It seemed like the right thing to say when someone is showing you their work in progress.

"You already have" is all he says before he starts playing.

I close my eyes and listen as he starts singing with that beautiful voice of his.

> I'm searching for a light, to guide my way
> A love so pure, that will stay
> No judgment, no fear, just love and grace
> A sanctuary, a safe place

Instant fucking chills. I open my eyes and watch him through the screen.

> I'm lost and alone, in this vast unknown
> Seeking a heart, to call my own
> Someone to love, without a trace of doubt
> Someone to find me, when I'm lost and out

"That's all I have so far."

I set my phone down and slowly look up. How the hell am I supposed to have dinner with him now?

*****

THE ONE

Today was the longest day of my life. Jeff was in court most of the day, and I was caught up on all my work, so it dragged on and on. I had lunch with Colbie and got her up to speed on everything I neglected to tell her last week. Thankfully, she's no longer mad at me.

After that, I sent Greylan my address, and then I locked myself in my office until it was time to go. I didn't need any backhanded comments made to me because it would just put me in a bad mood, so I stayed far, far away from Tracey.

As soon as I get home, I take a quick shower and change into something more comfortable. I have approximately twenty minutes until he gets here, so I wipe down the counters, make my bed, and pour myself a glass of wine. As soon as I take my first sip, there's a knock at the door.

I open it, and holy hell, does he look good. He's rocking sweatpants and a backward hat. I can't even explain how hot that is to me. Sweet lord.

I try to play it cool. "Come on in."

He steps inside, setting the bag down that he was carrying, and takes off his shoes.

"How considerate of you." I laugh awkwardly.

He stands tall and raises an eyebrow. "You look nervous."

I am friggin' nervous. I have a hot-ass country superstar in my living room with a bag of groceries so he can cook me fucking quesadillas.

I start to sweat.

"I'm good. Shall I give you a tour of my palace?"

Jesus Christ, Miley. Shut the fuck up.

"I'd love a tour."

He picks up his bag and walks into the kitchen, placing it on the counter.

The house I rent is a very modern open-concept home where the living room and kitchen connect. It's super cute and cozy. The entire place was renovated last year. And although it's a bit on the smaller side—two bedrooms, one bathroom flat—I love it.

"This is the kitchen," I say and then point toward the couch, "and that's the living room where I sat and watched *Halloween* last night. Also, that movie is scary as fuck."

"Oh yeah?" Greylan says with a deep chuckle. That low beautiful chuckle that rumbles in my chest as much as it probably does his.

"Yup," I say, popping the *P*.

I walk down the short hallway and gesture to the room with the door open and light on. "Here's my bathroom."

It's plain Jane in there, but at least it's all fresh and sparkling clean from my Sunday fun day scrub down.

I open the door to the room adjacent to the bathroom and flip on the lights.

"This is my office slash storage room."

He peeks inside and looks at the rack on the far end of the room. "You have a lot of shoes."

I laugh out loud. Yes, I do have a lot of shoes. And two closets full of clothes. I love them both equally.

"I love fashion. I can't help it."

I close the door and walk across the hall and flip on my bedroom light, the door already open.

"Here's the last room on the tour, my bedroom."

It's a big bedroom. Not quite a master because I don't have a bathroom, but it's pretty close. I have a nice bedroom set, everything matching, and a large mirror in the corner with a chair and bookshelf nearby.

"Where's Sutton's room?"

Oh god.

"Oh, this is weird," I say awkwardly again.

"What's weird?"

I shut my bedroom light off and walk back to the kitchen. "Sutton staying here is very temporary so she bunks it with me. I offered her the spare room and to buy a bed, but she refused. It's only for a couple weeks until she saves enough money to get her own place. Everywhere around here requires the first month's rent, last month's rent, and a security deposit."

Greylan interrupts, "It's all good. I was just wondering."

THE ONE

As he begins to unload the bag of groceries, I grab my wineglass and take a small sip. "Would you like some wine?"

"Yeah, that sounds good."

I top mine off, just a little bit more to take the edge off, and pour Greylan a glass.

"Where are your pans?"

I point to the cabinet behind him.

I give him his wine, dig out a spatula, and then watch him work his magic while sitting on the countertop.

I don't know if it's the wine or what, but I physically cannot stop staring at this man. He's so handsome. So fit. And so goddamn talented, singing along to every song my Alexa plays while he cooks for me.

I pour us each another glass of wine as he plates the food.

"Thank you, they look and smell amazing."

I grab the squeezable sour cream and add a mountain of it onto my plate.

"Thank you for finally having dinner with me." He winks at me and smiles as he takes a bite from his chicken quesadillas.

Oof...okay, things are getting acutely sweaty over here. The back of my neck feels dewy; my upper lip also seems to have a sheen to it.

"You knew I'd finally cave."

I know he did. I could tell you the exact moment he knew he had me. And that was the second he walked into Trixies.

"I knew I'd finally win you over," he corrects and then finishes a piece of his quesadillas.

Okay, what's happening? What is actually happening? Is he flirting?

I dunk the rest of my quesadilla in the sour cream and finish it. "These are really good."

"Thank you."

"Wanna play a game?" I ask stupidly.

He takes a bite of his food, smiling, and mumbles, "Sure."

"KFM."

"What's that?"

I laugh out loud, very loud actually. "Kill, fuck, marry."

I'm now laughing like a hyena. Too much wine.

"I name three famous people. You have to choose which one from the three would you kill, would you fuck, would you marry."

He shakes his head back and forth but says, "Fine."

"You can go first," I tell him as I finish my second quesadilla and take a gulp of my wine.

"Okay. The Rock, Bradley Cooper, and…me."

He eats his food and washed it down with some wine as well.

"You can't choose yourself." I laugh, wiping my mouth and placing the napkin on my finished plate.

"You said three famous people."

Right, I forgot about that. Touché.

"Easy. I'd marry Bradley Cooper, fuck the Rock, and kill you." I laugh at myself because I think my joke is hilarious. I take my plate to the sink, disposing of my napkin and scraps on the way. "Now my turn. Angelina Jolie, Kim Kardashian, and me."

I rinse my dish, and as I shut off the faucet, Greylan walks toward me, smirking. "Easy. I'd kill the two of them then fuck and marry you."

He pulls me into him, and his hand begins to trace a path along my arm, the touch sending shivers down my spine. His fingers pause at the hollow of my collarbone, then dip lower. I feel a tremor run through me.

He pulls back slightly, as if giving me space to breathe, but I reach for him.

"Mils…" His voice is rough with desire. "You're shaking."

"Okay," I admit, my voice barely a whisper.

"Okay?"

"Yeah."

His hand finds my waist, pulling me closer. Our bodies are pressed together, the heat between us intense. I can feel his heart pounding against my chest, a rhythm that mirrors my own.

His lips brush against my forehead, then my cheek, teasing the corner of my mouth.

THE ONE

"Can I kiss you?" he asks, his breath warm against my skin.

"Yes."

His lips meet mine, soft and gentle. The kiss deepens slowly, a dance of longing and anticipation. His hand moves up my side, lingering just below my breast.

I trace the contours of his body, feeling the hardness of his muscles beneath my fingertips. I pause just above his waistline, my heart pounding against my chest like a warning. He leans in, his breath catching in his throat. Our lips meet again, a desperate, hungry kiss.

Greylan's thumb traces a path beneath my bra, a shiver running through me as it brushes against my nipple. A moan escapes my lips as he circles the tender bud. Then as suddenly as it began, he pulls away, leaving me breathless and wanting more.

I lean in and place a small kiss against his exposed neck, showing him that I want more.

Greylan

That one little kiss is all it takes. My lips collide with hers again as I walk us backward toward her bedroom. Our kiss intensifies, desperate and hungry. Our breaths are uneven, our bodies craving for more. With one hand, I unhook her bra, sending it slipping down her shoulders, but it catches under the sleeves of her shirt. My fingers find her breast once more, kneading it gently.

When the back of her legs hit the edge of the bed, she breaks our kiss and sits down and slides backward toward the center, resting on her forearms once she's where she wants to be.

"You're perfect," I tell her, my voice thick with desire. I climb onto the bed, hovering over her, and kiss her again before pulling away. I look into her eyes, and I can see that she wants this just as much as I do. I kiss her lips once, and then her cheek, down to her neck, finishing at her chest before I tug the hem of her shirt up and dip my head, capturing her nipple with my lips. I can feel the jolt of pleasure shoot through her as I flick my tongue. "So, so perfect."

She wraps her leg around my hip, bringing me closer, my hardness pressing against her. The second she grinds against me, I go fucking lightheaded.

I place a single kiss on her breast before crawling up to lean my forehead against hers. "Tell me what you want, Mils."

"You," she whispers as she sits up and lifts her shirt over her head, removing her unfastened bra in the process. "I want you."

I lean in to kiss her before I stand up. I toss my hat, then reach my arm behind my head, grabbing the back of my shirt, pulling it off, as I watch her eyes follow my body up and down.

This girl is breathtakingly beautiful. Everything about her. I return to her, relishing every curve of her form, every inch of her skin.

The second her hand reaches out between us and palms my length, I lose it, letting out a heady moan as she glides her hand up and down my cock.

"Christ."

My hand slides down between her legs, and I rub her through her pants before dipping it inside and tracing a long line with my middle finger along her slit through her underwear. Her back arches as she lets out the sexiest moan I've ever heard.

"Greylan," she whispers against my ear, causing me to grind against her palm even harder.

I move her underwear to the side and slide my finger up and down her wetness before entering her. A second finger joins the first, curling and pumping. I've never felt so nervous but so filled with energy in my life.

"Not shaking now, are you, Mils?"

She's finally relaxed, falling into me as I kiss my way down her torso. I hook my fingers into both her pants and underwear, tugging them down as my lips meet her hip bone.

I pause for a moment, making sure that she's all right with what I'm about to do.

"Is this okay?"

"It's better than okay."

THE ONE

Once I get the green light, my head disappears between her legs, and I kiss the inside of her thigh.

"Perfect," I tell her before my tongue rolls over her wet center over and over again.

"Oh my god," she murmurs, and the sound of it has my heart skyrocketing into my throat.

When I steal a glance, I'm stunned by the sight of her watching me as I indulge, licking, sucking, and moaning. It's both vulgar and breathtaking—the way she consumes me. A thrill shoots through me with each flick of my tongue as I pin her down with one hand and slip two fingers inside her again. Her moans echo in the room.

Once I feel her start to clench, I slow down and turn to soft kisses against her thigh.

She reaches out and runs her hand over my cheek and against my jaw. I turn into it and kiss the center of her palm.

"I need you."

"You can have whatever you want," I whisper as I make my way back up to her slightly parted, plush pink lips.

I trace my thumb over the curve of her cheek and kiss her deeply as she explores my body, her hands moving with purpose. The feel of her touch is electric. She dips her palm underneath my waistband and strips me bare. I hover over her, forearms on either side of her head, my desire burning. I slide a hand between her thighs, dipping a finger in. She's soaked.

"Greylan..." The way she says my name sends shivers down my spine. I can feel my cock jump forward. "Please."

There's a moment of trust between us. Our eyes locked, asking all the questions we need answers to. Both of us somehow knowing that one would speak up if protection was needed.

She slides her hands up my chest, to my shoulders, keeping her eyes locked on mine, and begs again. "Please, I need you."

God, if that doesn't almost make me come on its own.

Taking myself in my hand, I center in front of her, teasing the head between her legs. And after a moment or two of her squirming beneath me, trying to scoot closer—the greedy girl—I start to dip in. I slowly thrust in and out, watching her beautiful face as she responds to my movements. I press deeper, but she's so tight. I slide my palm up between her breasts. My fingers trace over her nipple, and it has her relaxing enough for me to give a final push, sliding enough so that our hips finally touch. It feels incredible, like heaven. And the angel beneath me looks like a gift from above. She's absolutely beautiful.

I move in and out slowly, trying to find a rhythm. She responds, moving with me. After a moment, we find our pace, and it feels natural. I pick up the speed, and she feels incredible. Her body moves with each thrust, her hands gripping the sheets. My hand goes up to her collarbone, trying to steady her. I can feel her heart beating fast. Maybe I'm going too far. But when I try to pull away, she grabs my wrist and pulls me back. Following her lead, I tighten my grip more, and she moans. "You're fucking perfect."

I hold her there as I thrust in harder, and what a gorgeous sight it is. There are so many things unsaid, but I don't need to say them. She's mine. I pump faster, breathing heavier, and she feels so good. Everything about her is intoxicating. Her long dark hair, her perfect lips and amazing eyes. How small she is beneath me, clutching at my arm.

"Miley, I'm not sure I'm gonna last much longer."

"I don't care," she says through rasping breaths. "Please."

She's going to end me on her politeness alone. But my real undoing is when I watch—actually watch—us fuck. I steal a glance below at my cock sliding in and out of her, her body squirming beneath me as I rub her clit with my thumb.

"Greylan—" She doesn't need to finish her sentence before I feel her tighten around me, a soft moan escaping her lips as my own orgasm surges through me. "Holy fuck," she whispers against my skin.

I chuckle. "Solid eight and a half?"

Chapter 25

Miley

Pushing myself up, I rake my fingers through his dark hair, feeling his heavy breathing against my damp skin. My fingers trace the stubble on his jaw as I hold his gaze. "Ten out of ten," I say simply before going to the bathroom to clean up. When I return, I jump into my bed and snuggle up against him.

"What are you thinking about right now?" he asks.

"How hot you are. How insane your body is. How sweet you are."

His smile is a shot straight to the heart. "I'm being serious."

I exhale nervously, not wanting to have this awkward conversation. "I'm on birth control. I should have told you that."

I completely ignore the fact that I let him inside of me, not knowing where his dick has been. But for some reason, I trust him. I trust that he would have stopped everything before it even started had there been an issue of some sort.

"I trust you, and I hope you trust me too," he says softly.

"I do."

There's several seconds of silence. But it's not awkward, it's comforting.

"Tell me something I don't know about you." It's his favorite question to ask.

I don't know. At this point, I feel as if he knows everything about me. The good, the bad, the ugly. I reply with the only thing that comes to my mind.

"I've never orgasmed like that before." I close my eyes tightly, awaiting his response.

"What do you mean?"

Ehh. How do I explain this...

"Like in that position. I've only had orgasms while on top."

Greylan grabs my hand as he shifts his position and gently pulls me on top of him as he kisses me passionately, softly sliding his tongue against my lips so that I open them for him. He grinds upward at my pelvis as he positions me on top of his hardness.

"Show me."

With his back against the headboard and his legs sprawled, I straddle him, still trembling from the aftershocks of my orgasm.

"Like right now?" I question.

"I'm ready whenever you're ready. I could fuck you all day, every day," he says matter-of-factly, leaving me speechless, but if I'm being honest, so could I.

With one hand propped on his round shoulder, I reach down between us, wrapping my fingers around his throbbing length, and place him against my entrance as I sink down.

Greylan sits up taller to press a kiss to the center of my chest, hands moving around my body, landing on my ass, gripping it tightly. "Fuck, you feel like heaven."

And with those five little words, I ride him like there's no tomorrow, rubbing my clit back and forth on his pelvis until I am tightening around him and unable to move much more.

This feels so different from anything I've done before. It's not forced whatsoever. He is so vocal and so intimate, it makes me feel amazing. Listening to his breaths and moans almost instantly makes me finish. It's like music to my ears, my new favorite song.

I've never had that before. Someone express themselves while having sex. It's all so new, and he isn't holding back. He doesn't give a fuck. He is loud, and he is heard. And just as I rock back and forth, faster and harder, rubbing against him, ready to come, he sits up taller and holds me to him, biting down on me as we finish together. What I am feeling right now as I combust is absolutely insane...and I don't know what to do.

THE ONE

After a minute, he releases his strong hold and stares at me with his piercing black eyes. "You're amazing, Miley."

Not knowing how to respond, I kiss the tip of his nose and climb off him to head to the bathroom to get cleaned up.

If I wasn't falling for him already, I sure as shit am now.

Everything about him.

When I get back to my room, ass naked, Greylan already has his sweatpants on and is grabbing his shirt from the floor.

I feel slightly uncomfortable and confused now, and a bit hurt, knowing that he's just going to up and leave. Maybe I was wrong about everything between us. I felt something, I know I did. And I still feel something. It's extremely strong, a magnetic pull, and he's just going to walk away.

I try to cover myself up and look for my clothes as he gets dressed, but he stops me, moving my hands away from my body, his shirt slung over him.

"You're beautiful," he says, taking his shirt from his shoulder and putting it over my head.

"What are you doing?" I ask as I hesitantly slip my arms through the sleeves.

He completely ignores my question, and instead, he walks back to my bed and slips under the covers and gets comfortable. "You coming?"

Um. What is he doing? I thought he wanted to leave? I'm so confused.

"What are you doing?" I ask again.

"I'm sleeping over. Now get in and cuddle me." He holds the covers up for me to join.

I crawl in and cuddle up against him as he holds me tightly.

"What are you thinking?" I ask him now.

He takes a deep breath in and kisses the side of my head. "That I just won the lottery."

I lightly slap his chest. "I'm being serious."

"I'm thinking that I really want you to come to the CMAs with me."

"When is it?"

"Two weeks from Wednesday, in Nashville."

"What if you have court then?" I ask, bringing up the sore subject that he likely doesn't want to talk about.

"We could fly in late and leave early. You can bring your friends too."

"Okay."

"Okay?"

"Yes. I'll see if we have any news on your case in the morning and ask the girls if they want to come. And I'll have to request the time off from work..." I keep rambling, and he lets me. "And get a dress, and book a flight and hotel—"

"I'll take care of all that."

I smile as he pulls me closer, and I rest my head on his chest. The beat of his heart is a soothing lullaby. The thought of Nashville and red carpets fades as the room grows dark, and I feel myself falling asleep.

*****

I silence my phone as soon as my alarm starts going off, hoping that it doesn't wake Greylan, and slip out of bed to start my day. I tiptoe to the bathroom, wrapping my hair up in a tight bun, and take a hot shower, attempting to process everything that has happened in my head.

When I get out, I turn on my curling iron and section it in three different layers and begin my regimen. After curling layer one, I set the iron aside and apply minimal foundation before beginning layer two. Once I'm done, I put on some mascara and a neutral eye shadow and then add a little blush with a tint of highlighter to my cheeks and face, keeping everything very natural looking.

When I'm finished with my makeup, I unclip the top layer of my hair and curl it, then brush my teeth before tiptoeing back into my room to my walk-in closet.

As always, I check the weather on my phone before picking out my outfit. It's going to be surprisingly nice out today, mid-sixties, so I grab fitted black ankle ponte pants and gray floral blouse and pair it with black block pumps. Super comfortable. Then I head back out to my bedroom where Greylan is still sound asleep.

Sitting on the edge of the bed, I run my hand over his hard chest and up to his shoulder where I gently massage it, waiting for him to wake up.

After several seconds, his eyes flutter awake, and he smiles. "Good morning, beautiful."

I get instant butterflies. I think I could wake up this man forever and never once get sick of it.

"Good morning"—I kiss the side of his cheek—"would you like a bagel for breakfast?"

That's the only option, unfortunately. I typically just drink a protein shake every morning.

"Sounds perfect."

We share a quiet breakfast, the morning light filling the kitchen. I feel lighter than I have in weeks, and I'm not sure I've ever felt this…happy.

"What time do you have to be at work?"

I glance at the clock and chuckle. "In five minutes."

He shakes his head and smiles as I gather my things.

We step outside, and he leans in, pressing a soft kiss to my lips. "Have a good day," he murmurs, his voice a low rumble. "I'll call you later."

"Okay," I reply, a small smile playing on my lips. With a final glance, I turn and head toward my car, the image of his smile lingering in my mind.

When I walk into the office, Tracey stops me immediately. "Mr. O'Connell needs to see you."

I nod and head down the hall, not giving her the time of day. I don't need her tarnishing my good mood.

I hang my jacket up and turn on my computer quick before going to Jeff's office.

His door is open, so I let myself in, taking a seat as he wraps up the call he is on.

"Can we have a conference call next week?" he asks the person on the other line and listens to their response. "Great, my assistant,

Miley, will email you and schedule that later today." He continues. "Thank you for your time, talk to you soon."

He ends the call.

"The court scheduled a preliminary hearing in the Asher matter for Thursday, November 11. Can you let him know?"

"Yes. What time is it scheduled for?" I ask.

"Ten. Also, schedule a call between me and the DA next week. I told him that you'd email my availability."

"Okay, anything else?"

"No, that's it for now. We have three consults today. The pencil files are on your desk."

I stand to leave, but then remember that I need to request time off. "Oh, before I go…I need to take off the sixteenth through the eighteenth. Is that okay?"

"Sure," he says, practically ignoring me. "Just email me the dates and add them to the calendar."

"Thanks."

I go back to my office and send two messages, one to my girls and one to my guy—I mean, Greylan.

> **Miley**: A preliminary hearing has been scheduled for Nov 11th. Sending you an email in a few minutes.

> **Miley**: Anyone want to take a spontaneous trip to Nashville in a couple weeks?
> **Colbie**: For…?
> **Sutton**: Imma need more details…
> **Peyton**: I feel like I am missing something.
> **Miley**: CMAs on Nov. 17th. Sutton, get Peyton up to speed.
> **Sutton**: Call you in a sec, Pey.

THE ONE

Colbie: I'm in. I have no further questions or comments. Just tell me when I need to be to the airport.

The group message goes silent for a few minutes, likely because Sutton is on the phone with her bestie, Peyton. But I trust my girls, and I trust that Peyton won't say a word.

I open Outlook and type out the email to Greylan with the details for the preliminary hearing and send it.

From: Miley Miller
Date: November 2, 2024 9:48 AM
Subject: Preliminary Hearing
To: Greylan Asher

Greylan,

    A Preliminary Hearing for your case has been scheduled for November 11th at 10:00 AM. The hearing will take place at the Saratoga Municipal Center.

    Attorney O'Connell has a call scheduled with the District Attorney next week to discuss the case further. We will provide you with an update after the call.

    If you have any questions or concerns, please do not hesitate to contact our office.

Sincerely,
Miley Miller
Executive Legal Assistant
O'Connell Law Office, LLC

I email the district attorney after with Jeff's availability and then attend to my four unread text messages instead of preparing for our consultations.

> **Sutton**: I will request the time off tonight when I go in but Peyton just checked the schedule and we are already short that day.
> Peyton: I'm coming over after work. I feel left out.
> **Colbie**: What time should I be there?
> **Sutton**: I'm off, come whenever. I have pulled pork in the crockpot and a case of claws in the fridge. Time for bed. Byeeee!

I roll my eyes and laugh at the same time. Help yourselves, guys, no problem. My phone vibrates again, but this time it's Greylan.

> **Greylan**: Thank you. I just sent it to Ivan. I should be good to go back to Nashville a couple days before the CMAs then, right?
> **Miley**: Yes!

Greylan

I'm struggling to get through the day without bothering Miley. I don't want to come off as obsessed, but I'm also okay with spending as much time with her as I possibly can.

Last night was one of the best nights I've ever had in my entire life.

The feeling I get when I think about her is insane, but it multiples it by a thousand when I'm actually with her.

Once all this shit is over, I'm making her mine. I'm determined. But in the meantime, I'm booking us both a much-needed vacation.

Typically, Ivan handles all my travel, but I've got this one on my own.

THE ONE

I book two nonstop flights to Hawaii and a four-night stay at a resort, then call Miley while I internally pray that she doesn't say no.

"Hello?" she answers.

"I was thinking…" I pause, not exactly sure how I should ask her to take off work to go to Hawaii with me and then to the CMAs. The words won't come out.

"What were you thinking, Greylan?"

"That we should go to Hawaii."

She giggles, and it hits me straight in the heart. "Tell me when, and I'll be there."

I'm so fucking nervous right now, I go silent.

"Hello?"

"After the preliminary hearing, let's go to Hawaii for a few nights and then fly to Nashville for the CMAs."

Now it her turn to go quiet. She says nothing.

"Miley?"

"Yeah, I'm here."

"Say yes."

There's what feels like a very long pause, and then finally…

"Yes."

I laid out the plans, and she's going to request the additional time off from work tomorrow. She also said that she invited her sister and two friends to the CMAs, but isn't sure if they can all go. She confirmed Colbie will go and said she'd let me know about Sutton and Peyton by tomorrow.

After we hang up, I go downstairs to talk to Ivan about everything.

"Did you see the email I forwarded you with the preliminary hearing date?" I ask.

"Yeah. My uncle called me about it too. Thank god it doesn't overlap with the CMAs."

"So…about that," I say as he stares at me, waiting for me to continue. "Miley is going to be my guest. Her friend Colbie is going to come too." I grin at him, waiting to get yelled at for not running it by him beforehand.

"And how is Colbie going to be getting in? You only get one guest."

"Don't you get a guest?" I hesitantly ask him.

"You're such a dumbass. I already responded without a guest. I will ask Brody if she can be his plus one."

Ah, fuck. What about her other two friends? Crap. Well, let's just see how it all plays out. I will beg for forgiveness later. I know if Peyton and Sutton want to come, Ivan will be able to work his magic, and everything will be just fine. In the meantime, I'm not saying a word.

"Thank you, bestie." I smirk.

He rolls his eyes at me. "You don't pay me enough to deal with your bullshit."

I laugh out loud because I honestly have no idea how much I pay him. He's the one who controls my money and who gets paid what. He could give himself whatever he wants, and I wouldn't bat an eye.

"Double your salary in January," I tell him, and he looks at me blankly.

"I'm being serious, you deserve it. And I am grateful for you."

He cocks his head to the side, looking very confused. "Why are you so chipper right now? What am I missing?"

I guess maybe I am happy. I finally have something to be excited about.

"Nothing, all good."

"I call bullshit. It's because of Miley, isn't it? What did you do, Greylan?"

Do I tell him? I probably should. He's going to find out either way.

"I like her a lot. She makes me happy, and she isn't fake. She hardly knows who I am, and I enjoy being with her. So, yes, I am finally happy. And she's coming to the CMAs with me, and I don't give a shit if your uncle finds out."

And I really don't. I am hoping all the shit is wrapped up at the preliminary hearing, and I can move on with my life. And I hope Miley follows.

"I'm not going to ask any more questions because I don't want to know the answers," he says, looking annoyed but also pleased with my happiness.

I decide to go in for the kill since he says he isn't going to ask any more questions and doesn't appear to be too pissed off, which I'm sure has to do with the fact that I just told him to double his salary.

"After the preliminary hearing, I'm taking her to Hawaii for a couple days and then flying back to Nashville for the CMAs. I already booked it."

"Jesus Christ. Anything else I need to know?"

Might as well keep going while I can.

"I'm going to clear out my mom's house this week and offer it to Miley's sister, Sutton, to rent."

"Okay." He pauses. "And if she doesn't want to rent it?"

"Then I will continue the maintenance and figure it out after."

I'm not ready to sell my childhood home. Too many memories. I'd rather hang on to it because frankly, I can. I don't need to sell.

"Do you want me to get you a storage unit?"

I don't know if I need a storage unit. Mostly everything is gone. I think I will just take the stuff that I actually want and then give the rest away.

"No, I'm going to only keep the sentimental stuff, and the rest can be donated."

Ivan's phone rings, and his face transforms when he looks at the screen. He answers it right way. "This is Ivan." He walks to the other room. I try to listen to what's being, said but he's silent. After a moment, he says, "You can go fuck yourself. Goodbye."

He storms back into the kitchen looking pissed as hell.

"Who was that?" I ask.

"Rob. He's looking for his hush money."

I don't care if I was the richest person in the world; I wouldn't give that guy twenty bucks if he needed it. I know he will buy drugs with it like the scumbag he is.

"He can sue me. I'm not giving that dirtball anything."

THE ONE

"Yeah, I told him that. He threatened to go to the media by the end of the week, so we need to come up with a plan. Do you have any dirt on him at all that we can use as leverage?"

That's a good question. I could probably do some digging and find something. Two can play this game. Let's fucking go.

"I think it's time to go through Jillian's bedroom." I pause. Am I really ready for that? I think I am. But I know I can't do it alone. "Will you help me tomorrow?"

Chapter 26

Miley

My night was full of surprises. A spontaneous girls' night, which included way too much alcohol and food, and to top it off, Greylan invited me to go to Hawaii with him before the CMAs, and I freakin' said yes. At this point, I don't care if Jeff finds out and cans me. I'm happy, and that's all that matters. What's the worst that can happen? I get fired and can't find a new job, so I blow through my savings just to pay my rent, and when I hit rock bottom, I have to move back home with my mom and dad? I'll take my chances at this point. Wanna know why? Because I'm falling. I'm falling hard for Greylan Asher.

I head to Jeff's office and knock on the open door. "Hey, do you have a second?"

"Sure." He doesn't look up from his computer.

"I actually need to take off a couple more days in addition to the ones that I requested yesterday."

He doesn't bat a lash. "Okay, just put them on the calendar."

"Okay, thanks. I also scheduled that call with the DA for next week. He just emailed me back a little while ago. It's on Tuesday and already on the calendar."

He finally acknowledges my presence and looks up from his screen. "Thanks." He changes the subject rather quickly. "Can you draft a Motion to Dismiss in the Yates case?"

"Sure. Anything else?" I ask.

"No. But if you could get me the draft before you leave, that would be great."

THE ONE

I'm certain I roll my eyes right in front of him. Because it's annoying that I do all his work, and he gets all the credit. Actually, I now find it comical. He depends on me. He hasn't drafted shit in years. And once I am finished doing his job for him, he makes me enter the time spent drafting the pleadings under his name so that the billable rate is higher. And that's how he got his nickname as O'Douchebag.

"Will do."

I lock myself in my office, but before I get to work, I put my vacation dates on the calendar and email them to the douche.

>From: Miley Miller
>Date: November 3, 2024 11:23 AM
>Subject: Vacation Days
>To: Jeffrey O'Connell
>
>Jeff,
>
>As per our conversation, I will be on vacation from Friday, November 12th through Thursday, November 18th. I will return to the office on Friday, November 19th.
>
>Please note that I will have limited access to phone and email during this time.
>
>Sincerely,
>Miley Miller
>Executive Legal Assistant
>O'Connell Law Office, LLC

"Going anywhere fun?"

I jump halfway out of my seat as I look up and see Jeff standing there. He came out of nowhere and startled me. You can bet your ass that I will never knock on his door before entering his office again so that I can scare the shit out of him randomly.

"Girl's trip with Colbie."

I internally freak out, praying he doesn't ask any questions and, thankfully, am saved by the bell when my work phone rings. It's Tracey.

"Hello?"

"Mr. O'Connell's eleven thirty is here."

"Okay, thanks."

I hang up and tell him.

"Your consult is here. Do you need me for it?" I ask, knowing that he doesn't. If he did, he would have forwarded me emails and given me the file prior.

"Nope. Yates's case takes priority."

As he leaves my office, I let out a breath, thanking the lord baby Jesus that he didn't inquire more about my trip to Hawaii. Then I text Greylan quickly before I'm drowning in drafts for the rest of the day.

> **Miley**: Approved. Hawaii, here we come!
> **Greylan**: You just made my day.
> **Miley**: Happy to help. What're you up to?
> **Greylan**: Heading to my house to go through some stuff.
> **Miley**: That's gotta be tough. I am here if you need me.
> **Greylan**: Thanks, I will text you after.
> **Greylan**: Oh, quick question. Do you know anyone that would be interested in renting the house before I list it?
> **Miley**: Yes. Sutton is actively looking and works near there. I will ask her when she wakes up. Touch base with you later?
> **Greylan**: Sounds good.

Greylan

I was good all day until I walked inside. I didn't panic or freak out, and I didn't overthink anything. I thought I was good to go;

however, now that I am here, I'm not sure that I can do it. Enter her bedroom. Go through her stuff.

My heart begins to race.

"You good?" Ivan asks.

I just need to push through. I need to close this chapter in my book. I need to find dirt on the scumbag that's to blame for my sister's death. I need to move forward.

"Yeah, I'll be fine," I say as I open her bedroom door and instantly get a whiff of her fragrance, which physically calms me. I breathe it in. I miss it. It's very subtle but still there.

I honestly couldn't tell you if my mom ever stepped foot in this room after Jillian died, but I can almost guarantee you she didn't. I lost my sister and couldn't open the door. Imagine what it's like losing your child?

I walk over to her bed and pick up the piece of paper that's on top. I guess I'm wrong, she has been back in this room.

Dear Jillian,

My dearest daughter, my heart breaks for the pain I have caused you. I deeply regret my failures as a parent. I allowed grief to consume me, leading to harmful choices. I neglected your needs and ignored your cries for help. I am so sorry for the alcoholic haze that clouded my judgment and prevented me from being the mother you deserved.

I fear I may never fully absolve myself of the guilt of shaping you into someone you were not meant to be. The weight of my mistakes makes it difficult to envision a future free from this burden. I have failed you and our family. I'm so sorry.

Love,
Mommy

THE ONE

My hands tremble as I hold the fragile paper. The ink is faded, but the words...they slice through me like shards of glass. I read them again and again, each syllable a fresh wound. My mother's confession echoes in the silence of this room.

A coldness spreads through my chest, a hollow ache that I recognize as a strange mix of grief and something close to...vindication? No, not vindication. A confirmation, perhaps. A confirmation of the unspoken truths that have haunted me.

I feel a strange detachment. It's like I'm watching a play, a tragic drama, where the characters are my own family. A ghostwriting to another ghost, and I'm the silent observer left to pick up the pieces.

My breath catches in my throat. I feel the weight of her guilt, her regret, pressing down on me, suffocating me.

I pass it to Ivan. "I just need a couple minutes. I'll be right back."

I practically run out of the room and try to focus on my breathing. I can feel the panic begin to rise, the bile in the back of my throat, and my heart pound in my chest.

It physically takes everything I have left in me, but I push the anxiety to the back of my head and focus on the task at hand, the reason that I am here, and go back in.

"Are you okay?" he asks, and he puts something back inside of a box.

"Yeah, I'm good. What's that?"

"A box of sentimental things that your mom must have collected."

"But what were you just reading?" I ask, not entirely sure that I want to know the answer.

"The eulogy you read at the funeral."

Instant flashbacks of that day fill my memory. Writing the eulogy wasn't hard; I wrote down everything I wanted to say to those who surrounded her...but saying it out loud for everyone to hear was almost unbearable.

I open the top to the box and look inside. The prayer cards, photos from the display boards, the book of signatures of everyone

THE ONE

who attended, and my eulogy. I unfold the paper and read it, almost ten years after I wrote it.

We need to remember
the good times with Jillian.
We need to collect these moments.
Life is not measured by time,
it is measured by moments.

Jillian wasn't perfect. But who is perfect?

Remind yourself that,
like roses, we all have our thorns.
But it does not make us any less beautiful.
The most beautiful things are never perfect.

Maybe Jillian's past wasn't pretty,
maybe it was a little messy
and complicated, so what?
She was still a rose.

The beauty of a rose is evident,
but its ability to bloom,
despite apparent imperfections,
is what makes it truly remarkable.

A Letter To:
<u>*Anyone Suffering from Addiction*</u>

Sometimes life feels heavy.
It feels messy. It feels chaotic.

You lost something. You lost your way.

Sometimes it feels like everything goes wrong.

THE ONE

*Sometimes it feels like you're stuck,
like you're motionless.*

*Just remember,
tomorrow is an entryway.
Tomorrow is a second chance.
Tomorrow is a new day.*

*A Letter To:
<u>My Mother</u>*

*Do not let situations replay over in your head.
Take a deep breath and make peace with it
and keep putting one foot in front of the other.*

*I hope you can learn that just because
something ends,
does not mean you have failed.*

*A Letter To:
<u>Jillian</u>*

*One thing I know for certain is that
life is unpredictable.*

*Sometimes in life there are losses
that can never be replaced.*

*Losing you has been the hardest thing
I've ever had to live with.*

I wasn't ready to say goodbye.

*I loved you then. I love you now.
Always did. Always will.
Forever in my mind. Forever in my heart.*

THE ONE

I remember that day like it was yesterday. Standing there, everyone watching me as I read those letters out loud to a group of over two hundred people. My mother never once said a single word about it afterward.

I take out the rest of the stuff in the box, seeing what else is in it, and at the bottom, I find the evidence bag from the night of the car accident. I pull it out and dump the contents on the bed without thinking twice. Her wallet, very little money, the jewelry she was wearing, and a phone.

"Is that her cell phone?" Ivan loudly asks as I pull it out and attempt to turn it on.

It's dead as dead can be.

"We need to charge it. I'm sure there are messages or something that we can use as leverage."

I pass Ivan the phone, and he looks at the port and raises an eyebrow. "We're going to need to Amazon Prime a charger for this ancient-ass phone."

I shake my head and smile because it's true. How much technology has evolved over the last decade is mind-blowing.

"Check the side of her bed, that's where she always left it," I tell him, remembering our arguments when I would steal her charger from her bedroom.

"Jackpot," Ivan says as he plugs in her iPhone 5 as my iPhone 16 vibrates, alerting me that I have a new message.

> **Miley**: Hey you. Just checking in. Are you okay?

I reply right away.

> **Greylan**: I'm good. Still here but I'm alright. Did you have the chance to ask Sutton about possibly renting the house yet? No pressure… just wondering
>
> **Miley**: Yes. She is very interested but, unfortunately for you, has a million questions. Is it okay to give her your number (or Ivan's if he's

the point person) so you can discuss? I can have her sign a NDA prior... just let me know.

I laugh out loud, only because she thinks I actually give a damn about the agreement. And don't get me wrong, I used to. I wouldn't cross paths with anyone who didn't sign one. But I trust her tremendously. The nondisclosure agreement she signed is moot. It doesn't exist to me.

Greylan: Unnecessary. I trust you.
Miley: Phew, because I gave it to her already and then I started to freak out once she replied "OMG, I have Greylan Asher's phone number." HAHA. I keep forgetting that you're famous.

She makes me laugh so uncontrollably loud, Ivan begins to look nervous. Note to self, Miley is oblivious.

Greylan: Hahaha. Thanks for the laugh.

And thank god for the distraction because Ivan holds up the phone and shows me that it's powering on.

Miley: Oh. One last thing... Sutton and Peyton can't go to the CMAs because of work so it will just be me and Colbie.
Greylan: Sounds great. She will be my friend Brody's guest. He's chill, don't worry. I'll have Ivan book her a flight.

"It's on," Ivan says, and my stomach drops.
I can't do this.
"Can you go through it for me?"
He just stares at me.
"Please, Ivan."
"Okay." He takes a deep breath and starts to go through it.

THE ONE

"I'm going to grab boxes from the car. I'll be right back." I leave the room as my phone buzzes.

Miley: I'm super excited. Just so you know ☺

Instant butterflies take over the panic that was starting to rise. Immediate relief with just reading those three little words. Miley is saving me. The more time I spend talking to her, the more alive I feel.

Greylan: I'm super happy.

I grab the empty boxes from the car so that I can start to pack up some things in Jillian's bedroom. When I go back in, Ivan's face is as white as a ghost, which makes me very worried.

"What's wrong?"

He hands me the phone so that I can read the messages between Rob and my sister from the night of the accident, but I can't do it.

"I'm not ready for that. Just tell me if it's enough to get him to go away."

"It's more than enough." Ivan takes the phone back from me. He lays it down on the bed before snapping a photo of the messages. Before he leaves the room with her phone, he says, "I'll handle it."

I put some of her things in a box, and once I'm done, I check my phone, and I have a new email from Miley.

> From: Miley Miller
> Date: November 3, 2024 2:13 PM
> Subject: Meeting re: Preliminary Hearing
> To: Greylan Asher
>
> Greylan,
>
> Are you available to meet with Mr. O'Connell on Wednesday, November 10th at 10:00 AM at his home office? This meeting would be to

THE ONE

prepare for the preliminary hearing on Thursday, November 11th.

Please let me know your availability at your earliest convenience.

Sincerely,
Miley Miller
Executive Legal Assistant
O'Connell Law Office, LLC

I respond as soon as I see it, confirming my availability.

From: Greylan Asher
Date: November 3, 2024 2:22 PM
Subject: Meeting re: Preliminary Hearing
To: Miley Miller

Works for me. Thanks, Miley.

-Greylan

Chapter 27

Miley

These past several days have been utterly chaotic. Between preparing for my weeklong absence at work and helping Sutton pack for her big move, I've had zero downtime. But I somehow managed to get through it. Now all I need to do is get through today and tomorrow then off to Hawaii I go.

I make a cup of coffee at home since I am going straight to Jeff's house this morning and throw a load of laundry in the wash. I will finish packing tonight when I get home, then after tomorrow's preliminary hearing, I will erase work from my brain until after I come home from Nashville.

"What time are you leaving on Friday?"

I'm startled right away. I didn't even see Sutton sitting on the couch.

"Super early. When did you get home?"

"Few minutes ago. What time do you come home on the eighteenth?" she asks.

"Early afternoon. I will email you all the information."

I know she is going to want it anyways. She is going to need to know my flight numbers, the name of the resort we are staying at, Greylan's address in Nashville, and the location of the CMAs. And if I don't give it to her before I depart, there will be hell to pay. I learned that the hard way once, and I won't make that mistake again.

"Thanks. Did you invite him over for Thanksgiving dinner?"

THE ONE

I haven't given that a thought. I wonder what he typically does during the holidays since he doesn't have any family. If I had to guess, he celebrates with his friends.

"I haven't. Should I?"

"Yes, you probably should. But ask him first, then tell Mom and Dad. If you mention it first and he already has plans, then they are just going to bombard you with a million questions over dinner."

She's got a point. I will ask him when we are in Hawaii.

"Okay, I will ask...but not until after the preliminary hearing."

"Smart." She stands. "I'm going to bed. Love you. See you later."

"Love you too," I tell her as I pack up my bag and get ready to go to Jeff's house.

I haven't seen Greylan in over a week, but I've talked to him every day. He seems okay but slightly stressed over cleaning out his mom's home and going through Jillian's belongings. I'm sure tomorrow's preliminary hearing isn't making the situation any better.

I'm not sure how Jeff's call went with the district attorney yesterday, but it couldn't have gone too bad since he was in a decent mood for the majority of the day.

I park in the driveway behind Jeff's car just as Ivan and Greylan pull up. It's going to be so hard hiding the fact that we have been involved with each other. I want nothing more than to run up to him and wrap my legs around his body while giving him a huge hug.

"Hey, guys. Good morning."

They walk up the stairs side by side just as Jeff opens the door before we even knock.

"Good morning, come on in."

Everyone enters then heads to the office to get started with our meeting. I take my usual seat.

"Thanks for coming in. I just want to update you on your case and prepare you for tomorrow's preliminary hearing."

Greylan takes the seat directly across from mine and acknowledges Jeff with a nod.

"I have been in contact with the prosecutor—"

Ivan interrupts, "What do you mean a prosecutor?"

THE ONE

Jeff looks annoyed but answers his question. "The district attorney who represents the government in criminal cases. We had a conference call yesterday, and it is my understanding that we have a great chance of having your case completely dismissed."

"That's great, thank you," Greylan says.

"The DA will present the main evidence to the judge tomorrow—"

"What evidence?" Ivan interrupts yet again.

"The footage from the patrol car when it pulls up with Greylan in the driver seat along with the Breathalyzer and police report." When no one comments, Jeff continues, "He may ask you some questions regarding the incident, you can answer them honestly. He will likely call the officer to the stand to testify."

"Okay," Greylan acknowledges.

"Once the DA is finished, I will present our evidence and cross-examine the officer and ask you questions as well, if needed."

"Our evidence are the surveillance videos, correct?" Greylan shifts nervously in his chair.

"Yes."

"What happens after that?" Ivan asks.

"If the judge finds probable cause, the case moves forward to a trial…but if he doesn't, the charges will be dismissed."

"And what are the chances that the charges will be dismissed?" Greylan asks.

"Very likely."

I didn't realize I was holding my breath until I could finally breathe again after he says that. Jeff is usually very optimistic when predicting the outcome of a case, but he doesn't typically give someone a guarantee that big.

"Let's have a quick coffee break, and then we can run through some of the questions that I have prepared for when you are on the stand."

"Sounds good, but before we do that, can I update you on the assault matter?" Ivan says.

"Please do. Miley, takes notes."

I uncap my pen and position it so that I am ready to write.

"Last week I received a call from Rob, who, by the way, sounded hammered. He threatened to go to the media if he didn't have fifty thousand dollars by the end of the week. I ended the conversation by telling him to go fuck himself."

Jeff takes a deep breath in and slowly releases it, trying to keep his composure in front of Greylan. If the two of us weren't in this room, I'm certain that Jeff would slap the shit out of his nephew.

"Keep going."

"Well, obviously, this all ties into Greylan's sister, Jillian's, death, so we did some digging to find leverage to use against him, and we found her phone and reviewed text messages prior to the accident."

I'm in complete shock right now. I don't know what to do, what to say, or where to look, so I keep my head down and keep writing.

"When did this happen?" Jeff asks.

"We found the phone last Wednesday."

"I'm going to skip over what the messages said and ask the question that gets us straight to the point. What happened after you found and read the messages?"

"I called Rob's bitch ass and told him what I found, and if he contacts us again, goes to the media, or interferes with Greylan's life in any way, shape, or form, I'd ruin him and bring the messages to the police department."

"And what was his response?"

"He hung up. We haven't heard a word from him. Even after the due date for hush money expired."

"If he contacts you again, direct him to me." He stands, which means the conversation is done and the boss needs coffee. "Miley, you're all set. You can go."

Thank god. Not that I don't want to be here with Greylan; I just need to tie up a few loose ends and finish a couple assignments before I leave for vacation. If I don't, I know I won't enjoy my time because I will be stressing about it.

"Okay." I pack up my bag and follow them out as they go to the kitchen for coffee. "See you tomorrow."

I walk to the front door but am cut short when Greylan steps to my side from behind and places his arm across my lower back, leans in, and kisses the side of my head. "I missed you."

I get instant panic when I realize where we are. "What are you doing?" I shimmy away.

"Ivan's distracting him. We have a solid sixty seconds. Hug me." He opens his arms and waits from me to enter, and when I finally do, I melt.

"I missed you more."

"Not possible," he responds with his chin resting on the top of my head. He slowly pulls away and looks into my eyes and smiles before kissing me on the forehead and stepping back to walk away. "See you tomorrow, Mils."

Greylan

Insomnia's grip tightens, tossing me from side to side. I'm counting down the hours until the night is over, when I can finally finish everything and hopefully start a new chapter, one I hope to share with Miley. I look at the clock, and it's three thirty in the morning. What the hell am I supposed to do for the next few hours? My mind is haunted by the texts I read on Jillian's phone from Rob. No matter how hard I try to distract myself, they keep replaying in my head. It's been eating away at me for a week. Miley can sense my distress, but I haven't told her exactly why, and she hasn't pressed the issue. I don't want her to feel like she needs to save me every time my head goes under the water. I need to try to figure it out on my own.

I get out of bed and quietly go downstairs to the kitchen to get some water, I don't want to wake up Ivan's parents or brother. I grab a glass and start to fill it when I'm suddenly startled.

"You okay?"

I jump and almost spill it everywhere.

"You scared the shit out of me, Mr. Stevens."

"Stop calling me Mr. Stevens, it's weird."

"Sorry, Kirk. I was just getting some water. I couldn't sleep."

I'm pretty sure I've never called him by his first name, and I've known him since I've been a teenager. He's been a father figure to me since then.

THE ONE

"Are you worried about court tomorrow?"

"I just want it to be done and over with."

"You're gonna be all right, kid."

I know I'm going to be. It just takes time, and I need to move at my own pace. As long as I keep putting one foot in front of the other and step forward, then I don't care how long it takes. With the right people by my side, I know I will finally find peace.

I finish my water and place it in the sink before making my way back upstairs.

"Greylan..."

I stop and turn to Mr. Stevens.

"Remember those words you read at Jillian's funeral?" he asks, and I acknowledge with a nod. "Read them again, but read them to yourself this time. I'm here if you ever need anything, son."

With that, I go back upstairs to lie back down. As I close my eyes, I repeat to myself the same words I told my mother, "Do not let situations reply over in your head. Take a deep breath and make peace with it, and keep putting one foot in front of the other."

I drift off to sleep.

*****

Preliminary Hearing
November 11, 2024

THE COURT:	Good morning, everyone. This is the preliminary hearing for the case of *State v. Greylan Asher* charged with driving while intoxicated.
PROSECUTOR:	Your Honor, the State calls Officer Baker to the stand.
THE COURT:	Please raise your right hand. Do you swear to tell the truth, the whole truth, and nothing but the truth?
OFFICER:	I do.

THE ONE

PROSECUTOR: Officer, on October 18, 2024, did you have occasion to observe a vehicle being operated in a manner that caused you to stop it?

OFFICER: The vehicle was already stopped when I arrived.

PROSECUTOR: When you approached the vehicle, what did you observe about the driver?

OFFICER: The driver, who I later identified as Greylan Asher, was in the driver seat of the running vehicle where I detected a strong odor of alcohol.

PROSECUTOR: Did you administer any field sobriety tests?

OFFICER: Not on the scene but back at the station.

PROSECUTOR: So you placed Mr. Asher under arrest?

OFFICER: Yes, I did. I placed him under arrest for driving while intoxicated.

PROSECUTOR: Did you transport Mr. Asher to the police station?

OFFICER: Yes, I did.

PROSECUTOR: At the police station, was a Breathalyzer test administered?

OFFICER: Yes, he submitted to a Breathalyzer test, which indicated a blood alcohol content of .22.

PROSECUTOR: No further questions, Your Honor.

MR. O'CONNELL: Your Honor, I would like to cross-examine the officer.

(Cross-Examination)

THE ONE

MR. O'CONNELL: Officer, please tell me why you were dispatched to the scene on October 18, 2024.

OFFICER: I was dispatched to the scene for a bar fight between Greylan Asher and another individual inside.

MR. O'CONNELL: And when you arrived, Mr. Asher was in a vehicle outside of the bar?

OFFICER: Yes. He was in the driver seat of the car, and the car was running.

MR. O'CONNELL: So Mr. Asher wasn't physically driving the car?

OFFICER: The car was on, and he was in the driver seat.

MR. O'CONNELL: But you didn't physically see him operating the vehicle?

OFFICER: No.

MR. O'CONNELL: Please tell me what happened next after you arrived on scene.

OFFICER: I interviewed him about the incident that occurred inside of the bar.

MR. O'CONNELL: And then what happened?

OFFICER: He admitted to the physical altercation.

MR. O'CONNELL: Did you interview the other individual involved in the physical altercation?

OFFICER: Yes.

MR. O'CONNELL: When?

OFFICER: After I interviewed the defendant, I went inside and interviewed the other individual.

MR. O'CONNELL: So you went inside, interviewed the other individual, and then, thereafter, you arrested Mr. Asher?

OFFICER:	Yes.
MR. O'CONNELL:	Do you personally know Greylan Asher?
OFFICER:	No.
MR. O'CONNELL:	Did you personally know the other individual involved in the physical altercation?
PROSECUTOR:	Objection.
THE COURT:	Sustained. Where are you going with this, Attorney O'Connell?
MR. O'CONNELL:	Your Honor, at this time, I move to dismiss the charges against Greylan Asher. We present to the court two videos supporting dismissal.
THE COURT:	Do you have any objections, Mr. Norris?
PROSECUTOR:	I do not.
THE COURT:	Proceed with the first video.
MR. O'CONNELL:	The first video is the surveillance video from outside of the bar. You will see Mr. Asher exit the bar and try to use his cell phone. When he realizes it is dead, he asks his friend for the keys to his car so that he can charge his phone while he waits for the police to arrive.

[VIDEO PLAYS]

MR. O'CONNELL:	As you can see, Mr. Asher did not operate the vehicle, nor did he have any intentions to operate the vehicle. He was simply waiting for police to arrive and charging his phone.
THE COURT:	What is the second video?

MR. O'CONNELL:	The officer's body camera footage.
THE COURT:	Do you have any objections, Mr. Norris?
PROSECUTOR:	I do not.
THE COURT:	Proceed.
MR. O'CONNELL:	As you can see—
THE COURT:	I would like to review the footage in its entirety without explanation, Mr. O'Connell.

[VIDEO PLAYS]

THE COURT:	Counsel, approach the bench.
THE COURT:	At this time, we are going to break for a recess so that I can review both videos again, and we will meet back in my chambers in twenty minutes. Before I do that, Mr. Norris, do you have any response to the defense's motion?
PROSECUTOR:	No, Your Honor.

(Court Decision)

THE COURT:	Having reviewed the evidence presented, the court finds the prosecution has failed to establish probable cause to proceed with the charges against Greylan Asher.
MR. O'CONNELL:	Thank you, Your Honor.
THE COURT:	This matter is hereby dismissed.

The judge's words, "Case dismissed," hang in the air, a fragile hard-won victory. I feel the tension drain from my body, leaving me weak but strangely light. Ivan's by my side instantly; his hand on my shoulder is firm and steady.

I nod, unable to speak—the weight of the past few weeks, the accusations, and the ugly insinuations still pressing down on me. "I...I can't believe it," I manage, my voice hoarse.

"Believe it," Ivan says, his eyes filled with an emotion that mirrors my own. "It's done. That...that whole nightmare...it's finished."

"Watching that video again nearly killed me."

"I know." He pulls me into a hug, a brotherly embrace that speaks volumes. "We've been through hell together. You and me," his voice muffled against my shoulder. "And I'm really sorry that I wasn't a better friend at the onset of this bullshit."

"Thanks, Ivan," I say, my voice full of emotion. "I don't know what I'd do without you."

"We're brothers, man," he says, pulling back, a playful grin on his face. "Always will be. Now let's go make sure you didn't fuck up any of your vacation plans with your girl."

Chapter 28

Miley

Finding out that Greylan's case was dismissed was probably the best news I've heard in years. He really deserves for that chapter to close in his book because, man, was that entire situation messed up. I still can't wrap my brain around it. But I'm now filled with apprehension. Because what comes next? What comes next for him? For us? What if this magical time in Hawaii and at the CMAs is all we get? What if he returns to his life, and I stay in mine?

My eyes dart to the wall. The clock reads almost five in the morning. A wave of anxiety washes over me. I meticulously check my luggage one last time before zipping it shut, the seconds ticking away as I wait for Greylan to arrive. As soon as his headlights sweep across my driveway, I grab my luggage and head out.

He steps out of his rental to help me, but not before giving me the biggest hug, which puts a permanent smile on my face.

"You look beautiful and very comfortable."

Comfy clothes are a must for a full day of travel. My coziest sweater found its way over leggings, and I completed the ensemble with a pair of easy-to-walk-in sneakers.

"You don't look too bad yourself," I joke back.

"Ready to roll?"

"Ready as I'll ever be."

He opens my car door for me and waits until I am seated and situated before shutting it. Such a gent. You don't find them like this anymore.

"Where's your dress for the CMAs?" he asks.

"Colbie is going to bring it with her. It's still having a few alterations done to it."

It was a tad too long, and I needed to have the straps adjusted a bit, but other than that, she fits just like a glove, hugging me in all the right places. I can't wait for him to see it.

"If you guys need to ship anything to my house, you can do that too."

"Okay, thanks. I will let her know."

A brief silence hangs in the air, but unable to contain the question swirling in my mind, I blurt it out. "So are there going to be tons of people running up to you for your autograph and pictures?"

"Where?"

Fucking everywhere, Greylan. That's where.

"Um…" I wave my hand in a circle, referring to everywhere. "The airport, the hotel, anywhere we go…" I think a little more. "At the CMAs. Everywhere."

He laughs. He friggin' laughs at me. So I cross my arms like a child and stare at him until he answers the question.

"We will be fine at Albany International. It's so small, not too many people will recognize me. Plus, we'll be first to board the plane and the first to exit. First class perks."

I roll my eyes. I've never sat in first class in my life. This is going to be a week full of new experiences.

"We have a short layover in LA and will need to switch terminals, so we might get some attention there, but nothing crazy."

"Okay." I wait for him to continue.

"No one should bother us in Hawaii at all. The hotel staff could lose their jobs if they did."

I nod in acknowledgment and to let him know he should keep going. I need to know what is going to happen at the CMAs.

"You'll be perfect at the CMAs. But let's discuss that after our vacation. One thing at a time." He smiles as he reaches over and places his hand just above my knee, giving it a light squeeze.

THE ONE

When we pull up to the airport, he parks off to the side near the entrance and puts his hazard lights on before getting out and opening my door.

"Let's go, beautiful." He reaches his hand out, and I take it just as a gentleman walks over to us.

"How was everything?" the man asks.

"Great, thank you." Greylan hands him the keys to the rental.

"We just need to grab our bags from the trunk quick," I interrupt.

"He's got it covered, Mils. Is your ID in your purse?"

"Yes," I answer hesitantly.

"Then we are good to go." He takes his hand in mine, and we take the escalator upstairs to TSA. It's a little busy here, but the first flights of the day are getting ready to board, so it's to be expected. We zip through TSA precheck and make our way to our terminal.

"I'm just going to use the bathroom fast before we board," I tell him before slipping in and doing my thing.

When I walk out, I see Greylan talking to two people, likely fans of his, but as I walk closer, I nearly die, stopping myself completely before I try to run as far away as I humanly can because... This. Is. Not. Real. Life. Right. Now.

Everyone just stares at me, but Derek's eyes go back and forth between me and Greylan.

I slowly walk forward, feeling thirty-seven different emotions all at once. I can't begin to tell you how fucking awkward and uncomfortable this is for me.

"Do you two know each other?" Derek asks out loud as Greylan reaches for my hand and lightly pulls me to him.

"This is my girlfriend, Mi—"

Derek cuts him off. "Miley Maston."

"Miley Miller." I stand my ground to the person who purposely hurt me for years. "I changed my name back the same day our divorce was finalized, you imbecile."

I look to Greylan and can already tell that he instantly put the pieces together.

THE ONE

"Let's go," I say, but as we go to leave, Derek adds, "Good luck dealing with her crazy ass. That one is a big crybaby at night."

Oh hell no, he did not just say that, I will fuck—

Greylan beats me to it, taking a large step toward him, towering over his stupid ass. "Say one more stupid thing about her, and you're leaving here on a stretcher. Are we clear?"

After Derek nods in response, Greylan takes my hand, and we walk away without another word coming out of his mouth.

Just as we get to our gate, they call group A, first class, for boarding. We enter the plane and once we are situated, the flight attendant brings over two blankets, two pillows, and two mimosas. An instant smile spreads across my lips as I take the glass from her.

"This is going to knock me out. I'm so tired from waking up early."

I planned on napping the entire first flight from New York to Los Angeles.

"It's the best way to get back to sleep," I hear the flight attendant say as she moves down the aisle.

Greylan holds his glass to mine. "Here's to you"—he pauses for a split second—"for making me the happiest I've been in years."

A million butterflies release in my stomach right before he taps his glass to mine.

He's incredible, and I'm completely and utterly falling for him—fast. With dizzying speed and intensity.

"Cheers." I take a small sip, testing the waters, and then finish it in three large gulps.

"You can lean your chair back with this button." He points to my far left.

"Does the middle armrest go up?"

He lifts it up and adjusts his seat back, then pulls me to him, closing the doors on either side with a click of a button, letting the flight attendants know that we do not require any further service right now, and we will call them if and when we need something.

"Wake me when we get to LA," I tell him right before I slip the mask over my eyes and sink into his arm and chest.

THE ONE

Greylan

I'm exhausted but unable to sleep. My blood is still racing hours after her ex-husband made that insulting remark. The instinct to protect her was immediate and overwhelming. There's no way I could have just stood by and let him disrespect her. There's a lot I want to know about what happened between them, but for now, I just want to be there for her.

As the plane makes its final descent into Los Angeles, I slowly start to wake her up from her deep sleep by lightly tracing her leg with my hand.

"Hey, are we there?"

"Just about it," I tell her as she sits up and gets herself situated.

"I think that was the best flight I've ever had. I'm not sure I can ever fly coach again."

I laugh. "I agree. I'm starving, wanna get food before flight number two?"

"Will we have enough time?" she asks.

"Yeah, we will have time to stop somewhere quick."

The pilot announces our imminent landing, and she leans in, her hand finding mine, and she holds it tightly.

"Are you okay?"

"More than okay." She smiles at me as the tires hit the runway and the plane begins to slow down.

As soon as we exit the plane, I realize I've been spotted by fans. Every phone is aimed our way. I pull my hat down and grab Miley's hand, trying to shield her from the attention and focus on making sure she's not overwhelmed by all this.

"Would you rather just swing by the mini-mart for snacks and then eat on the plane?"

"Yes, please. I'd rather not be photographed while shoving food in my mouth at an airport." She laughs.

We grab the essentials—iced Starbucks coffee, Celsius, gum, and chips—and head to the checkout.

"Are you his girlfriend?" I hear someone ask and look over to see a little girl talking to Miley, but before she can respond, her mother interrupts. "Leave them alone, honey. You don't bother people in public."

"I'm sorry." The girl looks to Miley. "You're just really pretty."

The smile that spreads across her face is contagious.

"She is, isn't she?" I interrupt. "I'm Greylan." I reach my hand out to shake hers. "What's your name?"

"Hazel. I know a song that you sing," she says.

"Oh yeah? Do you like it?"

"Yes, I love it!" she says as her mom stands behind her.

"If it's okay with your mom, you can take a picture with me before I have to get on my airplane."

"Can I, Mommy?"

"All right, then you have to leave him alone, okay?"

"Okay."

Her mom snaps the photo, then Miley and I head to our gate where we have a little time before we need to board. We find two seats in the back corner to hide out at until it's time to go.

I open my Celsius and take a sip before asking her the very same question the little girl asked her in the mini-mart.

"So, are you?"

"Am I what?"

She looks at me confused, then takes a swig of her iced coffee, then nearly chokes on it after I ask her, "Are you my girlfriend? You never answered the kid's question."

"I—I don't know…"

"Now boarding group A, first class passengers, for flight 710 to Honolulu. Welcome aboard!"

"We can talk about it later." I wink at her, then pull her from her seat and scan our boarding passes before entering the gangway.

After settling in, we look over the breakfast menu. We're already dealing with a three-hour time difference from the East Coast, and there will be another two-hour time change during the flight to Hawaii.

I hope I can fall asleep during this leg of the flight. I am running on empty and am going to need as much energy as possible when we get to our room because the things I plan on doing to Miley is making me hard just thinking about it.

After takeoff and enjoying French toast and mimosas for breakfast, we relax for a while until I fall sound asleep and am awakened by her in time for landing. "Hey," she rubs my knee. "We're here."

We touch down with a smooth, almost gentle, landing. The air that floods in as the door opens is thick and warm, heavy with salt. The heat hits me as we step onto the tarmac, and I squint against the blinding sunlight. The airport explodes with color—hula dancers and surfers painted in vibrant murals, leis draped everywhere, and the air hums with Hawaiian music. I feel a sudden, unexpected lightness as if a weight has been lifted.

*****

The shuttle turns into a winding driveway with bright hibiscus bushes on both sides. The resort is spread out, collection of bungalows and villas connected by stone paths.

"This place is amazing," Miley says, turning to me, a wide smile on her face.

The main lobby is open-air and a cool shaded space with polished stone floors and woven wicker furniture. A gentle breeze drifts through, carrying the sound of trickling water from a nearby koi pond. The scent of sandalwood and ginger fills the air—a subtle calming fragrance. Behind the check-in desk, a massive wall of windows reveals a breathtaking view of the ocean, the turquoise water stretching to the horizon.

The concierge, a woman with a warm smile and a colorful floral dress, approaches. "Aloha! Welcome to our resort," she says, placing leis around our necks. "Checking in for Mr. Asher?"

"Yes, that's us," I reply.

"Wonderful! If you'll just sign here." She gestures to a tablet. "And here are your keys. I'll show you to your room."

The presidential penthouse unfolds before us, and I quickly turn to Miley, anticipating her reaction. Her jaw drops. The sheer scale of the place, its rich decor, and the breathtaking ocean view leave her speechless.

"Is there anything else I can get the two of you, Mr. Asher?"

I tell the concierge no and thank her. As soon as she leaves, I lock the door behind her and find Miley on the balcony, gazing out at the water. I step out and gently draw her back against my body. She responds instantly, sinking into my hold as if she were melting, her head finding a comfortable resting place on my chest. A soft "Thank you" escapes her lips as she turns her head, breathing deeply and freely. I seize the moment, pressing a soft, passionate kiss to her exposed neck.

"I'm going to take a quick shower and change." My clothes are beginning to stick to me from the Hawaiian heat. I'm not sure how she still has on a sweatshirt and pants.

"Care if I join you?" She turns and smiles at me, and I can feel myself growing hard already.

I take her hand and walk us straight to the glass shower, turning the water on right away. She takes off her sweatshirt, leaving her in only a sports bra, the fabric falling away to reveal a breathtaking glimpse of her toned skin. With sudden ferocity, she undoes my belt, her gaze burning as her lips find mine in a heated, domineering kiss.

Once she pushes my jeans down with my boxers and they drop to the floor, I step out of them, kicking them to the side. My hands trace a path to her, and with a slow, deliberate movement, I peel the fabric away from her breathtaking body, removing my shirt in the process.

I step through the glass doors, the waterfall a private oasis. Miley follows, and as the water washes over us, a sense of shared intimacy floods me, a connection deeper than words.

I suck in a sharp breath as she sinks to her knees, a shock of electricity surging through me. Her hands, hot and insistent, grip my thighs, and I brace myself for the inevitable as she pushes her hair to the side, then, with a delicate touch, she presses the flat of her tongue against the underside of my cock. A jolt of pleasure shoots through me.

THE ONE

This is one thing we haven't done yet, and I'm quite intrigued. I definitely don't expect to receive this type of pleasure very often because she has to come first. I need Miley to know that she deserves to be completely satisfied during sex. I'm not, nor have I ever, been a selfish lover. Seems as though she has different plans right now.

I place one hand against the glass wall as she brings her mouth up to my tip and sucks in the rim, and that's where she stays, stroking, sucking, making me hard as stone.

"So fucking good," I mumble as my head drops forward, and I spread my legs wider, giving her more access.

Her hand plays with my balls gently, moving them back and forth, farther…and farther. My cock bobs as she plays dangerously close to my backside while sucking me in even farther.

"Yes, baby."

She opens wider and takes me deeper until I'm continuously hitting the back of her throat. She doesn't gag, she doesn't even flinch, so I thrust inside, and she takes it. The moment her mysterious gaze meets mine, I'm a goner. My balls begin to tighten, and I am unable to control the moans that escape my lips.

"*Fuck!*" I yell as my cock swells, and I come in her mouth, down her throat. I come so fucking hard that I have to brace against the glass of the shower with both hands so I don't fall. I pulse in her mouth as she pulls every last drop from me.

When I'm completely empty, she winks and then stands up and presses a kiss to my chest.

"That was fucking amazing," I say through heaving breaths.

Chapter 29

Miley

The sound of his moans send shivers down my spine, leaving me incredibly aroused. It was easily, by a mile, the sexiest thing I've ever heard. I've never had the opportunity to listen to the voice of pleasure because before Greylan, it didn't exist. Just that powerful form of communication alone indicates how much one appreciates you, and I find it to be electrifying. A thrilling confirmation of your power to ignite one's senses. It's an experience that will leave you breathless, and if you have yet to hear it, you need to reconsider your life choices because it's a feeling like no other.

I step back, giving myself a moment to soak in the incredible view. His shoulders move as he takes a deep breath and then looks up at me, determination in his eyes. My teeth dig into my lower lip as his eyes move over me, hovering over my hard nipples.

I feel my face heat up, and in this hushed moment, I can almost hear our hearts echo through the room.

"Your turn." Grabbing my hips, he guides me out of the shower and straight to the bedroom.

Gently closing the door behind him, he turns around and takes one large step toward me, closing the gap between us. I close my eyes and lean forward so our lips meet in a soft and passionate kiss.

Moving together, he lays me on my back on top of the bed as my tongue slides over his bottom lip and our kiss intensifies, becoming hot and desperate. I can't imagine myself wanting anyone else this much. My desire for him is extreme.

THE ONE

Without a word, he drags my hips to the edge of the bed and gets on his knees. His lips linger for a moment, a seductive tournament, before descending upon my inner thigh, slowly kissing closer and closer to my core, leaving me breathless with anticipation.

I trace his hair with my fingers, gently urging him closer. I feel him smile, laughing softly under his breath at my insistence. The second his tongue grazes over my center, I feel myself melt into the mattress.

A low and quiet moan escapes my throat as he continues, applying the perfect amount of pressure, my whole body buzzing with a feeling of insane pleasure.

"You taste so fucking good," he mutters before putting a finger in his mouth and sliding into me.

My gaze falls upon him, mesmerized by the sight of him between my legs. His eyes are closed in ecstasy, and his expression says he's loving every minute of this, relishing the way I taste and the way I move underneath him.

I drag my nails across his scalp and, in response, feel him groan. I want this moment to last forever, watching him between my legs, my fingers tangled in his hair. Another shock of arousal shoots through my body as he slips a second finger into me and closes his lips around my clit, sucking and massaging with his tongue.

My legs begin to tense, and I can feel myself getting closer and closer, so close to finishing that I can't avoid it, and just as I'm about to lose my mind, an orgasm rips through me, an intense physical sensation.

I can't control the noises I'm making as I rock my hips, crying out as he holds me down with his forearm around my waist, pushing me to the end of it, my legs falling limp onto the mattress after my orgasm subsides.

He glances up at me as I attempt to catch my breath, my chest heaving. "I'm not done with you."

I open my mouth to say something, but the way he moves his eyes up and down my body quickly derails my train of thought.

His face moves inch by inch even closer to mine, our lips nearly touching.

THE ONE

The feeling of his hardness against my body sends me reeling as he drags his mouth down to my neck.

"Then keep going," I whisper right before I grab his throbbing erection and drag the head up and down along my slit.

His teeth slowly sink into my collarbone as he groans, his length growing harder with each movement.

Once he's able to gather himself, he pushes up and hovers over me, and I swear, his pupils blow. I've never seen him look this hungry...hungry for me.

I lean in, my clit continuing to rub against him again while I stroke the head of his cock softly with my thumb. His head falls forward, and I hear him whimper at the sensation.

"Tell me what you want," he says, his voice husky and rough as his fists tightly grip the sheets.

"Anything and everything."

His mouth falls slightly open in awe before saying, "You're so fucking amazing. I hope you know that."

Taking himself in his hand, he lines himself up with me perfectly before thrusting in with a single powerful motion. The only thing I can feel is him throbbing inside of me as my body lights up with desire. He shifts forward to bury his face in the crook of my neck, and that simple movement makes my heart jump into my throat. My eyes fall shut as my body rides out the waves of pleasure crashing through it.

After I let myself adjust for a minute, he begins pushing in and out of me, every stroke a new sensation.

"You're so tight," he whispers, "and it feels so fucking good."

My heart feels like it's going to beat right out of my chest as his pace picks up, each surge of pleasure washing over me in a wave of euphoria. His words, whispered against my skin, ignite a fire within me, bringing me closer to the edge with every thrust.

As our bodies move, we moan together, the sound of our skin slapping against each other setting the rhythm. My hips rock against him, my stomach starts to tense, and my legs go completely numb.

"You're close, aren't you?" he asks.

"I...I'm so close." I start to clench as my pelvis flexes upward, my orgasm builds fast, and everything goes dark.

"Not yet." He pulls out. "On your beautiful stomach. Now."

His words send a shiver down my spine; I have to wait for it to stop before I can turn over.

"That's it." He smooths his hand over my ass before gripping it then slapping it lightly. "You're so fucking sexy." He plants a kiss over the soft sting that's lingering from his touch. "I want to own this body." He kisses in between my shoulder blades. "I want to fuck every inch of it. Come all over you, inside you." He drags his lips to my neck and softly kisses it before whispering, "Let me give you the best orgasm you've ever had."

After my moan gives approval, he moves his hand slowly up my back, pleasure vibrating through my bones.

"Just like that." He gently pushes my head down into the mattress.

He slides his length up and down me right before pushing in, bottoming out immediately. "Fuck yes, Mils." His hand finds its mark once more, and I let out a muffled scream as my pelvis tilts higher, and a wave of intense arousal floods my senses.

"Holy. Shit." My hands dig into the mattress as he thrusts with increasing intensity several times before slowing his pace.

"This sight," he says as he runs his hand over my ass, "it's the most beautiful fucking thing I've ever seen."

His voice is like a spark that ignites my feelings for him. It's hot and filthy and intimate and perfect, perfect in every sense of the word.

His thumb rubs over my backside, and I clench around him. Just the thought of his finger there turns me on.

"You fucking like that, don't you?"

"Oh my god," I whisper.

After a few passes, I begin to relax just as his thumb slips inside me, pleasuring me on all ends.

"Greylan!" I gasp as he holds it in while reaching his other hand around to massage me. "Fuck, I'm going to...oh fuck!" My body tips over the edge, and I start pulsating with pleasure under his touch.

"Greylan!" I scream as I convulse around him so much that everything around me fades to black.

Greylan

I can't last any longer. Not after I felt her squeeze around me as she screamed my name. I grip both of her hips as my stomach drops; a burst of pleasure shoots through my entire body, and an overwhelming wave of pure, searing ecstasy envelops me.

"Motherfucker!" I cry out as I pulse into her, coming over and over until there's nothing left inside. I slow my movements, savoring the moment as she continues to pulsate around me.

We both sink onto the bed, and I settle on top of her. I kiss her shoulder. Her neck. Her cheek. And when she turns just enough so I can find her mouth, I kiss her there too.

"Fuck," I whisper as I slowly pull out of her. I have never come that hard in my life. Never. Not even a comparison.

*****

These last few days have been nothing short of perfect. Honestly, I'm fighting back the urge to just…stay. Forever. I'm not ready to leave, not even a little.

We both made these lists, three must-dos each, and I was determined to make it happen. Mine were the adrenaline-pumping kind: snorkeling, where the coral looked like a surreal landscape; zip-lining, feeling like I was flying; and the powerful experience of Pearl Harbor. I wanted to see the history and feel the weight of it.

Miley, though, is all about the water, the sun, and the sheer joy of living. Beach days were her happy place. And swimming with dolphins… I swear, watching her face light up like that, it was like she was a kid again—pure unfiltered joy. It was contagious.

Every little thing she does—every laugh, every shared look—it's like a tiny earthquake inside me. I'm falling, and it's happening so fast. I catch myself staring at her, wondering if she feels it too. We've been talking more—those late-night conversations that stretch into the early morning, where we reveal pieces of ourselves that we don't usually show. I see a vulnerability in her, a softness, that makes my heart ache. I'm starting to see the layers underneath the easy smile, and it makes me want to know every single one. I'm hoping, praying, that this isn't just one-sided.

"Colbie is freaking out about her flight tomorrow." Miley talks to me while getting ready for our last night in Hawaii. Tonight, we're crossing the last adventure off our list, the Luau—a final vibrant celebration before we have to leave.

"Why? Does she not like to fly?"

"I mean, as her best friend, I know she's always said she was afraid to fly, but I didn't know it was this serious."

"How serious are we talking?" I laugh.

"She had to go to her primary and get a prescription for Xanax in order to even go to sleep tonight."

Well, this is going to be interesting.

"Anything we can do to help?"

"Nope." She walks to me, looking fine as hell, and gives me a kiss. "I'm ready."

I smile and open the door for her, then we walk toward the beach. She holds my hand as we make our way down the lit path, and when we arrive, the place is alive. The energy is contagious. There is live music, food, drinks, and, of course, hula dancing.

"Okolehao?" Miley smiles big while helping herself to two shot glasses. "Mahalo!"

"You can speak Hawaiian now?" I chuckle as she hands me the second glass.

"Just 'hello' and 'thank you.'"

"Cheers to a very memorable vacation." I wink and clink, then shoot it back.

The taste is very distinctive. I can't really compare it with any other spirits I've had. It's kind of sweet and earthy, with a hint of rum and a bit of a tequila bite.

"Damn good stuff." Miley giggles as she puts her glass down at our table. "Dance with me." She reaches out a hand and walks us to the crowded dance floor, her fingers tracing the line of my jaw as she pulls me close.

Our bodies move as one, a perfect harmony of rhythm and desire. I feel the warmth of her breath against my skin, the softness of her hair brushing against my cheek. Her perfume—so clean and pure—fills my senses, intoxicating me with its freshness. I lose myself in the moment, in the feeling of being completely and utterly enveloped by her.

When the music finally fades, we stand breathless, our foreheads touching, and our eyes locked. I can't tear mine away. She is perfect. She is beautiful. She is everything I've ever dreamed of and more.

"Let's go eat the pig now!" She laughs.

We make our way to the long communal tables and sit down, and the gentle sound of ukuleles fills the air. Hula dancers move gracefully, telling old stories with their hips and hands. The firelight makes their flower necklaces glow, and their shadows dance.

The food is amazing. Everyone is laughing and talking. People from everywhere are here, sharing stories and drinks.

Miley's face glows with pure wonder as the Samoan fire knife dancers begin their final act. It's breathtaking. The dancers spin those flaming orbs, painting streaks of light against the night. The drums pound, building to a crescendo, and the crowd roars its approval. It's a raw celebration of their culture, and watching her watch, it hits me. Hard. I know, with a certainty that steals my breath, that I am completely, utterly, and irrevocably in love with Miley Miller. I need her to know. I need to tell her.

"Wanna head back? We have to be up really early tomorrow."

"Yes, I am exhausted!" She stands and takes my hand, attempting to pull me to my feet even though I am twice her size.

Most of our stuff is already packed up because we have to wake up so early so when we get back to our room, we don't have to do much.

"What time is it in New York? I have a few missed calls from Colbie and Sutton."

I do the math quickly in my head. They are six hours behind us, I'm pretty sure. "I think it's dinnertime."

"Okay, I am going to check in with them fast to make sure all is good."

Miley calls Sutton back first, who called about the holidays and the move into the house I am renting to her.

I try not to eavesdrop on her conversation with Colbie, but from the sound of it, she isn't going to make it to Tennessee. After about twenty minutes of back and forth, Miley finally ends the call, changes, and crawls into bed.

"Sorry about that, she's still freaking out. She says she is going to drive because she can't fly. I had to talk her off the ledge."

"Is she okay?" I ask.

"Yeah, I think I calmed her down." She scooches closer, and I pull her to me, holding her tightly while I think in my head how I am going to tell her how I feel.

"These last few days have been perfect. Thank you."

"They have been pretty perfect, haven't they?" she sarcastically questions, knowing damn well that our time here has been a ten out of ten.

I don't respond. Instead, I kiss the top of her head, feeling a surge of emotions I can't quite name.

"Sweet dreams, Greylan."

My time is running out, so I'm just going to say and hope that she doesn't freak out.

"Dream sweet, Mils. I love you."

I legitimately feel her tense up and freeze as soon as I say it, but she doesn't respond. Instead, she buries her face into my chest and goes to bed. And now I can't sleep. What if I just fucked up?

It feels like an hour has passed by, and I've tried everything, counting sheep, counting backward, blinking one hundred times. Nothing is helping.

I hear a low, quiet sound followed by a sniffle. It takes me a second to register what's happening, but I'm almost certain Miley is crying.

I stay still and don't say anything as she gets up from the bed and goes into the bathroom.

Unsure what to do, I slowly crawl out of bed and softly knock on the door. "What's wrong, Miley?"

When she doesn't respond, I open the bathroom door and find her on the floor, up against the wall, hugging her knees, hyperventilating. I drop down immediately and bring her to me. "Mils, what's wrong? Talk to me."

She doesn't respond. She shuts down completely. I have no idea what to do. But I'm pretty sure she is having a panic attack. I know she's had them previously because she told me. And she's helped me through several of mine. But she's always told me that talking about her issues helped her. But she won't talk to me. She just buries herself deeper and deeper. I need help. I need guidance.

I pull out my phone and text the very person who knows the most about her and who I know who will be able to help me get her through this.

> **Greylan**: Miley is having a panic attack and idk what to do.

It feels like forever passes before she texts back, but it's only a couple minutes later.

> **Sutton**: Like a full blown panic attack? Are you sure? She hasn't had one in a while.
> **Greylan**: I'm not sure. She won't talk. I found her on the bathroom floor. What do I do?
> **Sutton**: Jesus Christ.
> **Sutton**: I need more info
> **Sutton**: What happened prior?

Shit. Do I tell her? Do I lie? God, I don't even know what to do. I just know that I need to be here for her and help her.

Greylan: We went to a luau and when we came back she called you then Colbie. Colbie was freaking out about flying.
Sutton: Has she been taking her medication?

Ugh, that's a great question. I think she has, but I haven't asked.

Greylan: Yes?

I lie because I'm honestly not sure. My phone starts ringing, and I see it's Sutton calling, so I answer it.
"Hello?"
"Has she told you about her panic attacks? What causes them?"
"She's afraid to die," I say honestly.
"She can't handle the fact that we *all* have to die. She needs to understand the science behind it. She needs to know what happens next. When she tries to formulate an outcome in her head, typically at night, it gives her anxiety, and then panic consumes her. Something must have triggered this. What aren't you telling me?"
I pause and take a deep breath before I step out of the bathroom and tell her.
"I told her I love her."

Chapter 30

Miley

Everything gets smaller, closer. My chest feels like it's being squeezed, and I can't seem to get enough air. It's like there's a wall in front of my lungs. My heart…it's pounding. Racing. Like a drum trying to burst out of my ribs as the band around it gets tighter and tighter. I'm sweating and shivering at the same time.

There is no stopping it. No talking myself down.

I keep my gaze fixed on an invisible point on the wall, desperately trying to anchor myself as fear grips me. Its silent, suffocating presence saturates every inch of me, leaving me utterly terrified.

Imagine a fear so intense, it disrupts the very rhythm of your being. Every organ within you seems to rebel, functioning in a chaotic frenzy. Nightly medication becomes a necessity, a tool to temper the storm within and allow for even a moment of calm, a chance to simply breathe.

"Let me help you." Greylan kneels in front of me as his hands run over my shoulders and down my arms.

I catch his hand and squeeze it, trying to tell him that, yes, I do need help, but I am unable to speak.

"Mils, baby, where is your medication?"

I try to answer, but my breath fails me. My lungs are completely deflated. No sound will escape my lips. Suddenly, he's lifting me and carrying me back to the bedroom. He sets me down on the bed, kisses my forehead, and then empties the contents of my cosmetics bag onto the bed beside me.

THE ONE

My mind races just as fast as my heart, the constant reminder that nothing in this life is permanent. The tears roll down my face uncontrollably.

"I found it," I hear him say. He's on the phone with someone, but I don't know who he is talking to. "I will text you in a little bit, thank you."

"Take this." He hands me my medication and a glass of water, but I can't grab it. I just stare at the water as it ripples in the glass. The glass he holds with his shaking hand. "Baby, please, you're scaring me."

Through a haze of tears, I see Greylan. With a trembling hand, I take the pill from him and chase it with the water. He gently sets the cup down and lifts me, holding me tightly. My arms and legs instinctively wrap around him as I bury my face in his neck, seeking comfort.

The only thing I can focus on right now is how to breathe. I haven't experienced panic like this in a long time. I thought I had overcome it. Why is it suddenly happening now? Was it his confession of love? Is it because I feel the same way? Because the idea of losing him is terrifying?

He holds me tightly until the panic subsides, never loosening his grip. When I finally regain my composure, I turn to him and apologize. "I'm so sorry."

"Stop, Miley. You have nothing to be sorry for." He brings me down to the bed. "Talk to me."

"We really don't have to talk about it. I'm fine—"

"How did it start?" he interrupts.

I know Greylan won't let this go. He'll want to understand what had just happened. But, to be honest, I'm not sure myself. These panic attacks just…happen. I can't predict them or control them.

"I freak out when I think about what happens after we die," I confess, taking a deep breath. "It usually happens at night when I'm trying to sleep. My mind races with a hundred unanswered questions."

"Tell me about it," he says, crawling into bed and pulling me close. "I want to know everything. I want to be able to help you."

THE ONE

I don't think I've ever truly opened up to anyone except for Sutton and my therapist. Colbie knows bits and pieces, but that's it. Derek never even bothered to ask over the years. He'd just leave me to suffer.

"When I was five, three people close to me died within a short time. I couldn't understand it. I needed answers. I still need answers."

"Who?" he asks.

"The first was my mom's only sibling, her sister. They were only two years apart. I still don't know exactly how she died, but from what I've gathered through the years, I think it was an accidental overdose. My mom still can't talk about it. She was ruined for years. It took her a long time to come back around and to be the mother that we needed." I pause briefly. "Anyways, when me and Sutton would ask her how our aunt died, she would always respond, 'I don't know, she just died when she was asleep,' and that's forever fucked with me."

"Jesus Christ. That's what your mom told the two of you?"

"Yeah, unfortunately. And then, soon after, my dad's brother died. Lung cancer. He was only thirty. At least we were able to understand what happened to him. He had an incurable disease, and it killed him."

Cancer wasn't a stranger to me. I'd overheard my parents whispering about it countless times. Their hushed conversations were filled with words like *treatments* and *hospitalizations*, and they always seemed to be on the phone, probably talking to other family members, trying to learn more.

"Who was the third person?"

"My kindergarten classmate. Haylee. She was actually my best friend. Colbie's too. The three of us were inseparable. She was diagnosed with leukemia halfway through the school year, and by June, she was gone."

I can still remember walking up the path to the school entrance and my mom stopping me, pulling back on my arm, and telling me. And I'm almost certain that is the exact moment I realized that we all have to die, including myself, and that we don't get a say as to when or how it happens. Haylee was an innocent child who had to suffer before she died. It didn't make sense. It still doesn't make sense.

"That was the first funeral I've ever gone to. I had zero idea what I was walking into."

And after that, for twenty-five years straight, I'd try to come up with answers in my head. I'd try to piece it all together. And when that didn't work, Sutton forced me to see a doctor.

"That's a lot for anyone to comprehend, let alone a five-year-old. Does anything else help?"

"I honestly just can't think about it at all. The medication distracts me most of the time. It keeps my brain from wandering off in the wrong direction. But sometimes, even that doesn't help."

"Do you know what caused it to wander tonight?"

"I think so."

"Was it because I told you that I love you?"

"No. It was because I realized that I love you too."

Greylan

I don't think I've ever witnessed anyone, other than myself, have a panic attack, and without exaggerating, it's some scary shit. Miley has a deep fear that she will forever live with, and I will do everything in my power to help her through it. No matter what. Because I would do anything for that girl. Because I am all in. I love her, and she loves me.

After she fell asleep, I checked in with Sutton, then packed up the rest of our things (including her stuff I dumped all over the bed in a frenzy), then finally closed my eyes for a couple hours before we had to head to the airport.

We slept through most of the first flight, but as soon as we are settled on this second flight, we need to talk. There are some important things to discuss, and my CMA performance tomorrow night is a big one.

I stop the stewardess as she walks by. "Two mimosas, please."

"Absolutely. I will be right back."

I look over to Miley as she fidgets with her seat, making herself comfortable. "Are you still tired?"

"No, not at all. Why, what's up?"

I suddenly get nervous. "I just thought we could talk about some things before we land in Nashville."

"I'm all ears." She half smiles.

The one thing Sutton told me over the phone last night is that Miley gets embarrassed over her actions following a panic attack, that I need to move on as if nothing happened. And that is what I 100 percent intend to do. I make sure she knows that I'm not going to bring it up in this conversation.

"So tomorrow at the CMAs, there's going to be a lot of press and cameras."

"Sounds typical for such an event." She giggles, relieved.

The stewardess returns with our drinks, and I thank her before handing a glass to Miley.

"I have three nominations. There will be a lot of focus on me." I take a sip as I try to gauge her reaction.

"Seriously?" She smiles.

"Seriously."

She laughs. She laughs so hard at me, I laugh.

"Stop it, you're joking." She hits her knee.

"Zero joking, Miley." I take another sip of my drink before placing it on the tray in front of me. "I'm performing too."

She turns to me and smiles. "Are you really?"

"Yes." I smirk.

"That's super cool, Greylan. Congratulations."

And that right there is why I am so deeply in love with her.

"What are your nominations for?" She sips her mimosa.

"Artist of the year, song of the year, and album of the year." I hold my breath.

"Can I still cast my votes?" She reaches for her phone to likely check online.

"I'm not sure." I watch her scroll for a moment.

"Oh my god! There's a picture of us in Hawaii. That's so fucking weird."

THE ONE

She turns her phone screen toward me. The headline reads, "Greylan's Gotta Girlfriend" with a picture of us at the beach and a short story about their findings while stalking my life.

> Country music heartthrob Greylan Asher has been enjoying a romantic Hawaiian getaway with a mysterious brunette, sparking intense engagement rumors. The singer recently canceled several shows citing "personal reasons," which were later revealed to be the heartbreaking loss of his longtime guitar player's father.
>
> With the CMAs just days away, where he's up for a coveted three awards and set to perform, all eyes are on whether he'll bring his stunning, long-haired lady to the red carpet. Will this be the debut of country music's newest power couple?
>
> Sources close to the singer suggest this could be more than just a casual fling. Stay tuned for updates as this captivating love story unfolds.

I swipe up to close out of the app and place her phone down on her tray. "Never read their bullshit." I finish my mimosa just as the stewardess walks over to collect our glasses.

"Thank you."

We hand them over.

"Did Colbie get on the plane?"

"I think so. Peyton said she made it through TSA and that she'd keep me posted. She was going to stick around until the plane actually departed. I haven't heard from anyone, so I think it's all good."

I really hope so.

*****

"Jesus Christ." Miley scrolls through her messages while we wait for the flight crew to finish the disembarkation process. "I have twenty-four messages and two missed calls. I don't think the Wi-Fi was

THE ONE

working." She leans in to show me her phone while reading them out loud.

Group Name: Core Four

Peyton: She made it past TSA
Sutton: Was she freaking the fuck out?
Colbie: Yes, I'm freaking the fuck out. Peyton, come back, I'm not going.
Peyton: You are going, everything will be fine. We love you.
Sutton: We love you and we're jealous! YOU'RE GOING TO THE CMAs!
Colbie: I just threw up

Peyton: I think she got on the plane. I watched it take off and she didn't come running back.
Peyton: I will text you if anything changes.

Colbie: I can't do it. I can't fucking do it.
Colbie: Sorry
Colbie: I am going to try to take another Xanax
Colbie: It didn't work
Colbie: White Claw 30
Colbie: Ok, I feel better

Group Name: Miller Time

Mom: Sutton, are you working on Thanksgiving?
Sutton: No. What time is dinner?

Mom: 3pm
Sutton: Tell Miley to invite her boyfriend
Dad: Miley has a boyfriend?
Mom: Answer your phone Miley

Sutton: Oops.

Colbie: I just landed.
Colbie: I hate you.
Colbie: I'll be at the bar in Terminal C waiting. Hurry up.

Well, this is going to be interesting.

We exit the plane and head straight to Colbie, who is drinking a seltzer and scrolling on her phone. Miley wraps her arms around her and gives her a big hug from behind. "I love you. Thank you for coming."

"I hate you both," Colbie says dramatically, and I laugh.

"Did you already get your baggage?" Miley asks.

"I thought you said someone was getting it for me?"

"The driver has everything already and is outside waiting," I interrupt.

Colbie finishes her drink, and we all make our way downstairs and outside to the Escalade that is waiting.

"Mr. Asher." He reaches his hand out and shakes mine before opening the door for us.

"Thank you."

My house isn't too far from the airport, so the drive is rather quick. When we get close to my gated entrance, I open it using my phone. He pulls around my circular driveway near the front door and puts the car in park before opening Miley's door. I let myself out on the other side and assist with grabbing the luggage. "You guys can head right in, the door is unlocked."

I grab two of the three and follow behind them.

Colbie is the first to walk inside. "Holy fuck!"

Chapter 31

Miley

A lot has happened over the last twenty-four hours, and I am having a little bit of trouble trying to process it all. Thankfully Colbie made it, and I have her to help me through it all.

Once we got back to Greylan's house, he made us a drink and then gave us a tour. His house? To die for. Seriously, I've never seen anything like it. The heart of the home is undeniably his kitchen—a real showstopper for sure. Top-notch appliances, a massive marble island, and floor-to-ceiling windows with breathtaking views. The whole place is open concept, with polished concrete floors and sleek furniture. It's just stunning. He has a formal living room that he clearly never uses, and then a smaller cozier one with a gorgeous fireplace, plush sectional sofa, and a collection of guitars. It's all very music-inspired. This isn't just a house, it's a mansion. Five bedrooms, seven bathrooms, a movie theater, a game room, a music studio, a pool, a hot tub, a library...I mean, his master bedroom is bigger than my whole house!

"I'm going to take a shower and let you two catch up. Make yourselves at home."

The two of us smile as he leaves, and as soon as he is out of sight, Colbie's unfiltered self comes out to play.

"Jesus H. Christ, Miley. If you don't marry that man, you're insane."

"Can we walk before we run? Good god, settle down," I say nonchalantly while I internally freak out.

"I really hope you didn't just tell me to 'settle down.' I'll kick you in the shin."

She's such an asshole sometimes. I'm not sure why she's my best friend, but she is, so here we are. Me getting lectured by someone who despises love and everything it means.

"Bee, I love you, and you know that, but I just need you to shut the fuck up while I try to wrap my head around everything."

"Noted. I'll shut up for now. Quick question though…"

I stare at her, waiting for her to ask her "quick question."

"Does he have any hot friends?"

I roll my eyes hard. "I don't know, but I think you're his guitar player's date tomorrow."

"I'm sorry, what?" she deadpans, and I laugh out loud.

"I mean you're his plus one. I've never met him, but he's your ticket in, so be nice!" I know how Colbie can be. She's a spitfire. Her words are as sharp as her temper, but they're always laced with a dry wit that could disarm even the most irate opponent.

"I'm not acting fake, Miley. I am who I am."

"Oh my god, I know. I didn't say that. I'm just asking you to play nice. Now let's go have another drink and wait for Greylan to tell us what the game plan for tomorrow is, okay?"

"Okay," she says sarcastically.

When I open up Greylan's fridge, there's a case of black cherry White Claw with our name written all over it. Figuratively.

We grab two cans each and take them over to his oversized sectional where we catch up on everything that's happened over the last week. She pretended to be interested in our vacation, but I can tell she is super stressed over work and the fact that she might be losing her job to a merger. She's definitely trying to push it to the back of her head though. It makes my heart hurt.

"You found the White Claw, I see."

We both look over to see Greylan, who's sporting sweats and a tee and looking hella good.

"Ain't no laws when you're drinking the—"

"Shut up, Colbie," I interrupt, and Greylan laughs.

"Whatever. Greylan, please tell us how our day is going to go tomorrow. I need every detail. Leave nothing out...because if you do, I am just going to ask you question, after question, after question...and I really don't want to do that, and I'm sure you don't want me to do that."

"I sure as shit don't want you to do that." I sip my seltzer and giggle, which makes Greylan smile.

"So tomorrow I need to be at the Bridgestone Arena by eleven for a quick run-through. I shouldn't be long. I figured we could all use a relaxing morning, I'll make breakfast and then go."

"I'll take a bacon and cheese omelet."

"Good god." I try to hide in his oversized couch.

"Noted. I will make you the best bacon and cheese omelet you've ever had."

"Doubt it. Anyhoo, what happens next?"

"My buddy, Brody, is going to meet us here around five thirty, and my driver will get here at six. We need to be at the arena by six thirty. The awards start at seven."

"Who's Brody?" Colbie spits out.

"My guitar player. You're his plus one," Greylan says as he pours himself some whiskey and takes a seat.

"I'm not holding his hand," she says seriously.

"You don't have to."

"Good. What happens when we get there?"

At this moment, I am thankful for all her questions because they are my exact thoughts and more.

"We will all walk the red carpet, take some photos, and then find our seats."

"Sounds like you're leaving some shit out." Colbie gives zero fucks right now.

"Honestly, this is only my third year attending. My first year, I was a nobody. My second year I was only up for New Artist of the Year, and this year I have three nominations and I'm performing, so I don't know what to expect."

"Did you write a speech?" I'm genuinely curious when I ask.

"Yes." He freezes and says nothing else, and the room goes quiet for a quick second.

"Am I supposed to coordinate with your friend? Because I only brought two dresses, which, by the way, Miley, I need you to help me decide."

"Okay," I say.

"I don't think it's necessary, but I am pretty sure Brody is wearing black with white."

Oh god. Is this a thing? Should I have told Greylan what I am wearing?

"Black it is." Colbie smirks at me, knowing that she's about to put us both on the spot and not giving a single fuck about it. "What're you wearing?"

He processes her question, and it takes him a second to respond, but when he finally does, my heart melts right then and there, all over his couch.

"I'm not sure yet. I was going to wait and see what Miley is wearing first."

"All black everything," I respond while drinking my drink and avoiding eye contact.

"Perfect," he says. "Do you guys need me to get anyone here to do your hair or makeup?"

Oh god. If I could run, I would. Poor guy just said the wrong thing to two females, and he has absolutely no idea.

"I'm going to pretend that you didn't just say that, you dipshit."

"I was just—"

"It's all good. No worries. Colbie and I can do our own hair and makeup. Thank you though. Quick recap though, we are all essentially wearing black, and we need to be ready by six?" I interrupt.

"Yes."

The night continues, a few more drinks in hand, and laughter fills the air before we decide to call it a night. I feel a surge of anticipation; I can't wait to see Greylan perform tomorrow.

*****

"Seven out of ten," Colbie says with her mouth full.

"You're full of it. Ten out of ten."

I sit back and watch the two of them bicker while they eat their omelets. I hate eggs, so I had a side of bacon with avocado toast, which, I must say, was pretty tasty.

"How about I cook breakfast tomorrow, and we can see whose tastes better?"

"Sounds good to me." Greylan finishes his food and puts all the dishes in the dishwasher. "I have to head out. I should be back in a couple of hours. I left the keys to my S4 on the dresser upstairs if you need to go anywhere."

"Stop it. You don't really have the same car as me." I honestly thought he was lying to me before.

"Why would I lie about that? It's in the garage. I will send you the code for that and the gate."

"I don't think we are going to go anywhere, but thank you though."

He walks over to me and gives me a kiss on the top of my head before leaving. "See you soon."

"See you soon," I respond as I watch him leave.

"He really loves you, I can tell," Colbie says.

"I know."

"What do you mean, 'you know'?"

Oops. Must have left that part out when we were talking about Hawaii last night. That or she wasn't listening.

"He told me he loves me."

"Do you love him?"

"I really do, Bee."

She smiles. "I'm really happy for you, I truly am. I'm actually a bit jealous. But you are so fucked once your boss finds out."

Yup. That's crossed my mind every single day for the last few weeks.

"He's not going to find out."

She looks at me like I am a dumbass. "You're going to the fucking CMAs, which is on live television, and you don't think he's going to find out about it?"

My stomach flips.

"I'm going to take the longest shower of my life and try not to think about that. Will you do my hair after?"

"Yeah. I'm going to read my smut then shower too. Meet in my room at two?"

"Sounds good."

I know Colbie needs some downtime, and I do too. I head upstairs to the glass shower and turn it on, allowing it to heat up.

After a minute, I get in and let the water cascade down from the wide shower head and pound against my back, the force both refreshing and relaxing. I try not to overthink everything and tell myself to just enjoy every second; this is a once-in-a-lifetime opportunity.

I exfoliate my entire body then wash my hair before shaving. I have very thick hair, so I let my conditioner hang out for a while in the process. Once I am finished, I hop out and lotion up with my signature scent and add my oil before heading over to Colbie's room.

"I'm ready to get ready."

Greylan

The second I see her, the room dissolves. I'm aware of nothing else. Miley's stunning, the black gown flowing around her, a masterpiece of fabric. The long sleeves and deep neckline tease, rather than expose, and the high slit reveals a glimpse of her leg with each step she takes towards me. I'm suddenly nervous. I went with a black suit and shirt (no tie) instead of a tux, but now I'm wondering if I made the right call.

"You're beautiful." I meet her halfway and kiss her, not caring that Colbie is watching.

"Thank you." She smiles just as Brody walks in. He is only one of the four people whom I gave the code to enter. Ivan, the cleaner, and Miley, just a few hours ago, are the other three.

Brody gets along with anyone, everyone. He's very outgoing but chill at the same time. I don't think there will be any issues with him and Colbie walking the red carpet together.

THE ONE

"Brody, this is Miley and Colbie."

He reaches his hand out to shake theirs. "Nice to meet you both."

"You too," Miley says at the same exact time Colbie says, "Ditto."

"The cars are already outside waiting for us. Traffic is pretty backed up. We should probably get going shortly."

"Um. How many cars are we taking and why?" Colbie asks.

I actually don't know the answer to that question. I just go with the flow and listen to whatever Ivan tells me to do.

"Great question. I'm not sure," I respond honestly.

"Ivan booked us each a car not knowing that we were meeting up beforehand."

Thank god Brody pays attention more than I do and knows what's going on.

*****

I can't describe what I'm feeling as the car pulls up to the venue. I know it's definitely a lot of nerves, but there's also a little bit of fear and a fuckload of excitement.

As the car door opens, I step out and immediately turn to take Miley's hand. The flashbulbs are relentless, momentarily blinding me as we make our way to the red carpet where Brody and Colbie are already waiting. The noise of the crowd is overwhelming—a mix of shouts, screams, and the constant *click-click-click* of cameras. I manage to smile and wave, trying to look cool and collected, even though I feel anything but.

"Do you two want to walk first, or would you rather we did?" Brody asks. He knows by now that these types of events make me a bit uncomfortable.

"We can walk it together, but you guys can go in front."

"Let's do the damn thing," Colbie says as she wraps her arm around Brody's so he can escort her.

I look at Miley, and she surprisingly seems fine. "Are you ready?"

She giggles. "Yeah, let's do the damn thing."

Hand in hand, we start the short walk for the media and fans. The lights are hot, and the air is filled with the scent of expensive

THE ONE

perfume and hairspray. Halfway there, we pause at the backdrop, and I release her hand and pull her close, my arm finding the small of her back. I've never been photographed with anyone before, let alone at such a big event. The flashes explode, and the fans roar. We take a minute to pose for the cameras before microphones are shoved in my face.

"How does it feel to be nominated for three awards?" someone yells.

"What song are you performing tonight?" another one shouts.

I answer as best I can, trying to make eye contact with the reporters, even though it's hard to focus with all the commotion. I tell them that everything feels surreal and that I am singing my newest hit...but it's honestly all a blur.

Once we finally reach the end of the carpet, I pause for a second, taking a deep breath. It's been a rush, totally exhilarating, but also completely exhausting. I look out at the crowd one last time. All those faces, all that energy...it's for them. This is my moment. This is what it's all about.

"We gotta go take our seats. The awards are about the start." Brody looks to me, and I acknowledge with a nod as we begin to walk inside.

I lean in to Miley. "Still good?"

"Still good. And I am proud of you no matter if you win or lose." She squeezes my hand.

I'm truly honored by the nominations, and honestly, that feels like a win in itself. I've seen the competition though, and I know where things stand. My music, my album...it's just not on the same level as the other artists. They're incredibly established, household names, so realistically, I don't see myself winning.

"Thank you," I whisper, kissing the side of her head.

We make our way to our seats where Ivan awaits. He's in the aisle, I'm next to him, and then Miley, Colbie, Brody, and the others settle in.

The show's a blast this year, and the hosts are surprisingly funny for a change. I actually enjoy their jokes, unlike the last two years where I had to force a laugh. And it's a relief to see Miley and Colbie having a good time; it makes the whole experience much more relaxed. My cue to head backstage is right after the Vocal Duo of the Year award. Thankfully, my nominations aren't until after my performance, so it works out perfectly. Still, the pressure of performing in front of so many talented artists is intense. I feel like every note will be scrutinized, but I'm trying to push that aside and focus on connecting with my fans.

"I gotta head backstage. I will see you in a little bit, okay?"

Miley's smile is so big. "I'm so excited to watch you."

Those six words mean everything to me. That's all I need. I stand after the award is presented, as does Brody, and we follow Ivan backstage.

"Ready?" Ivan asks.

I'm about to perform my biggest hit, the one nominated for Song of the Year, but it's just Brody and me acoustically. I love my band, but I gave them time off after I canceled the tour, and I wasn't going to go back on that just because I'd forgotten about the CMAs. Brody, being the brother he is, wouldn't let me do this alone.

"Sure am." Ivan brings my guitar strap up and over my head then we walk to our spot and await our introduction, which is almost instant.

"Now performing his newest single, 'A Helluva Lot,' give it up for Greylan Asher!"

I'm blinded by the lights as soon as I walk out. I follow Brody to the center stage, where we each take a seat on the stools that are set up for us.

I didn't want to do anything big or crazy. I just wanted to be me.

The music starts, and I find Miley immediately and begin to sing on my cue.

> Another day begins to dawn
> Gotta face it, gotta move on
> Gotta chase that dollar sign
> A helluva lot on my mind

THE ONE

It's a helluva lot, yeah, a helluva lot
The pressure's on, whether I like it or not
Gotta give it all I've got, every single shot
'Cause it's a helluva lot, yeah, a helluva lot

Seeing other musicians in the crowd singing along to my single completely blows me away.

I've got a helluva lot to prove
Gotta break these chains and make my move
Through the doubt and through the fear
I'll rise above and make it clear
I've got a helluva lot to give
Gotta show the world the way I live
With passion burnin' in my soul
I'll reach my goals and take control

Because it's a helluva lot, yeah, a helluva lot
The pressure's on, whether I like it or not
Gotta give it all I've got, every single shot
'Cause it's a helluva lot, yeah, a helluva lot

But when I look out and see Miley singing along to the chorus with Colbie, I'm on top of the world.

Yeah, it's a helluva lot, but I'll make it through
Gotta stay strong, gotta be true
To myself and the things I do
'Cause it's a helluva lot, and it's up to you

Because it's a helluva lot, yeah, a helluva lot
The pressure's on, whether I like it or not
Gotta give it all I've got, every single shot

After the last note rings out, the crowd goes wild. We head backstage, buzzing with adrenaline, just in time for the Album of the

THE ONE

Year announcement. I don't win, but like I've been saying, getting here is an achievement in itself. I don't expect to win anything.

During the commercial break, we are able to make our way back to our seats.

"I'm sorry you didn't win." She seems sad. Or maybe she thinks I'm sad. I'm not sure.

"I'm not upset about it, Mils. He deserved to win that award. It's all good." I give her leg a quick squeeze.

We catch a few more performances before the final two awards, Song of the Year and Artist of the Year. When they introduce Song of the Year and the clips from two of my music videos flash across the screen, my heart starts pounding.

"And the award for Song of the Year goes to…Greylan Asher, 'A Helluva Lot'!"

I am in an instant state of shock. They actually just said my name. Holy fuck. I don't even know what to do. I stand with the others surrounding me in my row as everyone claps. I lean in to kiss Miley, who looks so goddamn proud, and then I ask Ivan to come up with me.

The moment the award is handed to me, it hits me that I have to say something. Thankfully, I have my speech memorized—perks of being a singer/songwriter.

"Wow. Just wow. I'm truly honored and humbled to be standing here tonight accepting this award. It's…it's really hard to put into words what this means to me. This journey, this dream, it wouldn't be possible without so many incredible people in my life.

"First and foremost, I have to thank my manager, my rock, my best friend, Ivan."

I look at Ivan and finish what I have to say.

"You've been with me through the good and the bad, navigating this crazy world with me, and I wouldn't be here without your guidance and belief in me, even when I sometimes struggle to believe in myself. Thank you, man."

He nods at me, accepting and appreciating the acknowledgment.

"I also want to give a special shout-out to my incredible guitar player, Brody."

I point the award toward him and continue, speaking directly to him.

"Brody, your strength and dedication are an inspiration to us all. Losing your father just a few short weeks ago is unimaginable, and yet you poured your heart and soul into our performances."

The crowd cheers, likely knowing who his father is, the legend himself.

"And now, I want to dedicate this award to someone incredibly special."

I look at Miley who is smiling so big and speak to her and only her.

"Miley, this past month has been extremely rough for me, and honestly, I'm not sure I'd be standing on this stage tonight if it weren't for you."

I go off script and look out to the crowd, continuing.

"Several years ago, I lost my younger sister, and it's a pain that never truly goes away."

I look back to Miley, who is physically holding her heart.

"But, Miley, you came into my life and brought sunshine back into my world. You've shown me how to smile again, how to laugh again, and for that, I am forever grateful. Thank you for everything."

I pause briefly, trying to get back on track.

"Finally, to my fans. You guys are the heart and soul of everything I do. Your passion, your energy, your unwavering support…it fuels me every single day. Through thick and thin, tour or no tour, you've stuck by my side. Your loyalty and love mean the world to me. From the bottom of my heart, thank you."

The crowd roars as I walk backstage with Ivan, and then, after the final commercial break, we make our way back to our seats right before they announce Artist of the Year.

"You amaze me." Miley grabs my hand and holds it as they announce the last award.

"And the award for Artist of the Year goes to…Greylan Asher!"

No. Fucking. Way.

I stand, and Miley grabs my face and kisses me hard. I hit Brody's arm, asking him to follow me, and nudge Ivan with me too.

THE ONE

This wasn't the plan. I'm not prepared for this. I don't have a fucking clue what to say. I've already said everything approximately fourteen minutes ago.

"I honestly don't know what to say. I'm completely speechless. I truly did not expect this. I'm in shock. Disbelief. And more than anything, just incredibly grateful.

"I've said a lot tonight already about the people who have supported me, and I don't want to be repetitive. But it's worth repeating. I wouldn't be here without them. They've believed in me even when I doubted myself. They've picked me up when I've fallen, and they've celebrated every victory, big or small, right alongside me. To them, thank you.

"And of course, to my fans. You are the reason I do what I do. Your passion, your support, your belief in me… it fuels me every single day.

"Honestly, I'm still trying to process all of this. These awards, this night…it's beyond anything I could have imagined. Thank you to the academy, thank you to everyone who voted, and thank you to everyone who has been a part of my story. I am eternally grateful."

Chapter 32

Miley

I've never been the jealous type. I used to think jealousy was a foreign concept. I was genuinely secure in myself, content with my own reflection. But the night I walked in on my husband fucking another woman in our bed, everything shattered. I'll forever be haunted by the image of their intimacy. I'll forever feel as if I'm not good enough.

After the CMAs, the four of us make our way to the after-party, which is absolutely insane. Luxury drips from every chandelier, the floral arrangements are breathtaking, and the champagne never stops flowing. Gourmet food, custom cocktails—it's all here, and it's all incredible. I feel like I'm on top of the world.

We are all having a blast. Colbie has me out on the dance floor more times than I could count. But my eyes keep finding Greylan, always talking to someone different. Usually a woman. I try to ignore it, but Colbie, already well on her way, isn't so subtle.

"Every woman in this place has their eyes on your guy, and you're the one that gets to fuck him tonight, woohoo!" Her words slur slightly as she offers a high five, a clear sign she is well past tipsy but not quite "white girl wasted."

"You good?" I laugh.

"Actually no, not really. I think I need to puke."

Good god. If she pukes in the middle of this dance floor during the CMAs after party, I will die. I will seriously fucking die.

"Alrighty then, let's get you to the bathroom…"

THE ONE

After listening to her vomit for approximately six minutes, I realize that it's time for us to go. We can't stay here with her throwing up in a luxury toilet at a luxury event.

She stumbles out of the stall, hair all fucked up, looking like a hot mess.

"Bee, I think it's time we go. Sit here." I point to the velvet couch. "I'm going to tell the guys."

She actually listens for once, thank god, and I find my way out back to the bar where I see Greylan surrounded by women legitimately hanging all over him. It flips my stomach.

He breaks free as soon as he sees me, and I place my hand softly on his chest. "Colbie is super sick. I think I should leave with her."

"We'll come too." He looks to Brody.

"No, no...please stay. This is your night. You deserve this." I fake a smile.

"Are you sure?"

"I'm positive, but can we take one of the cars back, and you and Brody take the other when you're ready to leave?" I look back toward the bathrooms, ensuring she didn't escape.

"Okay, but I am walking you out."

At the car, Brody guides Colbie to the passenger side, his hand resting lightly on her arm. He opens the door and helps her in, a small smile playing on his lips. At the other passenger door, Greylan leans in and kisses me, his hand cupping my cheek.

"I'll be home in an hour," he murmurs, his eyes locking with mine.

As the car pulls away, I twist in my seat and look back. Greylan stands there watching us, his silhouette framed by the warm glow of the venue lights.

By the time we get back to Greylan's house, it's one thirty in the morning. I help Colbie up the stairs, then get ready for bed. I change, take off my makeup, and tie my hair up in a knot before climbing into Greylan's bed.

I'm so tired, but I can't fall asleep, so I just lie there, tossing and turning. I finally look over at the clock as it's almost three in the morning, and Greylan still isn't back.

THE ONE

A wave of nostalgia washes over me as I lie there alone, just as it had a hundred times before, waiting for Derek to come home. My heart starts to race, a nervous flutter in my chest. Why isn't he back yet? The question echoes in the silence, each tick of the clock amplifying my growing anxiety.

My hand instinctively reaches for my phone on the nightstand. The blank screen offers no comfort. The question of texting him hangs heavy in the air, but I can't bring myself to do it. Instead, I bury my phone beneath my pillow and close my eyes as tightly as I can, fighting back the tears as they try to make their way out.

I'm not sure how much time passes, but when I hear the bedroom door creak open, I freeze. I don't know why, but I stay still, pretending to sleep. My breath is held captive in my chest as I hear the soft click of the closing door and the sound of him making his way to the bathroom. When the bathroom door shuts, I finally allow myself to peek at the clock. Almost three thirty in the morning.

I close my eyes once more; the sound of running water is white noise to my ears. When he finally comes out, he quickly slips into the bed beside me, immediately wrapping his arm around my waist as his chest presses close to my back.

*****

If I had to guess how much sleep I got last night, I'd say a solid four hours maybe. I turn over in the bed, and Greylan isn't next to me. I look at the time, and it's after ten in the morning. We have to leave here by noon to get to the airport.

I hop out of bed and use the bathroom quickly before walking across the hall to the guest bedroom to check in on Colbie. She is still sleeping. Snoring and everything. I will let her be.

I make my way down the stairs as the smell of French toast hits me in the face. The first thing I see as I enter the kitchen is a shirtless Greylan looking like a snack as he flips the bread in the skillet.

I take a deep breath and try to play it cool because I can't help the way I'm feeling. I feel jealous. I feel unwanted. Hurt. And a little disrespected. I can't help it. It's out of my control right now. I need time to think. To think about us, to think about everything.

"Hey, you."

He turns around and smiles. "You hungry?"

"I am. Let me wake up Colbie quickly. We need to get going soon."

He glances at the clock. "But you don't have to be at the airport until noon."

"I know, but Colbie needs to stop for a souvenir shirt beforehand. It's a thing she does. Whenever she travels, she needs to get a souvenir for herself." I ramble before backtracking to the staircase to wake up Colbie, not giving him a chance to respond whatsoever.

I take the hall to the guest bedroom and knock twice before walking in. She moves a little in her sleep.

"Time to wake up, Bee. We have to go soon."

She squints her eyes open and looks at the time before letting them fall together again. "Wake me up at eleven."

"No, we have to stop for your souvenir. We have to go after we eat the breakfast Greylan just made."

She rolls to her side and looks at me. "What did I miss?"

"You didn't miss anything."

"You're a fucking liar. Tell me now, or I will go downstairs and ask Greylan myself." She suddenly perks up.

"Jesus Christ, chill. A bunch of girls were flirting with him all night. You got drunk and puked, so I took you home, and they stayed."

"Shit, really?"

"Yup." I pop the *P*.

"I'm so sorry. Did I make a scene?"

I smile because sometimes she does. "No, it was all good."

"Phew. Okay, sorry. Please continue."

"Wait, quick question." I pause. "How the fuck don't you ever get hung over?" This is a serious question. My head is pounding from the few drinks I had. This bitch never, ever, ever gets hung over. It's weird.

"A bottle of water and Tylenol before bed. I'm telling you, it works wonders! Now go on."

I roll my eyes. "I took you back, and he and Brody were only going to stay for an hour. But an hour turned into two hours, and—"

Colbie interrupts. "Two hours turned into three hours."

"No."

"No?"

"No. He came home two hours later."

"Um, okay," she says. "That's not that bad." She looks confused.

"Colbie, please. I just want to go. I don't want to answer a million questions right now. Can we just pack up our things quickly, then eat breakfast with them?"

She understands girl code. She knows that she just needs to let me lead at this very moment. "Okay." She sits all the way up and heads to the bathroom. "But we are talking on the plane."

"Deal. Meet downstairs in five minutes?"

I head to Greylan's room to change and brush my teeth, then throw everything in my suitcase as quickly as I humanly can. We both walk out of our rooms at the same time and carry our luggage down to the stairs and leave them off to the side before heading into the kitchen for breakfast.

"Smells like heaven." Colbie helps herself to one of the three plates that are already on the counter as Greylan adds French toast to a fourth.

"Hopefully it tastes like heaven," Brody says as he makes his way to the table with another plate, and Greylan places the other two down for me and him before grabbing us all something to drink.

Colbie shoves a piece in her mouth, eating it quickly. "Seven."

Good god, here we go.

"Nine," Brody chimes in.

"This is really good. Thank you, Greylan."

"You're welcome."

"What time did you guys get back last night? I mean, this morning?" Colbie asks with her mouth full, and I nearly choke on my coffee.

I give her the death stare as Greylan responds instantly. "Three thirty."

Colbie is incredibly intrusive. She enjoys putting people on the spot and thrives on creating uncomfortable situations, particularly when she's not involved.

"Thought you were only staying another hour."

Brody looks at me as I look down and take another bite of my food. Jesus fucking Christ. I can't right now.

"It was my fault," he interrupts. "Greylan wanted to leave, but I was talking to some of my father's friends."

The room goes quiet for a moment; no one says a thing. Just awkward silence until Colbie takes the last bite of her breakfast.

"Well, that was tasty." She talks with her mouth full as she stands to walk her dish to the sink. "So, how are we getting to the airport?"

I look at the clock, and it's almost eleven.

"I'll take you," Greylan responds.

Greylan

A knot tightens in my stomach. Something feels off. Miley doesn't seem right. And I'm not sure if it's because Brody and Colbie are here or if I did something wrong.

As we near the airport, Miley instructs me to pull up front, assuring me I don't need to worry about parking. I comply. As I round the car to open her door, I find that she is already halfway out. I shift gears, grabbing their suitcases from the trunk and setting them on the curb.

"Can I talk to you for a second?" I whisper.

Colbie grabs the handles of both bags, answering for Miley. "Take your time. I'll be inside looking for my souvenir."

When the automatic doors open and Colbie is out of sight, I turn to Miley. "I feel like you're leaving before we've even had a chance to talk about...what comes next."

"Well," she says matter-of-factly, "I'm leaving because I have a flight to catch, and I need to get back to my normal life, to my job."

THE ONE

Her response stings. I'm taken aback.

"Miley, what's wrong? Talk to me. We don't hide from each other."

I watch a single tear slip from beneath her sunglasses. She tilts her head back, drawing in a deep breath before meeting my gaze again. "I just…I need a minute to process everything. I have to go." She leans in, brushing a kiss against my cheek, and then walks straight into the airport, never once turning back.

I stand frozen, time stretching into an eternity as I wrestle with what to do. Do I just leave? Do I chase after her, create some dramatic scene in the middle of the airport? Confusion and conflicting emotions fill me.

"You gotta move your car, buddy!"

The shout breaks through my daze. I glance over and see a security guard gesturing and directing traffic.

I slide into my car, but instead of pulling away from the airport, I steer into the parking garage and find a spot. I have no plan, no idea what I'll say or do when I find her. All I know is that I *have* to find her.

I walk back into the terminal and head straight for the only store before security. A quick scan confirms she's not in here. I exit then check the TSA line, but she isn't there either. I step back, trying to think. I grab my phone from my pocket and dial her number. No answer. I try again. Still nothing. Giving up for the moment, I go back to my car and text her.

> **Greylan**: Please call me when you get home. I love you, Mils.

The drive home is a blur; I can't recall a single detail. I feel lost, a passenger in my own life.

When I get home and step inside, I find Brody about to head out.

"Home already?" he asks, snatching his keys from the counter.

"She didn't want me there," I mumble.

"What do you mean?" Confusion clouds his face.

"She needs space to think. She...she just left." The words feel heavy, and I desperately want to avoid the subject.

Gratefully, Brody senses my reluctance. Instead of pressing for details, he simply asks, "Wanna write?"

Definitely.

We spend the next few hours writing. We finished the song I started a few weeks ago then started a new one, a better one, and it's for Miley. And it's amazing. I can see it becoming a big hit. It was a great distraction. But now that he's gone and I'm alone again, I'm getting really anxious. It's nighttime, and she still hasn't replied to my text or called me back. I'm at a loss for what to do.

I cave in and call her again, but she sends it straight to voice mail, I can tell.

Greylan: Talk to me, Miley...

Gray dots dance along the screen before they disappear quickly. When she doesn't respond, I text again.

Greylan: Please.

I watch the dots again, but this time they don't go away. Then finally...

Miley: I will call you tomorrow.

That's it. That's all she writes.

Frustration boils inside me. I head to the basement and punish myself with a workout. Running, lifting, stretching, over and over until I'm empty. I shower and fall into bed. My bed. It still smells like her.

I check my phone again. Nothing. I open Instagram. The first picture I see is me on stage at the CMAs, giving my Artist of the Year speech. I tap through the other photos on the account and freeze. There we are. Miley and me. On the red carpet. She looks phenomenal.

THE ONE

I rewind the whole night in my mind, searching for a misstep, a clue. But I come up empty. I keep scrolling through the Instagram feed, and then I see it: a photo of me at the after-party surrounded by a group of women. It hits me like a ton of bricks. Jealousy. Was Miley jealous? Did I *make* her jealous? Shit.

None of those people mattered. It was all just surface-level conversation about my music. I was just being nice. She's the only one who matters to me, and I need her to understand that.

I swipe up and out of Instagram and text Ivan.

Greylan: Can I make a post on Instagram?

The fact that I have to ask permission to post on my account is absolutely mind-boggling to me, but it's just the way the industry works. It's annoying, but it is what it is.

Ivan: Possibly. Send me it beforehand.

Back on Instagram, I grab a screenshot of the red carpet photo of Miley and me. I have other pictures of us from Hawaii on my phone, but I wouldn't post those without asking her first. Because this one was a public shot, I'm hoping she'd be okay with me sharing it on my personal page.

I send him the photo and follow up with the caption I'd like to add.

Greylan: Two awards, and one incredible person by my side. Thank you for sharing this night with me.

I'm selective about what I share online, and Ivan understands that. While my label might prefer more frequent posts, I'm not comfortable creating content just for the sake of it. When I do post, it's because I genuinely have something meaningful to say.

Ivan: Approved. Lunch tomorrow?

THE ONE

Greylan: Thanks. & yeah, sounds good.

I keep it at that. Yes, Ivan is my best friend, but I am praying that this shit is just a hiccup.
I make the post on Instagram and finally call it a night.
Tomorrow is a new day.

Chapter 33

Miley

When I reach the seventh floor and walk into the firm for the first time in over a week, the first person I see is Tracey. *Just let me be.* The thought echoes in my head. I'm in a mood. I didn't get any sleep whatsoever, and I'm confused, I'm conflicted.

"Welcome back. Vacation good?" Her smile is plastic.

"Yeah, thanks," I mumble, eager to escape and tackle the inevitable email deluge.

As I walk to the kitchen to put my lunch bag in the fridge, I can sense her following me.

"Where did you go again?" She pauses for a half second before sarcastically adding, "Oh, that's right, Hawaii. I always wanted to go to Hawaii."

An instant chill runs down my spine. I didn't tell her where I was going. I didn't tell anyone here where I was going.

I shove my bag on the bottom shelf, shut the door, and escape before she can say anything else to me because if she does, I will likely lose my shit.

"I will let Mr. O'Connell know you're here. He's been waiting for you!" she practically yells down the hallway.

I am so fucked.

As soon as I get inside my office, I shut the door and hide behind my dual monitors, desperate to slow my racing pulse. The worst-case scenario replays in my mind: unemployment. Six months of savings offer a sliver of comfort, but the thought of job hunting without a good reference causes panic to rise in my chest. This job, besides college waitressing, is the only real one I've ever had.

I inhale deeply, then stand. No point in wasting time on emails if I'm about to be fired. I'm going to face this head-on. I open my office door and make my way over to Jeff's.

The second I knock on his door, he gestures to the chair, his face unreadable.

"Miley," he begins, his voice tight. "We need to talk."

My heart plummets. "Jeff, I—"

He cuts me off, a sharp flick of his hand. "Let's not. Let's just be direct."

Direct. Right.

"This isn't about your performance," he continues, his gaze fixed on some point over my head. "You've always been…efficient." That word, so clinical, so devoid of any warmth. It hangs in the air like a bad smell. "This is about professionalism. And trust."

My cheeks burn. Here it comes. "Jeff, about Greylan—"

"Don't," he snaps. "Don't insult my intelligence or yours. Dating a client, especially one as important as Greylan Asher, is a clear violation of company policy. It's a conflict of interest. A breach of trust."

My mind races. It wasn't like that. It wasn't calculated. It just… happened. But his face is a granite mask. He doesn't care about the *why*.

"So," I manage, my voice a whisper. "I'm fired?"

"Consider this your official notice," he confirms, his eyes finally meeting mine, but there's nothing there. Just coldness. "HR will contact you about severance and vacation time. I want your laptop and keys on my desk by the end of the day."

"Just like that?" I ask, the words laced with disbelief. "After seven years?"

"You knew the rules, Miley," he says, his voice flat, emotionless. "You made a choice. And now you're facing the consequences."

My legs feel like jelly. I stand, trying to hold my head high. "I understand," I say, though I don't. I don't understand how something that felt so real, so right, could be so wrong in his eyes. How seven years of hard work can be wiped out like this.

"One more thing," he adds as I turn to leave. "Discretion is paramount. I suggest you keep the details of your departure…private."

I nod, my throat thick. I won't give him the satisfaction of seeing me break. I go back into my office, grab my purse, and walk out, the click of the door echoing the finality of it all. My career, my reputation, everything…shattered.

As soon as I'm in my car, the tears I held back finally spill. It's not sadness for the job—I despised it. It's anger, frustration, and a sense of profound unfairness. I cry because I lost. I lost control. I lost my way. I wasn't supposed to fall in love. I wasn't supposed to get fired.

The drive home is a blur. The familiar streets look alien; the traffic lights seem to mock me with their constant red-yellow-green cycle, a relentless reminder of time marching on while my own life feels like it's screeching to a halt. I grip the steering wheel so tight, my knuckles ache, trying to anchor myself as the swirling chaos of my thoughts begin to take over.

When I finally pull into my driveway, I don't even bother parking properly. I just kill the engine and stumble out of the car and into the house. I don't even bother changing out of my work clothes. I walk straight to my bedroom, close the door, and collapse onto the bed. I bury my face into my pillow, trying to muffle the sobs that shake my body. Exhausted and emotionally drained, I eventually cry myself to sleep, the weight of everything pressing down on me like a physical burden.

*****

I wake up to pitch-black. My bedroom is completely dark. I must have been out for hours. But considering the stress, lack of sleep the night before, traveling, and still struggling with the time change from vacation, I'm not surprised.

I drag myself to the kitchen, and just then, someone knocks at the door. I *never* get unexpected visitors. Everyone knows I hate that. Panic flickers. I need to see who it is. I frantically search for my phone to check the Ring camera, but it's nowhere to be found.

THE ONE

Before I can look again, I hear the click of a key in the lock. The door swings open, and Sutton is there, a look of pure relief on her face.

"Jesus fuck, Miley. I called you like twelve times!"

"I was sleeping...sorry."

"Miley, what is wrong with you?" Sutton's voice is laced with concern as she stands in my doorway. I'm still in my work clothes, hair a mess, makeup long gone. The events of the last two days feel like a bad dream, but the lingering headache and the knot in my stomach tell me otherwise.

"Just...a bad day," I mumble, turning away from her. I don't want to talk about it. Not yet.

"A bad day that involves you ignoring twelve phone calls and looking like a wreck?" she pushes, stepping farther into my house, and closes the door behind her, a clear sign she's not leaving until I spill.

I sigh, sinking onto the couch. "Okay, fine. It was...worse than bad."

Sutton sits beside me, her expression softening. "What happened?"

I hesitate for a moment, then the words start tumbling out, a jumbled mess of frustration and humiliation. "I got fired, Sutton. Fired."

Sutton's eyebrows shoot up. "He found out?"

"Yup," I say, picking at a loose thread on the couch.

"What did Greylan say?"

"I didn't tell him."

"Why not?"

"It's complicated."

"Complicated how?" Sutton is nothing if not persistent.

"I don't know, I didn't leave on good terms. I told him I needed time to process everything."

We never had a chance to talk yesterday. By the time my plane landed, she was already at work.

"Elaborate."

"All these women were hanging all over him at the after-party. It just...it bothered me more than I thought it would."

"Really? You've never been the jealous type."

"I know, right? I thought I wasn't. But then Colbie, she was pretty drunk, pointed it out, and it just…it got to me. Then she got sick, really sick. I had to take her back to Greylan's."

"Oh god."

"Yeah, it was rough. So I left the after-party with her. I told Greylan and Brody to stay, that it was their night. But it was hard, seeing him surrounded by all those women. He said he'd be home in an hour."

"And he wasn't?"

"Nope. I got back to his place, helped Colbie, got ready for bed…and waited. He didn't get home until almost three thirty. It brought back…memories. Of Derek. Waiting for him to come home. It just…it was a really bad night." My eyes start to water.

"I'm so sorry, Miley. That's really tough."

"Thanks. Then when I got to work this morning, Jeff was…he was brutal. Said I breached his trust, compromised the company. It was humiliating."

"I can imagine," Sutton says softly, though I can see the "I told you so" lurking behind her sympathetic gaze. "But Miley, seriously, what did you think was going to happen?"

"I don't know!" I cry, tears welling up again. "I wasn't thinking. I just…I liked him. And he liked me. It felt…real."

Sutton takes my hand, her grip firm. "I'm not going to lecture you, Miley. You messed up. You know that. But what are you going to do now?"

I shrug, feeling utterly lost. "I don't know. Start looking for another job, I guess. But…the reference thing. Jeff said…" I trail off, the memory of his cold words stinging.

"He's not going to give you a good reference, is he?" Sutton finishes for me.

I shake my head, tears streaming down my face now. "He said… discretion was paramount. Basically, he told me to keep my mouth shut."

Sutton squeezes my hand. "Okay. We'll figure this out. First things first, you need a shower. And then we're going to brainstorm.

You're not going to let this derail you, Miley. You're stronger than this."

I manage a weak smile. "Thanks, Sutton."

"Anytime," she says. "Now, how about I order some pizza, and we can just…chill for a bit?"

I nod. The thought of comfort food and my sister's support is a welcome to my wounded pride.

Greylan

She still hasn't called. I waited and waited but nothing. The silence is deafening. Six o'clock rolls around, her usual time home from work, and I dial her number. No answer. I hesitate, wanting to talk to her, but also respecting her need for space. I don't want to push.

I need a distraction. I drive to Ivan's because being alone just isn't an option tonight.

> **Greylan**: I'm coming over. I'll be there in a couple mins.

Inviting myself over is nothing new; he's used to it. Besides, I know he's free tonight, he told me earlier when we had lunch. I didn't mention anything about Miley at the time. I didn't feel the need. But now I'm stressed out and need someone to talk to.

When I walk in, Ivan is watching hockey and drinking a beer. I help myself to one in the fridge, then sink into the armchair in his living room and stare at the screen, pretending I'm interested.

After a moment, he breaks the silence. "Everything okay?" His brow furrows slightly. "You seem kind of…off." He must see the tension radiating off me.

"It's Miley…"

He just looks at me, waiting for me to continue.

"It's just…the way she left. We didn't really get to talk about anything. I mean, about us, about…everything that happened."

"What do you mean? Didn't you guys talk at all?"

"We talked a little, but...it wasn't enough. I told her I felt like she was leaving before we even had a chance to figure things out, you know, what happens next. And she just said she had a flight to catch and needed to get back to her normal life."

"Ouch. That sounds...dismissive."

"Yeah. It kind of stung. I told her we don't hide things from each other, and then she started crying. Just one tear, but...it was there."

"And then what?"

"She just said she needed a minute to process everything, and then...she left. Just like that."

"Wow. That's...rough. I'm sorry. Is that why you wanted to make a post last night?"

"Yeah. I want her to know how important she is to me. I love that girl."

"Give her some time. She said she needed to process things, right? She'll reach out when she's ready."

"I hope so. I really do."

I tell him about our entire vacation and fill him in on what happened at the CMAs after-party that he skipped out on, and he listens patiently, his expression shifting from concern to understanding as I speak. He doesn't interrupt, doesn't offer any quick fixes or empty reassurances. He just listens.

Once I am done venting, I stand and grab his guitar that's in the corner of his living room and walk back to the couch.

"What're you doing?" he asks.

"I wrote a new song yesterday with Brody. Want to hear it?"

He glances at the TV, where the first period is nearly over and the Rangers are winning two-nothing. "Yeah," he says, muting the game.

I tune his guitar, which probably hasn't been touched since the last time I picked it up.

"Ready?"

He gives a quick nod.

THE ONE

Down in the dumps, my heart was low,
Lost and adrift, didn't know where to go.
Then you came along, like a sweet summer breeze,
Picked me right up, put my heart at ease.

You rescued me, you set me free,
Showed me what love truly can be.
My guiding star, my steady hand,
My love for you, forever will stand.

Hawaii's beaches, a memory so clear,
Holdin' you close, whisperin' in your ear.
The best damn time I've ever had, it's true,
Just me and you, nothin' else to do.

You rescued me, you set me free,
Showed me what love truly can be.
My guiding star, my steady hand,
My love for you, forever will stand.

Long black hair and eyes so brown,
The prettiest girl in this whole damn town.

I'll choose you always, that's a fact,
Ain't no way I'm turnin' back

"Wow. That's actually really good," he says, nodding.

"Thanks." Brody's music is the perfect counterpoint to my lyrics.

"Think you want to record it? I can talk to the label, see if we can get you in soon."

"Definitely."

"I'll try to get you in before Thanksgiving." He pauses, his gaze softening. I know what he's thinking. Thanksgiving. Ten years. The last time I saw my sister…

"When is it this year?" I whisper.

"November twenty-eighth."

THE ONE

The date echoes in my mind. The day I lost her. The day everything changed.

"Are you staying here or going home?" I ask.

"Home. I'll book your flight. You're coming."

It's always been that way with Ivan and me. Thanksgiving, no matter where it is, we're together. It's just how it is.

"Thank you."

We settle back into the hockey game, the tension momentarily easing. But as the final buzzer sounds, I glance at the clock. It's past ten already—a knot begins to tighten in my stomach. She still hasn't called or texted.

"I should get going," I tell him. "I'll give you a call tomorrow."

"All right. I'll reach out to Jake in the morning about recording that song and let you and Brody know what he says."

"Great, thanks."

As I drive home, the weight of it all settles back on my shoulders, heavier than before. I pull out my phone and dial her number, hoping against hope that she'll answer. When it goes straight to voice mail, disappointment washes over me.

The house is cold when I get inside. I feel alone. Lost. She's pushing me away without even a conversation, without talking to me like an adult. If she's feeling some kind of way, if she's jealous because of the attention that comes with my career, I'll fix it. I swear I will. I'll do whatever it takes. Because I love her. Because I need her.

Before I can spiral any further, I pull out my phone and text Sutton. I make sure to keep it casual, professional, like a landlord checking in on a tenant.

Greylan: Just checking in to make sure everything is good at the house.

It's late, so I don't expect a reply anytime soon. But almost instantly, the little dots appear beneath my message, indicating she's typing. A wave of relief washes over me.

Sutton: It's perfect. Thank you again.

THE ONE

I reply quickly, eager to keep the conversation going to gently steer it toward Miley.

> **Greylan**: You're welcome. I forgot to cancel the weekly cleaners and just got a notification that they will be there Monday morning. Sorry. This will be the last week unless you want me to have them continue.

Her response is quick.

> **Sutton**: Haha, I can handle it. No worries about Monday.

I text back, holding my breath as I hit send.

> **Greylan**: While I have you…have you heard from Miley? She was supposed to call earlier but hasn't, and her phone is going straight to voicemail.

The dots appear, then disappear, then reappear. Finally, a message:

> **Sutton**: Miley was fired today…

Chapter 34

Miley

Is this what it feels like when you hit rock bottom? Empty. Hopeless. Constantly tired. It's a struggle to even lift my head, let alone face the day. My limbs feel heavy, like they're weighted down with lead. My reflection stares back at me, a stranger with shadowed eyes and a mouth that permanently frowns. Even the simplest tasks, like showering or making a cup of coffee, feel difficult.

I crawl back into bed, pulling the covers over my head. The darkness is comforting, or at least it's better than facing the reality of my life. I close my eyes, but my mind races with worries and regrets, replaying every mistake I made.

A single tear escapes and trickles down my cheek, but I don't bother wiping it away. What's the point? I'm a mess. My life is a mess. And the worst part? I don't even know how I got here. Or how to climb out.

"Miley…" Sutton's voice drifts through the closed bedroom door, but I bury deeper under the covers, pretending to be asleep. The door creaks open. "Come on, you gotta get up. We're going to lunch with Colbie and Peyton."

My voice is muffled by the blanket. "You told them?"

"Yeah," she replies. "Remember? You told me to last night so they wouldn't pry and make things worse."

I vaguely recall the conversation.

I manage to haul myself out of bed and stumble into the bathroom. A quick lukewarm shower does little to shake off the lingering fog, but it's something. When I step out of the bathroom wrapped in a towel, I find Sutton rummaging through my purse.

"What are you doing?" I mumble.

"Looking for your phone. It's dead." She pulls it out from the depths of my bag and plugs it into the charger. "Now get dressed," she says, a hint of command in her voice, "and I'll blow out your hair."

I pull a pair of leggings from my drawer and an oversized sweater from my closet. Hopefully, wherever we're going isn't too fancy because this is it. This is what I'm wearing. No arguments.

Once dressed, I sit on a stool at the kitchen island while Sutton tackles my hair with a brush.

"Are you going to talk to Greylan today?" she asks, the question catching me off guard.

"I don't know. Why?"

A beat of silence hangs in the air before she answers. "He's worried about you."

"And how do you know that?" I ask with a flicker of suspicion.

"Because he texted me last night…"

"Why does he have your number?"

"He's my landlord, Miley."

"Right. I'm an idiot. Sorry," I admit.

"Just talk to him," Sutton continues, giving my hair a few more strokes. "Either call it quits or don't…but don't leave him hanging, giving him false hope."

"Okay," I say. "I'll call him after lunch."

Twenty minutes later, Sutton finishes my hair, and it's time to meet Peyton and Colbie for lunch. As Sutton drives to the restaurant, I stare out the window. The passing scenery is meaningless, a blurry backdrop to my thoughts. The last thing I want is to be in public right now.

Sutton glances over at me. "If you had a redo button," she asks, "a chance to choose a different career, a different path…what would you pick?"

I don't even have to think about it. The answer has been simmering in my soul for years, and I'm pretty sure she knows it too; I've probably mentioned it a million times. "I'd want to be an author."

THE ONE

"Then you should try it," she replies. "When you get home later, open your laptop or pick up a pen and just start writing. It'll be a good distraction."

Hmm. Maybe she's right.

She pulls into the restaurant parking lot and checks her phone. "They're already inside," she says, opening her car door, and I do the same.

We find Peyton and Colbie at a table tucked toward the back.

"I don't want to talk about it," I announce as soon as I slide into my chair.

They both nod, understanding. And they actually don't talk about it. Not a word. Nothing about Greylan, nothing about losing my job, nothing about the CMAs, and nothing about Hawaii. It's... refreshing.

But as time goes on, the traffic to and from the restrooms picks up. A steady stream of people pass our table, back and forth, back and forth. It's not until someone points directly at me that I realize what's happening.

Colbie, sensing my sudden shift in demeanor, turns just in time to see someone aim their phone in my direction to take my picture. Without a second's hesitation, she snaps, "Could you kindly fuck off? We're trying to enjoy our lunch. Thanks."

But it doesn't stop there. More and more phones come out; more and more pictures are snapped. I feel like crawling out of my skin. So many eyes, so many strangers capturing a moment of my life without my consent.

"Are you Greylan Asher's girlfriend?" someone sitting at the table behind me asks, and I freeze. I don't turn around. I don't respond.

"Don't engage," Peyton tells the three of us, but whoever it is that I have my back to continues.

"I just don't get it. You're two totally different people..." There's a brief pause. "He's so hot, and you're—"

"Say one more word, I dare you." Colbie stops her before she can finish.

"Can we go?" I ask.

THE ONE

"Yes," Sutton responds as she flags down our waiter and hands him her card. "We're all set."

The waiter returns with the check, and Sutton quickly adds a tip and signs the slip. "Ready?" she asks, sliding her chair back and standing.

Peyton, Colbie, and I follow suit.

As I walk out of the restaurant, I glance back at the table behind us. Two Barbie clones, all smiles and laughter as their judging eyes follow me out the door.

"What the fuck!" Colbie shouts the second we are outside.

"I love you guys. Thanks for always having my back." I give Peyton and Colbie each a hug before I leave.

Sutton's car is just a few steps away, but it feels like a mile. I just want to be home, in the quiet darkness of my home, where no one can see me, no one can judge me.

We climb into the car, the silence punctuated only by the click of the seat belts. Sutton starts the engine, and we pull out of the parking lot, merging into the flow of traffic.

"Do you want to talk about it?" Sutton asks softly, her eyes on the road.

I shake my head. "No," I whisper. "I just...I just want to go home."

She nods, understanding. The rest of the drive is quiet. When we finally pull into my driveway, I feel a wave of relief wash over me.

"Thanks," I say to Sutton as I open the door to get out.

"Miley," she says, pausing, "comparing yourself to others is a waste of energy. It won't get you anywhere."

"I'm not," I snap. "I'm never going to be one of those girls. I'm not a follower. I'm perfectly content walking my own road, and I'm not going to change to fit in with anybody."

I step out of the car and head straight inside. The moment I cross the threshold, my phone vibrates on the counter. Greylan's name, accompanied by a picture of us from Hawaii, lights up the screen.

Greylan

You know what's worse than being ignored? Not knowing *why* you're being ignored. What you did wrong. Having the opportunity to fix it. When Sutton told me Miley was fired last night, it was a cold splash of reality. Whatever she was already dealing with, this was the last straw—and it's my fault. She lost her job because of me, and I'm not sure I will ever be forgiven.

But I refuse to give up. She means everything to me. I have to fight for her. I have to keep trying.

I dial her number and listen to the ringing that seems to go on forever, then at the last possible second, she picks up.

"Hello?" Her voice is quiet.

"I'm so sorry, Miley. Let me fix this."

I hear a sniffle as if she's crying, but after a moment, she says, "I can't do this anymore."

"Do what? Be with me?" The question feels stupid even as I ask it.

"We're...we're two different people living in two different worlds," she continues, her voice cracking. "And we both know it will never work."

"Miley, what's changed?"

"Everything. I can't even go out in public anymore. Everywhere I go, there are cameras. People whispering, pointing, taking pictures."

Understanding dawns.

"I know it's hard," I say, my voice laced with helplessness. Because what can I do? I can't stop it.

"Hard?" Miley echoes, a bitter laugh escaping her lips. "It's suffocating. My life was quiet and predictable, Greylan. Now it's a whirlwind of flashing lights and constant scrutiny."

The silence that follows is thick with unspoken words. I can't speak. I can't find my words. I think it's because a part of me understands where she is coming from.

Miley takes a deep breath, trying to compose herself. "I'm so sorry," she whispers. "I truly am."

THE ONE

My heart clenches, a fist squeezing so tight, I can barely breathe. It feels like something inside me is fracturing. It's not just a dull ache; it's a physical tearing, like my ribs are cracking inward.

"Goodbye, Greylan," she says, her voice barely audible before she hangs up.

I collapse onto the couch. The cushions are soft, but they offer no comfort.

My life, my music—the things I pour myself into, the things she once loved—have become the reason she walked away.

The silence screams. I'm lost and disoriented. I don't know where to go from here. I feel completely demolished. My heart is destroyed.

My phone buzzes on, and I instantly check to see if it's her. But it's not. It's Ivan. I hit decline and look at the half-empty bottle of whiskey that sits on the coffee table next to it, a silent dare. I pour a generous amount of the amber liquid into a glass, then swallow. The burn in my throat is a welcome distraction from the ache in my chest.

My phone vibrates again, and I ignore it, allowing it to continue until it goes to voice mail. I don't want to talk to anyone.

I take another swig of whiskey. The warmth spreads through my veins, but it's not enough. Nothing will be enough.

My phone goes off for a third time. Grabbing it, annoyed, I yell, "What?"

"I'll be over in an hour to get you. The studio has availability for a few hours," Ivan says to me on the other end of the line.

I'm not interested in recording anyone. Not right now, anyways. "I'm good."

"What do you mean you're good?" he asks, confused.

"I'm not recording it. Also, your douchebag uncle fired Miley yesterday. He can go fuck himself."

I finish my glass and set it down on the coffee table in front of me before falling back and resting my head on the back of the couch. I just stare at the ceiling.

"I'm coming over" is all he says before hanging up, and within minutes, he's letting himself into my house.

THE ONE

"You gotta hear me out," he says as he sits across from me, his voice softer than usual. "I pulled some strings, bumped a session—we have to go to the studio."

I stare at my hands. "Ivan, I appreciate it, but I'm really not in the mood."

He sighs, a genuine expression of sympathy on his face. "I know, man. I know you're going through it. But this song…it's *insane*. It's got to be heard. People need to hear this, and more importantly, *she* needs to hear this."

My stomach clenches. "Don't, Ivan. Just don't."

"I'm serious! This isn't just some song, man. It's…it's *her*. It's everything you're feeling. It's the kind of song that could…I don't know…change things."

"Change what? She's gone, Ivan. It's over." The words feel heavy, hollow.

Ivan leans forward, his voice earnest. "No, man. No way. You don't give up on something like that. Not on someone like *her*. You wrote this song, right? About her, about how much you love her? Well then, don't just sit here moping. I know it hurts, I really do, but use it. Let it be your voice. Let it show her what she's throwing away."

I'm silent for a moment, picturing her face, the way she used to smile when I played for her. "I don't know, Ivan…"

"Look, I get it," he says gently. "You're hurting. I'm not saying this is some magic fix. But what's the alternative? Just…give up? Let her go without even trying? You poured your heart into that song, man. Now pour that same heart into fighting for her. This song…this could be your best shot. It's a way to show her, to remind her…"

He pauses, letting his words sink in.

"Let's go. We're laying this down, and then…then we figure out the rest. But step one is getting this song out there. It's your story, man. Don't let it go untold. And don't give up on her. Not yet."

But how can I create anything beautiful when my world just shattered?

Chapter 35

Miley

We hang up, and I stare at my phone for a moment, the image of Greylan and me in Hawaii still lingering on the screen. With a deep breath, I set the phone down and sit on the couch. The silence is deafening; the tears fall freely. I don't know how long I sit there, lost in my thoughts, but eventually, the tears subside, leaving behind a hollow ache.

I think back to what Sutton asked me in the car. *If you had a redo button, a chance to choose a different career, a different path… what would you pick?* The answer comes to me instantly, as clear as a day. I would be an author. I *want* to be an author. I've always loved reading, loved telling stories, loved the way words can transport you to another world.

I think I should just do it. Give it a try. At least I can say I started.

I stand from the couch and walk into my office, sitting at the desk before opening my laptop. I've had so many ideas pop into my head throughout the years, stories I've always wanted to write. But where do I begin? The question hangs in the air, heavy with possibility with a small touch of fear.

Taking a deep breath, I position my fingers on the keyboard, and then I just start typing. I type what I'm thinking, what I'm feeling, the raw, unfiltered thoughts that have been swirling inside me for so long.

THE ONE

Chapter 1

Have you ever woken up and thought, *What the actual fuck am I doing with my life?*

I'm thirty-one years old, recently divorced, and I hate my job with a burning passion. I absolutely despise walking through those doors every goddamn morning. My boss is an arrogant prick who I would love nothing more than to punch directly in the face. He's as pompous as they come. But I guess he can be with his award-winning streak as being one of the best defense attorneys in the country. His specialty, DWIs.

As I type, a strange sense of calm settles over me. It's as if I'm finally giving voice to the things that have been weighing me down, releasing them into the world. There's a flicker of excitement too, a thrill at the possibility of creating something new, something meaningful. It's just a beginning, a first step, but it feels…right.

Hours melt away as I lose myself in the writing, the glow of the laptop screen illuminating my face in the otherwise dark room. My fingers fly across the keyboard, barely able to keep up with the words pouring out of me. It's as if a dam has broken, unleashing a flood of emotions and experiences that I've kept bottled up for far too long.

I write about the heartbreak, the confusion, the crushing weight of expectations. I write about the feeling of being lost and alone, of not knowing who I am or where I belong. And somewhere along the way, I start to write about a girl named Sara, a girl who, like me, is struggling to find her place in the world. Sara's story begins to take shape, her struggles and triumphs mirroring my own, yet also becoming something separate, something unique.

As the first rays of dawn peek through the blinds, I finally stop typing. My fingers ache, my eyes are blurry, and my head is pounding. But there's also a sense of accomplishment, a feeling of having created something real, something tangible.

THE ONE

I look at the screen, at the words I've written, and a small smile touches my lips. It's messy, it's raw, it's probably full of typos and grammatical errors, but it's mine. And in that moment, it's enough.

Greylan

I sit on a stool in front of the microphone. The headphones feel heavy on my ears, isolating me in a bubble of my own anxiety.

"All right, man, just relax," Ivan says through the talkback mic, his voice booming in my headphones. "Take a deep breath. You know the song inside and out."

Easy for him to say. He's not the one pouring his heart out to an empty room, knowing *she* might never even hear it.

"Just…play it like you mean it," he continues. "Like you're playing it for her and only her."

I close my eyes, trying to capture her image. Her smile, the way her eyes crinkled at the corners when she laughed. The memory stings, a fresh wound. I strum a chord, testing the sound. It rings out clear and resonant in the headphones, but it feels hollow.

"Ready when you are," Brody says.

I nod, my throat suddenly tight. I take a deep breath, just like he said, and begin to play. The opening chords fill the room, a melody that echoes the ache in my chest. I try to focus on the music, on the intricate fingerpicking patterns, on the way the notes blend together.

My voice comes in, rough and strained at first, then gradually gaining strength as I lose myself in the lyrics. Every word is a confession, a plea, a desperate attempt to bring us back together.

As the song builds, my emotions spill out, raw and unfiltered. My voice cracks, and I almost stop, but Ivan's voice in my headphones urges me on. "Keep going, man! You got this!"

I push through, pouring every ounce of my being into the final verse. The music swells, the guitar soaring, my voice ringing out with a desperate hope that maybe, just maybe, she'll hear this, and she'll understand. Brody's guitar echoes mine, adding another layer of emotion to the track.

The last note fades, leaving a silence that feels heavier than any sound.

I open my eyes, blinking against the bright lights of the studio. Ivan's face is beaming. Brody gives me a thumbs-up.

"Dude," Ivan says, his voice filled with emotion. "That was... that was incredible."

"We should totally record a video of this," Brody chimes in. "Just a simple one. Post it on social media. Get it out there."

Ivan nods enthusiastically. "Yeah, man! That's a great idea. It'll give the song even more impact."

I don't say anything. I just sit there, my fingers still resting on the strings of my guitar, the silence ringing in my ears.

"What do you say, Greylan?" Brody asks.

"Okay." I just agree because I know they will just keep pestering me if I don't.

"All right, let's do this. Same energy, same passion. Let it all out," Ivan says.

We get into position again, this time with a small camera set up in the corner of the room. Brody gives me a nod, and I close my eyes, take another deep breath, and begin again. This time, there's a different kind of focus. Knowing we're filming adds a layer of pressure, but it also fuels me. I channel all the raw emotion, all the longing, into every note, every word.

When the final note rings out, I know we've got it. We've captured something real, something that just might make a difference.

Chapter 36

Miley

I fell. I rose. I wrote. And in those words, I found it. My purpose. My passion. I open the laptop again, eager to dive back into the narrative. I reread what I've written, the words flowing smoothly, connecting in ways I hadn't planned. I work for hours, getting lost in the world I'm creating, the characters becoming more real to me than the people I pass on the street. Her journey mirrors my own in ways I hadn't anticipated, the fictional struggles and echoing battles I've fought within myself.

I reach the part of the story where she falls in love. The tentative first touches, the whispered secrets, the undeniable pull that draws two people together. I write about the buildup, the slow burn of attraction that ignites into a flame. And as I write, I realize something else. Something profound and undeniable. I don't think I'm capable of *not* loving Greylan Asher.

But the memories are double-edged. Alongside the warmth and affection, the flashbacks flicker to life: the whispers, the stolen glances. The image of Greylan surrounded by adoring women, a constant reminder of the insecurity that gnaws at me. *He's so hot, and you're...* The words from the restaurant echo in my ears, a cruel whisper of doubt. *Am I enough?*

I close my eyes, trying to push the thoughts away. I love him. I really do. But the fear, the lingering shadow of my past, holds me back. But the pain, the struggle, the darkness...it's transforming into something beautiful, something powerful. It transformed into words.

I pick up my phone, the screen still displaying Greylan's picture. A wave of emotion washes over me, a complex mix of sadness, longing, and a dawning realization. It's true. I can't live without him. He's not just a part of my story; he *is* my story. The thought of a future without him stretches out before me, empty and meaningless. I can't let pride or fear or uncertainty keep me from him.

I set the phone down, my hand trembling slightly. I can't call him. Not yet. Not until I can reconcile the love I feel for him with the fear that consumes me. I need to be sure. Sure of myself, sure of him, sure of what I want. And right now, I'm not.

But maybe, just maybe, if I keep writing, I can find the answers I'm searching for. Maybe this story will show me the way.

And then maybe I will share this story with the world. Maybe I'll publish it. The idea is both exhilarating and terrifying. The thought of putting my work out there for the world to see, to judge, to critique…it makes my stomach churn. But the fear is quickly overshadowed by a surge of excitement. What if people connect with my story? What if it inspires them, gives them hope? What if it's the beginning of something bigger than I ever imagined?

I close the laptop, a sense of purpose filling me. I know the road ahead won't be easy. There will be rejections, setbacks, and moments of crippling self-doubt. But for the first time in a long time, I feel like I'm on the right path. I'm doing what I'm meant to do. And I'm not sure where I'm going next, but I know one thing—I'm not the same person I was yesterday.

Greylan

Brody sprawls out on the couch, scrolling through his phone, while Ivan hunches over his laptop, his fingers flying across the keyboard as he edits the video footage. I pace restlessly, my insides a knot of anxiety.

"Dude, chill," Ivan says, glancing up at me. "It's almost done. Just give me five more minutes."

I grab us a couple more beers from the kitchen, and as I walk back, he says, "It's done." He clicks a button, and the video fills the laptop screen.

The concept is straightforward but moving. The camera finds me, my face an open book of emotion as I sing, my fingers *creating* melodies from the strings. Brody is visible in the background, his guitar adding depth and texture to the music. The lighting is dim, creating a personal, almost confessional atmosphere.

"Damn," Brody says, whistling low. "That's some powerful stuff, man."

I watch the video, a strange detachment settling over me. It feels like I'm watching someone else, someone who's pouring out their heart in a way I never could in person, someone capable of such raw emotional expression.

"All right, it's ready," Ivan declares, clicking the mouse. "Time to unleash it upon the world." He uploads the video to YouTube, Facebook, Instagram—every platform he can think of. Then we sit back and wait, the tension in the room thickening with every passing minute.

"Crack open your beer, man," Brody says as he sips his. "We've done all we can do now. Time to just let it be."

I pop the tab and take a long swig, the cold beer a welcome distraction. But two beers turns into three, then four, and the alcohol starts to loosen the tight knot of anxiety in my chest. It also loosens my tongue.

Hours crawl by. We talk about music, about life, about anything but the video that was posted. But with each beer, the conversation gets heavier, more personal.

"You know," I say, my voice heavy with emotion, "this whole thing with Rob...it just brings everything back, you know? Losing someone you love..."

Ivan and Brody exchange a concerned look.

"I miss her," my voice strains, the words tumbling out before I can stop them. "I miss Jillian so goddamn much."

THE ONE

The room falls silent. I can feel their eyes on me, but I can't meet their gaze. I stare at the empty beer can in my hand as the memories flood back, sharp and painful.

The phone call, the panicked drive to the hospital, the sterile smell of the waiting room, the doctor's somber expression.

"The worst part is," I tell Brody, my voice barely above a whisper, "the last text she ever got…it was from Rob…" It was the last message she ever read. The last thing anyone said to her before she died. Because four minutes later, she hit a pole going 45 mph.

I can't finish the sentence. The words catch in my throat, so I pull out my phone, my hands shaking as I navigate to my photos until I find it. A picture of the last message. I hand it to Brody.

"This," I say, my voice thick with tears, "this is the last thing anyone ever said to her."

Brody takes the phone, his brow furrowing as he reads the message. It's short, brutal, and utterly disrespectful: "No $$, no blow u dirty skank. The only thing u will ever be 2 me is a customer. Idc what happens 2 u."

He looks up at me, his eyes filled with a mixture of shock and anger. He doesn't say anything, but he doesn't have to. That message speaks for itself. It's the kind of message that makes your stomach drop, the kind of message you'd instantly regret sending, the kind of message that could haunt you forever.

We sit in silence for a long moment, the weight of the message hanging heavy in the air. The video, the song, the desperate attempt to win back Miley. It all seems insignificant now compared to the gaping hole in my life where my sister used to be and the cruel, callous words that was the last thing she ever read.

Chapter 37

Miley

The story consumes me. I write obsessively, driven by a force I can't explain. Food, daylight, even basic hygiene become secondary. My world shrinks to the confines of my laptop screen.

There are still gaps in the narrative, missing pieces that need to be filled in, but within a few short days, something miraculous has happened. I have a story. A beginning, a middle, and an end. It's rough, unfinished, a diamond in the rough, but the foundation is solid. It's there. And it's good. Really good.

As night falls, I finally crawl into bed, exhaustion weighing heavily on me. Pulling out my phone, I quickly craft a message to Sutton, Colbie, and Peyton, the excitement bubbling up inside me. "Guess what?!" I type, then attach the draft of my manuscript. "I wrote a book!"

Group Name: Core Four

Sutton: OMG! I'm staying up all night to read this.
Peyton: That's so exciting.
Miley: It isn't completely finished but the foundation is there. I need to make it bigger and better. Add more details, yah know?
Colbie: Hell yeah! The first line has me sold!

THE ONE

Miley: Yay! Let me know what you guys think. I'm headed to bed.
Colbie: Don't forget about Friendsgiving tomorrow!!
Miley: I won't. Still picking me up?
Peyton: I'll scoop you both around 4.
Sutton: Wait, before you go... you should watch this...

Forever Will Stand | Greylan Asher

I click the link and press play without giving it a second thought. It's a new song from Greylan, uploaded just last night. The video is simple yet profoundly moving. It's a single shot focused entirely on him as he sits on a stool in the center of the recording studio. There are no fancy effects, no elaborate staging. It's just Greylan, his guitar, and his voice, laid bare for the world to see. He looks...broken. Haunted almost. Yet as he begins to sing, his voice is powerful, filled with an emotion that resonates deep within me. It's as if he's inviting the viewer into his most private thoughts, sharing a piece of his heart with each note, each word.

I listen closely to the lyrics, my breath catching in my throat. He's singing about me. About us. He's telling our story, our love, our struggles, through music, just as I'm telling it through words.

The realization hits me with the force of a physical blow. He's not just a musician; he's an artist pouring his heart and soul into every lyric, just as I've poured mine into my writing. And in that moment, the wall I've built around my heart begins to crumble. Tears stream down my face as I listen to the song. It's as if he's reached inside my soul and pulled out the very essence of our love, transforming it into music. By the time the song ends, I'm sobbing uncontrollably, a flood of emotions I can no longer contain.

The song is over, but the feeling remains. I swipe the video away, my focus now solely on Greylan. I open my contacts and find his number, my thumb hovering over the call button for only a second before I press it. It rings and rings, but he doesn't answer. I try again, the anxiety rising in my chest with each unanswered tone. Where is he? Why isn't he answering? The doubts creep back in, whispering deceptive lies. *Maybe he's with someone else. Maybe he's moved on. Maybe he doesn't want to talk to you.*

I hang up, my heart sinking. I need to talk to him, to tell him how I feel, to apologize for pushing him away. But how can I when he won't even answer his phone?

Frustrated and heartbroken, I throw the phone onto the bed. I need to do something, anything, to distract myself from the overwhelming emotions swirling inside me. I can't just sit here and wait for him to call back. I need to move, to act, to create.

I grab my laptop and open the document, the words on the screen a welcome distraction. I start to write, not about Sara and her fictional love story, but about my own. I write about the passion, the pain, the fear, the hope. I write about the song, about how it made me feel, about how it opened my eyes to the depth of my own feelings. And as I write, a new sense of clarity emerges. I know what I have to do.

Greylan

I spent the entire next day in bed. I just lay there in the darkness, letting the sadness wash over me, letting it consume me. I've completely shut down. I'm numb. I'm empty. And frankly, I don't care. I don't care about anything.

As the plane ascends off the runway, I close my eyes, trying to block out the world, the pain, the memories. But they're relentless, clinging to me like shadows; they won't go away. I see my sister's face, her bright smile, her infectious laughter. I hear her voice; it's telling me everything will be okay. But it's not okay. It hasn't been okay for a long time. And I don't know if it ever will be. I'm lost, and I don't know how to find my way back. I just…I just want the pain to stop.

Tomorrow it'll be ten years. Ten years since I last saw my sister. Thanksgiving 2014. The day before…the day before everything changed. The day before my world shattered.

The flight to New York is a blur. I look out the window, but I don't really see anything. I feel like a passenger in my own life, just going through the motions.

The plane finally lands, and I'm jolted back to reality. My phone buzzes, reconnecting to the network. A bunch of notifications pop up, but the one that catches my eye is the missed calls. Two missed calls.

I stare at the screen, my thumb hovering over her name. Miley. A part of me, a small, foolish part, wants to call her back, to hear her voice, to…to what? To beg her to come back? To explain everything? But the larger part of me, the part that's buried under layers of grief and self-loathing, just…can't. It feels too big, too complicated. Too much.

I shove the phone back in my pocket and grab my bag. I just want to get out of here, get this whole Thanksgiving thing over with. But as I walk through the airport, the missed calls keep flashing in my mind.

*****

The house is quiet when we arrive. Everyone's already asleep.
"You hungry?" Ivan asks.
"No, I'm good. I'm tired. I'm going to go to bed."
"All right, man. Night."
I escape upstairs to the spare bedroom and sit on the bed, the mattress sagging a little under my weight.

I pull out my phone again. The two missed calls are still there, mocking me. I hesitate, then finally press the call button. It goes straight to voice mail.

"Hey, Miley," I say, my voice hoarse. "It's me. I…I got your calls. I don't know…I don't know what you want. But…I'm here. In New York. I'm at Ivan's parents' house. Call me back."

I hang up, feeling a little lighter, a little less alone. But the feeling doesn't last. The truth is, I don't know what I want from Miley. Or from anyone. I'm just reaching out, grasping at anything that might fill the emptiness inside me.

I lie on the bed, staring at the ceiling, waiting for her call. The silence in the room is deafening, amplifying the frantic beating of my heart. But it doesn't last long…because my phone rings. I snatch it up, my hand shaking as I answer.

"Hello?"

"Greylan?"

It's her. Her voice sounds… different. Worn-out, maybe? I can't tell.

"Miley?"

"Yeah, it's me."

There's a pause, a beat of silence where neither of us speaks. It's like we're both holding our breath, waiting for the other to say something.

"I…I got your message," she finally says. "I didn't know you were in New York."

"Yeah, I…I came back for Thanksgiving," I say, the words catching in my throat.

"Oh," she says. "Right."

Another silence. It's excruciating.

"Greylan," her voice is even softer now. "I…I saw your video."

My stomach clenches. "And?"

"And…it was beautiful," she says. "Really beautiful. It…it made me think."

"Think about what?"

"About…about everything," she continues. "About us. About… about what I lost."

THE ONE

My heart skips a beat. Is it possible? Is there a chance?

"I...I don't know what to say."

"Me neither," she replies. "But...can I see you? Tomorrow maybe?"

Tomorrow. The tenth anniversary. The day my world shattered.

"Yeah," I say. "Yeah, okay. Where?"

"I...I don't know," she says. "Do you want to come here?"

"Okay."

"Okay," she echoes.

We hang up, the phone feeling strangely light in my hand. I sit on the edge of the bed, my mind reeling. She saw the video. She misses me. She wants to see me. Is it really happening? Is it possible that after everything, after all the pain, there's a chance for us?

A flicker of hope fires within me, a tiny spark in the darkness. But it's fragile, easily extinguished. I know better than to get my hopes up. I know that tomorrow is going to be hard, harder than I can even imagine. And I know that even if Miley and I...even if we...it won't bring her back. It won't erase the pain.

But for now, I allow myself to feel it. Hope. A tiny fragile sliver of hope. It's enough. It has to be.

Chapter 38

Miley

    The anticipation builds with each passing hour, a nervous flutter in my stomach. I spend the entire morning cleaning my house, not wanting him to see the mess I've been living in for the past few days. I change into something comfortable but cute, something that makes me feel confident. I even put on a little makeup, a small attempt to erase the signs of the emotional roller coaster I've been on.

    When the doorbell rings, my heart leaps into my throat. I take a deep breath, trying to compose myself as I reach for the doorknob. But when I open the door, Greylan stands there, his gaze fixed on the ground. He looks up, and his eyes meet mine. The weariness in them is deep; he looks tired, a bit sad, and…nervous. It's a look I've rarely seen on his face, and it makes my heart ache.

"Hey," he says softly.

"Hi." I step aside to let him in.

    As he crosses the threshold, his cologne fills the air. The door clicks shut behind him, and without a word, I step closer to him, close enough to feel the warmth radiating from his body. Then I do what feels most natural, most right. I wrap my arms tightly around his waist, burying my face against his chest. The same way I hugged him the very first time, a desperate plea for connection.

    His arms wrap around me, strong and secure, pulling me closer. The warmth of his body chasing away the lingering chill of doubt and fear. The silence that follows is comfortable, a quiet understanding passing between us. I can feel the steady beat of his heart beneath my ear, a reassuring rhythm that soothes me.

We stand there for a long moment, wrapped in each other's arms, the world outside fading away. When we finally pull apart, it's a slow, reluctant separation. Greylan looks down at me, his eyes searching mine as if he's looking for an answer to a question he hasn't asked yet. Then he tilts my chin up gently, his thumb brushing against my cheek, sending a shiver down my spine, and kisses me. It's a kiss that makes my heart soar, that makes my knees weak. It's a kiss that erases all the darkness, all the uncertainties, all the insecurities. It's a kiss that tells me he loves me, that he wants me, that he's here, and he's not going anywhere.

"Greylan," I begin, my voice a little shaky, "I need to explain some things."

And I do. I tell him about the way I felt, seeing him surrounded by women, the pang of jealousy that twisted in my gut. I tell him about the flashbacks to my ex-husband, the betrayal that haunted me. I tell him about the insecurity that was eating at me when he wasn't back when he said he would be, the fear that I wasn't enough, that I couldn't compete with the attention he received.

"Miley," he whispers, "I get it. I understand why you're scared. But I'm not him. I would die before I hurt you like that. Those women don't matter. You're the only one I see. The only one I've ever seen."

My eyes begin to fill, but I try to compose myself.

"But why me? You could have anyone…" My breath hitches, and a single tear escapes, tracing a path down my cheek.

"Because you make me feel whole, feel alive. You make me happy. Definitely because you're smoking hot," he adds with a playful grin, "and because you enunciate your swear words perfectly." His smile fades, replaced by something more intense. "Miley, I literally couldn't breathe before I met you. You are everything, my everything, and I will always choose you. Because you are my person, and I can't imagine a life without you in it."

His words heal me. The fear, the insecurity, the jealousy…they begin to recede, replaced by a wave of relief, of trust, of love.

THE ONE

"And I know it's hard," he continues. "This life...it's not easy. But I promise you, I'll do everything I can to make it work. If...if this is what you want."

I look at him, really look at him, and I see the sincerity in his eyes, the love that shines through. And I know, without a doubt, that this is what I want. I want him. I want this. I want a future with him, no matter how challenging it might be.

"It is," I say, my voice filled with conviction. "It's what I want more than anything."

The future is uncertain, a winding road with unseen turns, but for the first time, I don't feel afraid. I know there are challenges ahead, but I also know that I'm not alone. I have him. I have us. I will cherish this feeling, this connection, and face whatever comes next together.

Greylan

When Miley said she wanted to make it work, I swear, I felt like I was floating. I won the girl of my dreams over, and the feeling is just...indescribable. This day, which used to be a painful reminder of the last time I saw my little sister, has now been completely transformed. It's the day I got my forever girl, and for the first time in a long time, I feel whole. Tomorrow, I'm meeting her parents, starting a new chapter, and becoming part of a family that loves her as much as I do—a family that will someday be mine too. Because I'm telling you right now, I'm locking that shit down. I'm all in. I'll be staying with Miley for the rest of the month, and we're going to figure out our future together. But tonight? Tonight, we're celebrating Thanksgiving with her closest friends, and I'm dragging Ivan along for the ride.

The familiar scent of my childhood home wraps around me as I sit at Mom's dining room table. But surprisingly, I don't feel sad. I feel grateful, thankful even. Without the obstacles and challenges I've faced throughout my life, I wouldn't be here. I wouldn't have met Miley, and I definitely wouldn't be watching her and Sutton do a handstand contest at Friendsgiving on the eve of my sister's tenth anniversary.

"Did you tell him?" Sutton's voice cuts through the air.

"Tell him what?" Ivan's interruption is like a pebble in still water.

I can tell Sutton is annoyed. But she ignores him, speaking to me upside down. "Did Miley tell you about her plans? About her book?"

A flicker of guilt pricks me. We talked about her job loss, but not beyond. We got lost in the comfortable flow of conversation, and now I feel like I've missed something important.

"This is the first I'm hearing of it," I admit.

Miley abandons the handstand. "It's just a rough draft, nothing serious."

Colbie's voice booms across the table. "You're kidding, right? It's a masterpiece."

"It's really good." Peyton smiles as she passes out the pie.

"Five fucking stars, Greylan. Your girl is going to create her own fame." Sutton lands gracefully. "Also, I win! Sucks to suck, Miley."

"When did this even happen? And what is it about?" I ask curiously.

"Life, laughter, and happily ever after." Colbie laughs at her own joke.

She's actually hilarious after a few drinks. Sober Colbie and nonsober Colbie are two totally different people. But both have grown on me tremendously. Either she likes you or she doesn't. She's definitely not a people person. Watching her interact with a stranger is basically torture, but if you give that girl a longneck and some freedom of speech, you're gonna have a good fucking time, I'll tell you that.

"It's about love and loss and second chances. It's a romance," Miley says shyly.

"Is it…is any of it about…us?" I ask, not caring who is around and listening.

Her eyes flicker away. "Some of it is inspired by things I've experienced," she admits. "But it's fiction. It's not…exactly…me."

THE ONE

I smile at her, listening as she and her friends excitedly discuss details. I'm so proud of her, and if writing is her dream, I'll be right there beside her, every step of the way.

*****

As we drive back to her house, I can't help but think about her book and her plans. I want to learn more. I want to be a part of her journey, and I very much want to read it. And I will tell you right now, I haven't, nor have I ever wanted to, read a book in my *entire* life. But now I want to.

"Can I read it?" I ask as I exit off the interstate.

She smiles but doesn't try to make a big deal over it. I'm not sure why though. This is something she poured herself. Just like me with my music. I'm sure that very ounce of energy she had is in there.

"I'd love for you to read it."

"I already know it's incredible," I tell her as I park in her driveway.

She tries to dismiss the attention as we walk inside her house, but this...this is huge. It's her dream, and she's actually doing it. I want her to find the person she's meant to be. I want her to be happy, truly happy, doing what she loves. Just like I want that for myself. And I want her to know, deep down, that I'll support her no matter what.

Miley sets her things on the counter, and I can't resist the pull to be closer to her. I move behind her, gently trapping her between my body and the cool surface. "Miley...," I murmur, my breath warm against her neck as I kiss it.

"Yeah?" she breathes, tilting her head and offering me more.

I tighten my hold on her waist, the simple touch sending a shiver through me. "Is this it? Writing. Is this your dream? What you want for the rest of your life?" I need to know. Her happiness, her fulfillment, it matters more than anything.

Her breath hitches, a tiny vulnerable sound that makes my heart ache with tenderness. "I...I think so."

I pull her back against me so our bodies are flush. She leans into me, a soft sigh escaping her lips.

"Then you should do it," I whisper, wrapping my arms around her, holding her close. "Finish your book on the road. Come on tour with me. Be with me."

The words tumble out, fueled by a longing I can no longer contain.

She turns in my arms, her eyes searching mine, but I don't let her speak yet. I need to get this out. I need her to understand the depth of what I feel.

"I can't be without you, Mils," I confess. "I fucking love you. I want to spend every single day, every single night, every single moment of my life with you. Because you're…you're everything. You're perfect. You're *the one*."

A tear slips down her cheek, and she nods, her expression a mix of emotions.

I pull her close, wrapping my arms around her.

"Is that a yes?" I murmur, kissing her forehead.

"Yes."

Epilogue

One Year Later

Miley

The world feels...different. Brighter somehow. My book, *Love, Loss, and Second Chances*, is no longer just my story. It belongs to so many others now, resonating with people I've never met, echoing the whispers of their own hearts. It's surreal, this whole author thing. Sometimes I still pinch myself. The insecurity that used to cling to me like a shadow? It's mostly gone now, chased away by the unwavering belief Greylan has in me and by my own slow, hard-won self-acceptance.

Greylan's music...it's breathtaking. He pours his soul into every note, every word. The pain he carried for so long, the grief that threatened to consume him, it's all there in his music, transformed into something beautiful, something healing. He's found his peace, I think. Or at least a kind of peace. He understands now that some wounds don't fully heal. They just become a part of you, a reminder of the love that shaped you.

Our life together? It's not some fairy tale. It's real. Messy, sometimes chaotic, but always real. We still have our moments, flashes of old fears, old insecurities. But we face them together, hand in hand. We've learned that love isn't about pretending the past didn't happen. It's about building a future, one shaky brick at a time, on a foundation of honesty, trust, and the kind of support that makes you feel like you can conquer anything.

THE ONE

Greylan

This past year has been nothing short of incredible. We've had our share of challenges, but Miley and I both achieved what we'd dreamed of. She wrote a masterpiece, a book that's touched so many, and I...well, I still get to sing to her every time I take the stage. Last night, playing my hometown was pure magic. It was perfect. And now, standing here today, overlooking these acres, the crisp scent of fall leaves and fresh-cut wood in the air...I know I did everything right.

I watch the sunlight filter through the colorful autumn leaves, illuminating the ground where our house is being built—our dream taking shape on my family's land. It feels surreal, watching the walls go up, the roof being fitted, a symbol of the love we share, a future we're building together.

Miley stands beside me, her hand resting on my arm, her presence a constant source of strength and comfort. She's changed so much this past year. Her confidence radiates like the autumn sun. She is happy. Truly happy. And seeing her like this, her heart finally whole, makes me feel like the luckiest man alive.

"It's beautiful," she murmurs, her gaze sweeping over the breathtaking panorama.

"It is," I agree, my voice husky with emotion. I turn her to face me, my eyes searching hers. "Miley," I begin, my voice catching slightly, "I never thought I'd find this kind of happiness. This kind of love. You...you've given me everything I never knew I was missing."

I reach into my pocket, my heart pounding against my ribs, and pull out the small velvet box. I open it, revealing the ring before dropping down to one knee.

"Miley," I say, my voice heavy with emotion, "will you marry me?"

Her eyes wide with surprise, her hands instinctively cover her mouth as she nods up and down to me.

"Yes," she whispers, her voice thick with tears. "Yes, Greylan. A thousand times yes."

THE ONE

Relief washes over me in a wave, followed by an overwhelming surge of love. I slip the ring onto her finger and pull her close, my lips finding hers in a kiss that is both tender and passionate, a promise of forever sealed with a touch.

A distant cheer erupts from Sutton's porch, followed by clapping.

"It's about goddamn time!" Colbie yells.

"Way to ruin the moment!" Brody barks back.

Our laughter bubbles up, breaking us apart. And in that moment, I know, with a certainty that settles deep in my soul, that this is where I belong, with this woman, in this place, forever.

Acknowledgements

Writing this book has been a journey, and I couldn't have done it without the love and support of some truly special people.

To Sandra, my twin, my constant companion. Through life's twists and turns, we've always been each other's anchor. Thank you for your unwavering support, not just in life, but throughout this book's journey. Your willingness to lend an ear, offer advice, and read countless drafts was invaluable. I love you.

To my dearest friend, Amanda. Thirty years of friendship speaks volumes. You're my rock, always there to lift me up, both figuratively and literally. Thank you for believing in me, for your constant encouragement, and for pushing me to keep going even when I wanted to give up. Forever & 2 days.

To Ashley, thank you for your grounding perspective. Your honest feedback, even when it was hard to hear, was essential to this process. You're truly the best.

To Shelby, your enthusiasm has been a tremendous gift. Thank you for taking the time to read my book chapter by chapter and for your incredible support. It meant more than you know.

My deepest gratitude goes to my husband, Seany B. Your patience during this writing process was truly remarkable, a testament to the support you offer in everything. Our journey hasn't always been easy, but you've consistently transformed the difficult into something brighter, more meaningful. Thank you for being an amazing father to our girls, for your steadfast love, and for seeing me through the good, the bad, and the downright ugly. I love you more than words can say.

About the Author

Sara is a paralegal by day and a storyteller by night. Her Communications degree provided the foundation, but life experience—including raising two daughters and her nephew after the loss of her sister—has fueled her storytelling.

Core Four: The One is her debut novel and a dream come true. While the story is fictional, it captures the heart-wrenching and heartwarming moments that shape us, including some of her own.

When she's not working or writing, Sara cherishes time with her family. She's known for her straightforward personality and unfiltered sense of humor—qualities that often find their way into her writing.

www.ingramcontent.com/pod-product-compliance
Lightning Source LLC
Chambersburg PA
CBHW021728310725
30391CB00001B/24